EVERYMAN,
I WILL GO WITH THEE,
AND BE THY GUIDE,
IN THY MOST NEED
TO GO BY THY SIDE

MIKHAIL LERMONTOV

A Hero of
Our Time

Translated from the Russian by
Vladimir Nabokov in collaboration
with Dmitri Nabokov

Foreword and Notes by Vladimir Nabokov
Introduction by T. J. Binyon

EVERYMAN'S LIBRARY

78

This book is one of 250 volumes in Everyman's Library
which have been distributed to 4500 state schools
throughout the United Kingdom.
The project has been supported by a grant of £4 million
from the Millennium Commission.

First included in Everyman's Library, 1992
Copyright © 1958 by Vladimir Nabokov and Dmitri Nabokov
This edition published by arrangement with the Estate of Vladimir
Nabokov. All rights reserved.
Introduction, Bibliography and Chronology © David Campbell
Publishers Ltd., 1992

ISBN 1-85715-078-3

A CIP catalogue record for this book is available from the
British Library

Published by David Campbell Publishers Ltd.,
Gloucester Mansions, 140A Shaftesbury Avenue,
London WC2H 8HD

Distributed by Random House (UK) Ltd.,
20 Vauxhall Bridge Road, London SW1V 2SA

A HERO OF OUR TIME

CONTENTS

———

Introduction xi

Select Bibliography xxiii

Chronology xxiv

Translator's Foreword 1

The Author's Introduction 15

A HERO OF OUR TIME

    Bela 17
    Maksim Maksimych 56
    Introduction to Pechorin's Journal 67
    Taman 69
    Princess Mary 82
    The Fatalist 164

Translator's Notes 175

INTRODUCTION

Much in Lermontov's life and work can be traced back to the events of his childhood. His mother, consumptive and unhappily married, died in 1817, two and a half years after his birth. His grandmother, Elizaveta Arsenev, who had disapproved of her seventeen-year-old daughter's engagement to a far from well-to-do neighbouring landowner, a retired army officer with a reputation as a *bon viveur*, was rich, powerful and determined to bring up her grandson. She brought financial pressure to bear on her son-in-law, forcing him to place the child in her care, and endeavoured during the following years to keep the two apart: Lermontov saw his father only rarely before the latter's death in 1831. To the pain caused by the rancorous enmity between the two sides of the family was added that of a serious childhood illness, which left him permanently stoop-shouldered and bow-legged. His grandmother took him on three occasions to convalesce in the Caucasus, later the setting, not only of *A Hero of Our Time*, but also of a number of other works, including the narrative poems *The Novice* and *The Demon*.

The family moved to Moscow in 1827, where Lermontov entered a preparatory school attached to the university, and then, in 1830, the university itself. Two years later, frustrated in an attempt to transfer to the university in St Petersburg 'owing to domestic circumstances', he became a cadet at a military academy there, and in 1834 was commissioned as a cornet in the Life Guards Hussars.

Lermontov had been writing poetry since adolescence. It was his poem on Pushkin's death in a duel in 1837 ('The Poet's Death'), however, which made his name and caused him to be looked upon as the elder poet's successor, at the same time bringing him unfavourably to the attention of the Tsar, Nicholas I: the poem concludes with a powerful invective, directed against those

> ... standing in a greedy crowd around the throne,
> Hangmen of Freedom, Genius and Fame

xi

who are accused of complicity in the poet's death. Seen as a revolutionary tirade and an act of *lèse-majesté*, it led to Lermontov's arrest and exile: he was transferred to a dragoon regiment stationed in the Caucasus and left the capital in March. After recuperating from severe rheumatism in the spa town of Pyatigorsk to the north of the Caucasus, he travelled widely throughout Transcaucasia, visiting Tiflis, the capital of Georgia, and, like Pechorin, Taman. By the spring of 1838, however, thanks to the intercession of his grandmother, he was back with his old regiment in St Petersburg. Turgenev, who met Lermontov only twice, both times in the space of a few days in the winter of 1839–40, has left in his reminiscences a striking picture of the writer glimpsed at a party given by Princess Shakhovskoy:

He sat down on a low stool in front of a sofa on which, in a black dress, sat the Countess Musin-Pushkin, one of the capital's beauties at that time, a really lovely creature. Lermontov was dressed in the uniform of the Life Guards Hussars; he had taken off neither his sabre nor his gloves, and, hunched up and frowning, gave the countess from time to time a sullen look. She said little to him, speaking more often to Count Shuvalov, another hussar, who was sitting next to him. There was something ominous and tragic about Lermontov's appearance; some gloomy, unfriendly force, a meditative contempt and passion emanated from his swarthy face, his large, immobile dark eyes. His heavy gaze was strangely out of accord with his almost childishly tender, pouting lips. His whole figure, squat, bow-legged, with a large head on wide, hunched shoulders, aroused an unpleasant feeling; but it was impossible to ignore the power within him.

A few days later an imprudent remark at a New Year's masked ball again drew the Tsar's attention to him; and when, in February, he fought a duel with the son of the French ambassador (neither participant was seriously wounded), he was arrested and exiled to the Caucasus for the second time, being transferred to an infantry regiment garrisoning forts on the Black Sea coast. Evading this duty, he joined an expeditionary force and was recommended for two decorations and for reinstatement in his old regiment as a result of his conspicuous bravery in a number of skirmishes with the native tribesmen. Both recommendations were turned down by the

Tsar. At the beginning of 1841, thanks again to his grandmother, he had two months' leave in St Petersburg, but in
April he was ordered to return to the front. On pretence of
illness, he again broke his journey at Pyatigorsk. Here he
met a former fellow-cadet, Major Nicholas Martynov. They
quarrelled and met in a duel: a curious re-enactment of the
encounter between Pechorin and Grushnitsky in this novel –
which would be even more curious were those commentators
correct who believe that Lermontov based Grushnitsky on
Martynov. Lermontov, saying 'I'm not going to shoot that
fool', apparently did not fire; Martynov's bullet was fatal. 'A
dog's death for a dog,' Nicholas is reported to have exclaimed,
on hearing the news.

*

Lermontov's literary career was extremely short; much of
what he wrote remained unfinished; much consists of juvenilia.
His reputation rests on a hundred-odd lyrics, the narrative
poems *The Novice* (1839) and *The Demon* (1841) and the novel *A
Hero of Our Time* (1840). The latter is not Lermontov's first
attempt at a novel: in 1833 he had begun *Vadim*, an historical
novel set, like Pushkin's *The Captain's Daughter*, against the
background of the Pugachev rebellion of the 1770s. A grotesque
blend of Romantic emotion and Gothic melodrama, stuffed
with hyperbolic simile, it remained unfinished. *Princess Ligovskoy*, begun in 1836, but also never completed, was a large step
forward. It is a society novel, set in St Petersburg, which has
close links with the 'Princess Mary' episode of *A Hero of Our
Time*: there is a similar three-cornered relationship between
the hero and two women, a similar male rivalry, while Lermontov even carries the names of the main characters over
from one novel to the other. However, although the eponym-
ous heroine of *Princess Ligovskoy* bears the same name as
Princess Mary's mother, she is in fact a preliminary sketch for
the character of Vera in the later novel. Both women are
undoubtedly portraits of Varvara Lopukhin, with whom Lermontov fell in love in the early 1830s, and who remained his
most enduring attachment: a number of his poems are
addressed to her. In 1835 she, like her fictional counterpart,

married a man seventeen years older than herself. And though the hero of *Princess Ligovskoy* is a young officer called Grigory Aleksandrovich Pechorin, with his 'irregular countenance' and 'unfavourable appearance' he is physically a self-portrait of the author himself, and in no way resembles the handsome Byronic figure described by the narrator in 'Maksim Maksimych'. It might be noted here that by choosing the name Pechorin Lermontov obviously wished to suggest some kinship between his character and the hero of Pushkin's *Evgeny Onegin* (1833): both take their name from rivers in northern Russia, the Onega and the Pechora.

Lermontov may have begun *A Hero of Our Time* in the Caucasus in 1837, but the main part of its composition took place in 1839–40, when three of the episodes, 'Bela', 'The Fatalist' and 'Taman', were published as separate stories in three issues of the journal *Notes of the Fatherland*. 'Maksim Maksimych', 'Introduction to Pechorin's Journal' and 'Princess Mary' were added in the first edition, published in 1840; 'The Author's Introduction' was a last-minute addition to the second edition of 1841.

In his foreword Vladimir Nabokov points out that the chronological sequence of the five stories in the novel differs from the order in which they are presented. The effect is to bring the reader gradually closer to the enigma of Pechorin's character. We see him first at two removes, through the narrator's rendition of Maksim Maksimych's story; then at one remove, when the narrator comes face to face with him in 'Maksim Maksimych'; and are finally admitted to his intimacy in the passages of self-analysis in 'Princess Mary'. The technique is surprisingly sophisticated, given the late development of the novel in Russian literature. But Lermontov does not only dislocate chronology to achieve this result; in equally brilliant fashion he reinforces the effect by employing, in succeeding stories, different contemporary literary genres which move from objective description to intimate portrayal to create, in the end, a unified whole.

'I was travelling post from Tiflis': the narrator begins 'Bela' *in medias res*, a manner typical of the many travel notes, by officers and others, published in Russian journals of the 1830s.

Indeed, on its first appearance in *Notes of the Fatherland*, the story carried the subtitle *From an Officer's Notes on the Caucasus*, and the narrator himself calls attention to the genre he is employing when he remarks, 'it is not a novella I am writing, but travelling notes'. He emphasizes his intention by following the remark with a description of the journey past the Mountain of the Cross and a scholarly gloss on the legend that the cross was placed there by Peter the Great. And he is only conforming to a convention of the genre when he inserts into his travel notes a story told by a chance-met companion.

With 'Taman' we move into the genre of the romantic tale. The characters – the strange blind boy, the fearless boatman Yanko, who lives beyond the law, and especially the wild and beautiful girl, Pechorin's 'water nymph', his 'undine' with her 'serpent nature' – are highly romanticized figures, and the aura of mystery that shrouds their actions is heightened by the descriptions of the surroundings. Lermontov has, however, set the romantic tale in a realistic frame. The opening sentence, 'Taman is the worst little town of all the seacoast towns in Russia', links the story to the earlier travel notes, and the conclusion, in which the characters are prosaically revealed to be a band of '*honest smugglers*', who have made use of Pechorin's self-deluded infatuation to rob him of his belongings, casts an ironic light on the earlier proceedings.

Though Pechorin describes his actions in 'Taman', he tells us little about his motivation. This is remedied in 'Princess Mary', which has the form of an intimate journal, through which is refracted the content of a society novel set in the spas of Pyatigorsk and Kislovodsk, some forty miles to the west. The use of the journal form for confession and self-analysis was, of course, a well-established tradition in Lermontov's time: the narrator makes the point when he compares Pechorin's journal, to its advantage, with Rousseau's *Confessions*. But Lermontov is perhaps innovative in extending the form to embrace two further elements: self-analysis alternates with the professional seducer's cynical analysis of feminine psychology, in a manner which goes back to Laclos' *Les Liaisons dangereuses*. At the same time Lermontov, by moving the plot of *Princess Ligovskoy* from St Petersburg to the Caucasus, uses the journal form as a vehicle for a story of love and rivalry culminating in a duel. The employment of Pyatigorsk as the setting for the episode was no doubt motivated by Lermontov's own experience of the town: Doctor Werner is an undisguised and accurate portrait of a well-known local character, the army doctor N.V. Maier (1806–46). But Lermontov, who read Scott (as we know from the fact that he gives Pechorin *Old Mortality* to read on the night before the duel with Grushnitsky), might also have been struck by the arguments set out in Scott's introduction to his *St Ronan's Well* (translated into French and Russian some ten years before the writing of *A Hero of Our Time*) concerning the advantages to be derived from choosing a watering-place as the setting for a novel. However, the use of an intimate journal to narrate a story of love and intrigue does have certain disadvantages, as Nabokov points out in his foreword, where he comments on Lermontov's excessive use of eavesdropping to further the plot in 'Princess Mary'. Lermontov is not the only Russian author to violate verisimilitude in this manner: excessive eavesdropping is also a characteristic of Turgenev's *Rudin* (1856) and his *Fathers and Sons* (1862).

The final section of the novel, 'The Fatalist', is a short, tersely and objectively narrated story, which, from an artistic point of view, is perhaps the most successful of all the episodes. Like 'Taman', it contains little introspection, but it also lacks the heavy romantic atmosphere which is the predominating feature of the earlier story. Its important position as the conclusion of the novel presents something of a puzzle. The final paragraph of 'Princess Mary' with its return, closing the circle, to the setting of 'Bela' – 'this dull fort' – and Pechorin's summation, in an extended simile, of his character – 'I am like a sailor born and bred on the deck of a pirate brig ...' – would seem to be a more natural point at which to close the narration. One might almost suspect that Lermontov, having written the story and being loth to abandon it, could find no place for it other than as the coda to the novel. There are, however, arguments, reviewed below, for considering the story as an essential key to an understanding of the novel and its necessary conclusion.

Commentary on *A Hero of Our Time*, in particular that of

Russian critics, has often concentrated on Pechorin's significance as the representative of a literary type, that of the so-
called 'superfluous man', a term which became current after
the publication in 1850 of Turgenev's *Diary of a Superfluous
Man*. In very general terms, the superfluous man can be
described as an individual who is in conflict with the world
about him, either rejecting it or being rejected by it. As a
psychological type such characters are, of course, not confined
to Russian literature: Nabokov points out that the 'bored and
bizarre hero' belongs to a long literary tradition, beginning
with Rousseau's Saint-Preux and Goethe's Werther, and continuing through Chateaubriand and Constant to Byron. The
specifically Russian superfluous man, however, is seen primar-
ily not as a psychological, but a sociological type. The failure
of the Decembrist revolt of 1825 dashed all hope of the
emergence in Russia of a freer political régime, which would
have more in common with those of Western Europe; instead,
the generation to which Lermontov belonged found itself
beneath the heel of Nicholas I's harshly repressive and
isolationist autocracy. Young men such as Pechorin, deprived
of the multiplicity of opportunities to make a career for
themselves which Western society offered, and rejecting with
repugnance the idea of serving the state, could find no outlet
for their energies, no hope of self-fulfilment. It was these
circumstances, it is thought, which gave rise to the line of
'superfluous' heroes who populate Russian literature between
the 1830s and 1860s: together with Pechorin, they include
Pushkin's Onegin, Goncharov's Oblomov (*Oblomov*, 1859), Turgenev's Rudin and Lavretsky (*A Nest of Gentlefolk*, 1859).

The title of the novel together with the comment on it in
the introduction and the concluding sentences of the 'Introduction to Pechorin's Journal' do give some licence for this
interpretation. But it is impossible to go further and agree
with those Soviet critics who see a concealed political message
in *A Hero of Our Time*: an example of this approach is Irakly
Andronikov's patently ludicrous contention that the smugglers
in 'Taman' are not 'honest' but 'honourable' – the same
Russian word denotes both concepts – because 'they are
secretly supplying the tribesmen with arms – honourable

contraband, since it assisted the freedom-loving peoples of the Caucasus in their struggle against the Tsarist autocracy for independence and honour'. Against the sociological approach and even more the political stands the argument implicit in the novel's construction and its method of narration: its stage by stage penetration into the psychology of the hero. As the narrator remarks, in his introduction to Pechorin's journal: 'The history of a human soul ... can hardly be less curious or less instructive than the history of an entire nation.'

The chief character of almost all Lermontov's verse is the poet himself. Through the persona of his lyrics, the protagonists of his longer poems, he charts the inner movements of his psyche, cries out against the lot which has been given him, or turns viciously against a corrupt society to accuse it of having corrupted him. Only in *A Hero of Our Time* does he succeed in establishing an ironic distance between himself and his alter ego. Yet, though he offers us an objective analysis, almost a psychological case history of his hero (as Pechorin offers himself to Werner as a case for physiological observation), and though in physical appearance Pechorin bears little resemblance to his creator, the passions which impel him and the questions which obsess him are still recognizably those of Lermontov himself.

'I have an unfortunate disposition: whether it is my upbringing that made me thus or whether God created me so, I don't know.' With these words Pechorin begins his reply to Maksim Maksimych's reproach that he has been ill-treating Bela. The alternative explanations he offers for his behaviour have wide implications. They contrast nurture and nature, necessity and free will, the avoidance and acceptance of responsibility for one's actions. And the question as to which explanation is correct is one which constantly preoccupies Lermontov in his verse, where he oscillates between the two extremes. On the one hand, with images of a boat caught in a storm, a leaf borne by the wind, he sees himself as the plaything of fate, tossed hither and thither by the vagaries of existence. On the other, the granite cliff, the oak tree stoutly resisting the gale, convey the idea of the poet as the master of his fate, controlling his destiny and imposing his will upon life as Napoleon, together with Byron, one of his heroes, imposed his will on history. The two great narrative poems, *The Novice* and *The Demon*, provide the fullest examination of the opposing hypotheses. The novice is a young, orphaned Circassian boy. Taken into a monastery, he is brought up by the monks. But he yearns for his native land, for reunion with his kinsmen. One night he escapes, and begins to make his way home. He revels in the beauties of nature; proves his manhood in battle with a snow-leopard. But his natural instincts have atrophied in confinement; he loses his way, wanders in a circle, and is brought back, dying, to the monastery. The demon, expelled from heaven, is an eternal exile. Flying over the Caucasus, he catches sight of Tamara, a Georgian princess, and falls in love with her. He brings about the death of her betrothed and, when she retires to a monastery, follows her there. He feels within him the possibility of redemption, wishes 'to pray, to believe in good' again. But the kiss with which he seals their love is poisonous to her: she dies and her soul is carried up to heaven; the demon is left alone for ever, 'without hope, without love'. Both heroes fail, but for different reasons. The novice fails because of external circumstance, the demon through his innate character: together they represent the two poles of Pechorin's speculation.

In fact Pechorin, unlike Lermontov, never seriously contemplates the possibility that his character can have been formed by external circumstance. He resorts to this explanation only either as an excuse for his behaviour, when speaking to Maksim Maksimych, or as another conscious tactic of seduction. On the expedition to The Hollow, on the slopes of Mount Mashuk, he relates to Princess Mary, in phrases which might have been culled from Lermontov's early verse, how the experiences of childhood and the influences of society have made him what he is. The artificiality of the recital is made clear by its introduction: 'I thought for a moment and then said, assuming a deeply touched air ...' But he is as successful here in arousing her sympathy as he was earlier in arousing her interest through the tactic of ignoring her.

'Contradiction is, with me, an innate passion'; 'There is no man in the world over whom the past gains such power as it does over me'; 'I look upon the sufferings and joys of others only in relation to myself as on the food sustaining the strength of my soul'; 'Within me there are two persons: one of them lives in the full sense of the word, the other cogitates and judges him': Pechorin is far too fond of the uniqueness of his character, glories far too much in the peculiarities of his individuality, ever to accept that he is the product of social conditioning. To do so would, in addition, deny the independence of the mainspring of his character, his will to power: 'my main pleasure ... is to subjugate to my will all that surrounds me'. Like Lovelace in Richardson's *Clarissa*, Valmont in *Les Liaisons dangereuses*, or Julien Sorel in Stendhal's *Le Rouge et le Noir*, the objects he chooses for domination are women: Bela, Princess Mary, Vera. The maintenance of his power is essential to his self-esteem. His one moment of genuine, unfeigned emotion is evoked by the failure, through the death of his horse, of his pursuit of Vera. Following this, he returns to Kislovodsk and sleeps 'the sleep of Napoleon after Waterloo'. His defeat lies not in the loss of Vera, but in the fact that he has not been given the choice of ending the relationship.

'If predestination actually exists, why then are we given free will and reason, and why must we account for our actions?' The question posed by the unnamed infantry officer on the first page of 'The Fatalist' contains the key to the novel. There are two episodes in the story. In the first, Vulich offers a proof of predestination by putting a loaded pistol to his head and pulling the trigger; in the second Pechorin repeats the experiment – 'It occurred to me to test my fate as Vulich had' – by capuring the drunken Cossack who has murdered Vulich. The earlier stories in the book are suddenly revealed in a new light. Pechorin, in kidnapping Bela, interfering with the smugglers, seducing Princess Mary, fighting a duel with Grushnitsky, is not acting in arbitrary fashion with the aim of dissipating for a moment the tedium of existence: in each case he is testing his fate, seeking a final proof of predestination.

Belief in predestination can lead to two very different conclusions. On the one hand stands Pechorin's comment, speaking of a time when men believed that their actions were controlled by the influence of the stars, 'what strength of will they derived from the certitude that the entire sky with its countless inhabitants was looking upon them with mute but permanent sympathy!' On the other the remark of the unnamed officer, for whom predestination negates free will and responsibility. Pechorin himself oscillates between the two views. At times he is as superstitious as those ancient sages he derides, with his belief in the old woman's prediction that his death will be caused by a 'wicked wife', his presentiment of the quarrel with Grushnitsky, of Vulich's death. 'What if my star at last betrays me?' he exclaims on the eve of the duel: it is his belief in his star, his destiny, which impels him to action. He is forever seeking an answer to the question he poses himself in the same passage: 'Why did I live, for what purpose was I born? ... And yet that purpose must have existed, and my destination must have been a lofty one, for I feel, in my soul, boundless strength.' But once involved he swings to the other extreme, seeing himself a mere tool in the hands of fate and thus absolving himself from responsibility for the consequences of his actions: 'What business did fate have to land me in the peaceful midst of *honest smugglers*?' he asks disingenuously at the end of 'Taman', turning himself from active agent – 'I ... left, firmly resolved to find the key to this riddle' – to passive instrument – 'Like a stone thrown into the smooth water of a spring, I had disturbed their peace.' The same reversal of roles is to be seen in 'Princess Mary', expressed by a series of metaphors linked by the comparison between life and drama:

'We have the beginning of a plot!' I cried with delight. 'The dénouement of this comedy will be our concern.'

Ever since I have lived and acted, fate has always seemed to bring me in at the dénouement of other people's dramas, as if none could die or despair without me! I am the indispensable persona in the fifth act; involuntarily, I play the miserable part of an executioner or a traitor.

... how many times I have played the part of an axe in the hands of fate! As an executioner's tool, I would fall upon the head of doomed victims, often without malice, always without regret.

'*Finita la commedia!*' I said to the doctor.

As Lermontov deflated the romanticism of 'Taman' with a prosaic conclusion so too does he deflate the philosophical pretensions of 'The Fatalist': Pechorin is brought down from metaphysical speculation by stumbling over the carcass of a dead pig, and in the final paragraphs Maksim Maksimych sees Vulich's experiment as of interest only in as much as it illustrates the unreliability of Asiatic pistols. Of course, he is right. No attempt to test fate can offer a conclusive proof of predestination. All Pechorin's exploits, in the end, misfire like Vulich's pistol. But Maksim Maksimych's final comment on Vulich is significant:

'Yes, I'm sorry for the poor fellow ... Why the devil did he talk to a drunk at night! ... However, this must have been what was assigned to him at his birth!'

The observation takes us back to 'Bela', reminding us of his warning on the danger of consorting with drunken Circassians. At the same time it echoes the remark he makes in that story to the narrator about Pechorin:

'You know, there really exist certain people to whom it is assigned, at their birth, to have all sorts of extraordinary things happen to them.'

Here Maksim Maksimych is not only concurring in Pechorin's view of himself, he is also identifying the character with his creator: it was of himself that Lermontov wrote, in a poem of 1832 ('To *'):

I was born, so that the whole world might be a spectator
Of my triumph or my doom.

T. J. Binyon

SELECT BIBLIOGRAPHY

There is little on Lermontov in English; his work, and its significance in Russian literature, are discussed in two recent excellent histories of the subject: *The Cambridge History of Russian Literature*, edited by Charles A. Moser, Cambridge University Press, 1989; and Victor Terras, *A History of Russian Literature*, Yale University Press, New Haven and London, 1991.

D. M. Mirsky's comments, in *A History of Russian Literature*, Routledge, London, 1949, are interesting and stimulating, if sometimes idiosyncratic. Lermontov's verse has been well translated, and furnished with an informative commentary, by Anatoly Liberman: Mikhail Lermontov, *Major Poetical Works*, Croom Helm, London, 1983. Works which deal wholly with Lermontov include the following:

GARRARD, JOHN, *Mikhail Lermontov*, Twayne, Boston, 1982, is a scholarly study of the writer's life and work which is possibly of more interest to the specialist than to the general reader.

KELLY, LAURENCE, *Lermontov: Tragedy in the Caucasus*, Constable, London, 1977, is a lively and very readable biography, which is particularly strong on the Caucasian background to Lermontov's life.

LAVRIN, JANKO, *Lermontov*, Bowes & Bowes, London, 1959, is a short, somewhat impressionistic introduction to Lermontov's work which concentrates mainly on the verse.

CHRONOLOGY

DATE	AUTHOR'S LIFE	LITERARY CONTEXT
1812	Marriage of Yuri Lermontov and Maria Arsenev, the former an ex-army captain, whose family, landowning gentry, claimed descent from the Learmonths in Scotland, the latter from a wealthy aristocratic family who disapprove of the match.	Byron: *Childe Harold* begins publication (to 1818). Zhukovksy: *Svetlana.* Vostokov: *Experiment in Russian Versification.* Birth of Herzen.
1813		Byron: *The Giaour, The Bride of Abydos.* Batyushkov: 'To Dashkov', 'On the ruins of a castle in Sweden'.
1814	Mikhail Yurievich Lermontov, only child of the marriage – which turned out to be both brief and unhappy – is born in Moscow (2/3 October). The couple shortly afterwards move to the country estate of Maria's mother at Tarkhany in the province of Penza in Central Russia.	Narezhny: *A Russian Gil Blas.* Batyushkov: 'Ghost of a Friend'. Scott: *Waverley.* Byron: *The Corsair, Lara.* Wordsworth: *The Excursion.* Southey: *Roderick; the Last of the Goths.* Jane Austen: *Mansfield Park.* Hoffmann: *Tales* (to 1815).
1815		Griboedov: *Young Married People.* Scott: *Guy Mannering.* Byron: *Hebrew Melodies.* Wordsworth: *Poems.* Hoffmann: *The Devil's Elixir* (to 1816).
1816		Byron: *The Prisoner of Chillon.* Coleridge: *Christabel and Other Poems* (includes 'Kubla Khan'). Scott: *Old Mortality.* Constant: *Adolphe.* Karamzin: 12-vol. *History of the Russian State* (to 1829).

HISTORICAL EVENTS

Fall and internal exile of Speransky, architect of the liberal reforms of the first part of Alexander I's reign. End of Russo-Turkish war; Russia gains Bessarabia (May). War between France and Russia. Napoleon marches on Moscow (June). Battle of Borodino; fall of Moscow; burning of the city (September). Unable to make peace, Napoleon orders the retreat from Moscow (October); destruction of French army through cold, hunger and disease.

War of Liberation. Combined Allied armies defeat Napoleon at battle of Leipzig. Treaty of Gulistan: Persia cedes Russia a wide area of Kahnates in the eastern Caucasus, but Russo-Persian hostility in the region continues.

Alexander insists that the Allies continue to Paris, which falls in March 1814, the Tsar riding in triumph through the streets. Abdication of Napoleon and banishment to Elba. Restoration of Louis XVIII. Congress of Vienna (to 1815): Alexander presses for generosity towards France. The hated reactionary, Arakcheyev, is given charge of Russia's internal affairs (to 1825).

Napoleon's 'Hundred Days' and defeat at Waterloo. Second Bourbon restoration. At the Tsar's instigation, the three autocracies, Russia, Prussia and Austria, form Holy Alliance to protect European status quo. Quadruple alliance (includes Britain) formed to safeguard postwar settlement. Russia obtains central Poland including Warsaw; Alexander grants Poles a constitution. First steamship in Russia, on the Neva.

Ermolov appointed commander-in-chief in the Caucasus (to 1828), where he establishes a line of fortified Russian bases, the most important being Fort Grozny in 1818 (Lermontov is stationed there in 1840). Ermolov annexes Shirvan (1820) and Karabagh (1822); inflicts severe defeats on the tribes but does not succeed in pacifying the region.

DATE	AUTHOR'S LIFE	LITERARY CONTEXT
1817	Lermontov's mother dies of consumption. After a bitter contest, his grandmother, Elizaveta Arsenev, acquires control of his upbringing. He continues to live with her at Tarkhany and is rarely allowed to see his father.	Byron: *The Lament of Tasso*, *Manfred*. Tom Moore: *Lalla Rookh*. Griboedov: *The Student*. Keats: *Poems*.
1818	His grandmother takes 'Mishka', as he is known, to the Caucasus for the first time – a perilous 1000 kilometre journey. They spend the summer on the estate of Madame Arsenev's sister.	Byron: *Beppo*. Scott: *The Heart of Midlothian*. Jane Austen: *Northanger Abbey*, *Persuasion*. Mary Shelley: *Frankenstein*. Birth of Turgenev.
1818 –28	The young Lermontov is educated at home by a series of foreign tutors. Learns French, and later English and German. Reads widely, especially Romantic literature. Byron becomes his literary hero.	
1819		Byron: *Don Juan* (to 1824), *Mazeppa*. Goethe: *East-West Divan*. Hoffmann: *The Serapion Brothers* (to 1821). André Chénier: *Poésies*.
1820	Second expedition to the Caucasus. Lermontov becomes captivated by the region, its landscape and people. Stays once more with his great-aunt, also visiting the spa town of Pyatigorsk during the 'season'. Lifelong love of horses begins.	Shelley: *Prometheus Unbound*, 'Ode to the West Wind'. Keats: *Poems* (includes the Odes). Lamartine: *Premières méditations poétiques*. Hegel: *Philosophy of Right*.
1821		Pushkin: *The Prisoner of the Caucasus*. Ryleev writing his historical songs (to 1823). Byron: *Cain, Sardanapalus*. Goethe: *Wilhelm Meister's Travels* (to 1829). Death of Keats. Birth of Dostoevsky.

CHRONOLOGY

HISTORICAL EVENTS

Serfdom in Russian Estonia abolished. Arakcheyev engaged in implementing Alexander's hugely unpopular system of military colonies, involving the conscription of peasants as part-time soldiers, while billeting soldiers on them as part-time labourers. Mutinies among colonists, and within army, savagely suppressed.

Congress of Aix-la-Chappelle: France readmitted to the 'Concert of Nations'; Allied troops withdrawn. Alexander I instructs Novosiltsov to prepare a draft constitution for the empire and Arakcheyev to draw up a scheme for the emancipation of the serfs. Both are drafted but neither pursued.

Massacre of Peterloo in Britain, followed by repressive Six Acts. Assassination of conservative playwright August von Kotzebue by student Karl Sand in Mannheim. Metternich responds by repressive Carlsbad Decrees, designed to stamp out liberal opposition throughout the German Confederation.

Conference of Vienna: Metternich succeeds in eliminating constitutional control within individual German states. Congress of Troppau: Great Powers agree to check revolutionary movements in Spain, Portugal and the Two Sicilies. In Britain, death of George III and accession of Prince Regent as George IV. In Russia, purging of the universities by Golitsyn and Magnitsky begins.

Greek War of Independence against the Turks. Foundation of the Northern and Southern Societies in Russia. Like the Union of Salvation (1816) and the Union of Welfare (1818), these were secret societies of officers and noblemen disappointed by the waning of the Tsar's liberalism. All supported the abolition of serfdom and agrarian reform but their political aims diverged. The Northern Society, led by Colonel Nikita Muravyov, favoured a constitutional monarchy and a federal system; the Southern Society, led by Colonel Pavel Pestel, a democratic republic.

DATE	AUTHOR'S LIFE	LITERARY CONTEXT
1822		Pushkin: *The Fountain of Bakhchisaray*. Mickiewicz: 'On Romantic Poetry'. Death of Shelley.
1823		Pushkin begins *Evgeny Onegin* (first complete edition, 1833). Tom Moore: *The Loves of the Angels*. Scott: *St Ronan's Well*.
1824		Griboedov: *Woe from Wit*. Vigny: *Eloa*. Death of Byron at Missolonghi.
1825	Third and last summer in the Caucasus.	Pushkin: *Boris Godunov*, 'Winter Evening', 'To Friends', 'Tempest', 'I recollect a wondrous moment'. Scott: *The Betrothed* and *The Talisman* (*Tales of the Crusaders*). Delvig: 'Bathing Women'. Kozlov: *The Monk*. Polezhaev: *Sashka*.
1826	The Tarkhany household is touched by the aftermath of the Decembrist conspiracy. Neighbours in Penza are arrested and interrogated; Elizaveta Arsenev's brother, General Dmitri Stolypin, a friend of the ringleaders, dies in January, before he can be incriminated.	Scott: *Woodstock*. J. F. Cooper: *The Last of the Mohicans*. Heine: *Travel Pictures* (to 1831). Vigny: *Cinq-Mars*. Bestuzhev-Marlinsky: *Blood for Blood*. Death of N. M. Karamzin.
1827	Moves to Moscow with his grandmother in anticipation of his entrance to school and university. First meeting with Varvara Lopukhin, to whom he becomes romantically attached during the early 1830s – an attachment which lasts for the rest of his life, in spite of her marriage and his other love affairs.	Pushkin: *The Blackamoor of Peter the Great* (to 1828), 'The Poet'. Mérimée: *Guzla*. Heine: *Book of Songs*. Manzoni: *The Betrothed*. Baratynsky: 'The last death'. Death of poet Dmitri Venevitinov, aged 22.
1828	Lermontov enrolled at the 'Noble Pension' in Moscow, leading school for the children of the aristocracy. Begins writing	Pushkin: *Poltava*, 'The Upas Tree'. Pogorelsky: *The Double*. Baratynsky: *Eda*.

CHRONOLOGY

Congress of Verona. Suicide of Castlereagh, British Foreign Secretary: Britain's disengagement from Metternich's European (Congress) system.

French invasion of Spain. Meeting of Emperors Alexander and Francis at Czernowitz.

Death of Louis XVIII; accession of Charles X.

Death of Alexander I at Taganrog (19 November), and succession of his brother as Nicholas I. Disaffected army officers organize a demonstration in support of Constantine (another brother), hoping thus to secure constitutional reform and the abolition of serfdom; the new Tsar orders the artillery to be turned on them. A strict authoritarian, Nicholas becomes personally involved in the investigation of the conspiracy. Some 3,000 arrests are made. In 1826 five 'Decembrists' are hanged on a bastion of the Peter and Paul Fortress – their martyrdom to provide a source of inspiration for future Russian revolutionaries – and many hundreds exiled to Siberia. Nicholas develops system of autocratic government based on militarism and bureaucracy. Extends his personal Chancery: a Second Section, under Speransky, deals with legal reform; the notorious Third Section under Count Alexander Benckendorf acts against subversion and revolution, controlling censorship and employing a widespread network of spies.
Protocol of St Petersburg between Russia and Britain, the two powers agreeing to mediate between the Sultan and the Greeks. Russia and Persia at war (to 1828), the Shah hoping to reclaim Georgia and Azerbaidjan: the Russians narrowly avoid losing Tiflis.
The war carried into Persian territory: Russians capture Erivan and Tabriz. In Daghestan Kazi Mulla proclaims holy war (*ghazavat*) against foreign invaders, winning support from Avar and Chechen tribesmen, and carrying out damaging raids into Kakhetia and the Terek valley.
Battle of Navarino: British, French and Russian navies destroy Eyptian fleet of Mohammed Ali, the Sultan's vassal, after failure to persuade the Turks to agree to mediation in the Greek war.

Start of peasant revolts in Russia, averaging 23 per year to 1854.
Russo-Persian treaty of Turkmanchay gives Russia Erivan and Nakhichevan – i.e. Persian Armenia. The main Caucasus massif is still unconquered, and centres of resistance remain in Circassia to the west, and in Daghestan to

DATE	AUTHOR'S LIFE	LITERARY CONTEXT
1828 *cont*	poetry (200 pieces between 1828 and 1832).	Polezhaev: 'The Song of the Shipwrecked Sailor'. Yazykov: 'Waterfall'. Mickiewicz: *Konrad Wallenrod*. Casanova: *Mémoires*. Birth of Tolstoy.
1829	Under an English tutor at home, reading Tom Moore and Sir Walter Scott, and making his own translations of Byron. Also reading Russian poets assiduously. Makes first sketches for his narrative poem *The Demon*.	Zagoskin: *Yury Miloslavsky* (first Russian historical novel). Bulgarin: *Ivan Vyzhigin*. Pushkin: 'I used to love you'. Tyutchev: 'A Vision'. Baratynsky: *The Ball*. Delvig: 'The Retired Soldier', 'The End of the Golden Age'. N. Gnedich's Russian translation of *The Iliad*. Hugo: *Les Orientales*.
1830	Tsar visits the Pension, and, considering the atmosphere subversive, demotes it to grammar school status. Lermontov enrols at Moscow University in September, first in the Ethico-Political Department, but soon changing to Literature, where fellow students – from whom he holds himself aloof – include Herzen and Belinsky. Among poems written this year are the lyric 'Hope' and the narrative poem 'The Lithuanian Woman'.	Pushkin: *The Tales of Belkin*, *The Little House at Kolomna*, four 'Little Tragedies'. Bestuzhev-Marlinsky: 'An Evening at a Caucasian Watering Place in 1824'. Stendhal: *Le Rouge et le Noir*. Hugo: *Hernani*.
1831	Death of his father. First draft of *The Demon* dedicated to Varvara Lopukhin. Writes 'A Wish' and 'The Angel', 'The 11th day of June 1831', 'Aul Bastundzhi'.	Pushkin: *The Tale of Tsar Saltan*. Gogol: *Evenings on a Farm near Dikanka*. Zagoskin: *Roslavlev*. Lazhechnikov: *The Last Novik* (to 1833). Baratynsky: *The Concubine*. Bestuzhev-Marlinsky: 'Lieutenant Belozoi'. Kalashnikov: *The Daughter of the Merchant Zholobov*. Koltsov: 'Song of the Ploughman'. Hugo: *Notre-Dame de Paris*. Barbier: *Iambes*.

HISTORICAL EVENTS

the east. War between Russia and Turkey (to 1829), fought in the Balkans and in Transcaucasia.

Treaty of Adrianople ends Russo-Turkish war. Russia restores most of her conquests in Europe and Asia to Turkey, but gains free navigation of the Danube and tree trade within the Ottoman Empire. Cholera epidemic begins in Russia, reaching Moscow in 1830 and St Petersburg in 1831, resulting in more than 100,000 deaths.

July Revolution in Paris; Charles X overthrown and Louis Philippe becomes 'King of the French' under new constitutional Charter. Nicholas I reluctant to give him official recognition. Belgian revolt against the Dutch.
Speransky's codification of the law completed: the new code replaces that of Tsar Alexis Mikhailovich in 1649, and lasts until 1917. First metalled road between Moscow and St Petersburg.
1830s: Proliferation of discussion groups influenced by German idealistic philosophy, particularly in and around Moscow University.

Failure of Polish rising against Russia: Poles lose their constitution and most of the autonomy granted them in 1815. In Russia, a revolt of military colonists following a cholera epidemic is brutally put down. Russia, Austria and Britain recognize Greece as an independent kingdom. With French support against the Dutch, an independent Belgium is secured.

DATE	AUTHOR'S LIFE	LITERARY CONTEXT
1832	Disenchanted with the University, Lermontov quarrels with various professors, and leaves in June. Enters School of Cavalry Junkers and Ensigns of the Guard at St Petersburg as an officer cadet. Writes 'A Sail', 'No, I am not Byron', and *Ismail Bey* (narrative poem set in the Caucasus).	Bestuzhev-Marlinsky: 'Ammalat Bek'. Polevoy: *The Oath at the Lord's Tomb*. Mickiewicz: *Forefathers' Eve*, Part ; Irving: *Legends of the Alhambra*. Sand: *Indiana*. Lenau: *Schilflieder*. Goethe: *Faust*, Part 2. Death of Goethe and Scott.
1833	Writing a historical novel, *Vadim*, which he never completes.	Pushkin: 'The Queen of Spades'; *The Bronze Horseman*. Tyutchev: 'Silentium!'. Baratynsky: 'Death'. V. Odoevsky: *Motley Fairy Tales*. Katenin: *Princess Milusha*. George Sand: *Lélia*. Balzac: *Le Médicin de campagne*; *Eugénie Grandet*.
1834	Lermontov's anti-authoritarian spirit notwithstanding, he survives his cadetship and is commissioned as a cornet in the Life Guards Hussars. Sets up in grand style in a St Petersburg flat, and proceeds to enjoy a lively social life. Writes 'Hadji Abrek'.	Pushkin: *History of Pugachev*. Mickiewicz: *Pan Tadeusz*. Belinsky: *Literary Reveries*. Baratynsky: 'The last poet'. Arrest and internal exile of Herzen and his circle.
1835-6	In May 1835 Varvara Lopukhin marries Nicholas Bakhmetiev. Lermontov's bitterness and disappointment inform the play *Masquerade*, the unfinished society tale *Princess Ligovskoy*, and the melodrama *The Two Brothers*. Also writing *Sashka*, a satirical narrative poem inspired by Byron's *Don Juan*.	Gogol: *Mirgorod, Arabesques, Taras Bulba*. Pavlov: *Three Tales*. Lazhechnikov: *The Ice Palace*. Koltsov: 'Harvest'. Balzac: *Le Père Goriot*. Musset: *Les Nuits* (to 1837). Vigny: *Servitude et grandeur militaires, Chatterton*. Hugo: *Les Chants du crépuscule*.
1836	Poems include *The Boyar Orsha*, 'The Dying Gladiator', 'The Mermaid', 'A Branch of Palestine'.	Pushkin: *The Captain's Daughter*. Gogol: *The Government Inspector*, 'The Nose'. First of Chaadaev's *Lettres philosophiques* published in Russia. Tyutchev: 'As the ocean embraces the globe of earth', 'Dream of the Sea'.

CHRONOLOGY

HISTORICAL EVENTS

Russian army invades Kazi Mulla's territory with 10,000 troops: Kazi Mulla is killed.
First Parliamentary Reform Act in Britain.

The Sultan, now threatened by Mohammed Ali, makes treaty of alliance (Unkiar Skelessi) with Russia – opposed by Britain and France. Russia is given the right to request the Straits to be closed to foreign warships. Doctrine of 'Official Nationality' – Orthodoxy, autocracy and nationality – formally proclaimed by Tsar's minister of education, Count Sergey Uvarov.

Uvarov extends and modernizes education system (to 1849), while at the same time declaring his intention to construct a 'dam' to 'hold up the flow of new ideas into Russia'. Full-time inspectors introduced into Russian universities to watch student activities in the classroom. Shamil, Kazi Mulla's son and an inspired military leader, takes up the Caucasian war where his father left off; his raiders are soon posing a serious threat to the Russians.

Michael Pogodin becomes first professor of Russian history at the University of Moscow. Death of Emperor Francis I of Austria: the mentally ill Ferdinand I rules with the help of a regency council dominated by the chancellor, Metternich.

Pratasov becomes Supreme Procurator of the Holy Synod (to 1855) and proceeds to bring the church more thoroughly under government control. Metternich clamps down on liberal/nationalist movement in Hungary: imprisonment (to 1839) of Kossuth and Wesselényi. Chartist Movement begins in Britain (to 1848).

DATE	AUTHOR'S LIFE	LITERARY CONTEXT
1837	Lermontov's elegy for Pushkin, 'The Poet's Death', earns him instant fame and the Tsar's displeasure for his denunciation of court intrigue; he is transferred to a dragoon regiment in the Caucasus (February). Other poems this year include 'Borodino', 'When billows the yellowing grain' and 'Do not mock my prophetic anguish'. Taken ill on the journey south; recuperates at the Military Hospital at Pyatigorsk (May–August). Among his fellow exiles are many former Decembrists. Travels to the Black Sea, then across the Caucasus to join his regiment in Kakhetia. Finding the life pleasantly sociable, he is not overjoyed to receive a pardon from the Tsar and orders to transfer to the Hussar Guards. Visits Tiflis (November) en route north.	Death of Pushkin. Baratynsky: 'Autumn' (mourning the death of Pushkin). Gogol writes most of the first part of *Dead Souls* (published 1842) in Rome (to 1838). Balzac: *Illusions perdues* (to 1843). Hugo: *Les Voix intérieures*. Stendhal: *Les Cencis, Vittoria Accoramboni*. Dickens: *The Pickwick Papers*. Carlyle: *History of the French Revolution*.
1838	On leave in Moscow and St Petersburg. Joins Grodno Hussars near Novgorod, with the rank of lieutenant (February), but thanks to his grandmother's influence is reinstated in the Life Guards (April). Introduced to St Petersburg literary circles through the salon of Ekaterina Karamzin, widow of the historian; is taken up by Zhukovsky, editor of *The Contemporary*, and Krayevsky, editor of the newly founded *Notes of the Fatherland*, who help push his poems past the censors. Zhukovksy publishes the romantic ballad *The Song of the Merchant Kalashnikov*, written at Pyatigorsk, and *The Tambov Treasurer's Wife*. Lyrics this year include 'A Meditation' and 'The Poet'.	Evdokia Rostopchina: 'Rank and Money', 'The Duel'. Dickens: *Oliver Twist*. Stendhal: *La Duchesse de Palliano*. Hugo: *Ruy Blas*. Charles de Bernard: *Gerfaut*.

CHRONOLOGY

Count Paul Kieslev begins re-organization of state peasants in Russia. His reforms include shifting of taxation from persons to land.

First public Russian railway, between St Petersburg and Tsarskoe Selo.

Nicholas I visits his forces in the Caucasus, hoping to obtain personal submission of Shamil. But Shamil, driven by religious fanaticism, love of liberty, and a determination to protect the social and cultural traditions of the tribes, continues the fight until his capture in 1859.

Death of William IV and accession of Victoria in Britain.

Meeting of Tsar with Austrian Emperor at Teplitz: declaration reasserts opposition to Egyptian designs on Turkey.

Severe fighting in Caucasus region: General Grabbé leads expedition into Chechnya.

DATE	AUTHOR'S LIFE	LITERARY CONTEXT
1839	Lermontov writing the novel *A Hero of Our Time* and the poem *The Novice* (to 1840), both inspired by his experience in the Caucasus. Also continues work on *The Demon*, which circulates widely in MS. Begins an uncompleted ballad, *A Fairy Tale for Children*. Lionized by St Petersburg society but becoming increasingly dissatisfied with life. Joins secret society 'The Sixteen' and is viewed by his military superiors as a potential troublemaker. Poems include 'Duma', 'Prayer', 'The Three Palm Trees, an Eastern Legend' and 'The Gifts of the Terek'.	Stendhal: *La Chartreuse de Parme*. Lamartine: *Recueillements poétiques*. Dickens: *Nicholas Nickleby*. Poe: *Tales of the Grotesque and Arabesque*. V. Odoevksy: 'Princess Zizi'. Death of Decembrist poet Alexander Odoevsky of malaria at the Lavretsky fortress on the Black Sea: commemorated by Lermontov in 'To the Memory of A. I. Odoevsky'.
1840	*A Hero of Our Time* serialized in *Notes of the Fatherland*, then published in book form in April. A series of incidents – including the publication of his poem 'The First of January' – bring him once more to the unfavourable notice of the authorities. A duel fought with the son of the French ambassador (in which neither is harmed) proves the last straw: Lermontov is arrested (March), and again sentenced to join an infantry regiment in the Caucasus. Writes the lyric, 'Clouds', about his exile. Travels via Moscow (where he meets Gogol). Arriving in Stavropol in June, he volunteers to join expedition from Fort Grozny against rebel leader Shamil. Writes 'The Battle of the Valerik' (at which he was present) and 'The Dream', the thoughts of a wounded soldier on the battlefield. Takes part in other sorties and skirmishes and is commended for bravery.	Shelley's *Defence of Poetry* (1821) first published. Hugo: *Les Rayons et les Ombres*. Mérimée: 'Colomba'. Cooper: *The Pathfinder*.

CHRONOLOGY

HISTORICAL EVENTS

Grabbé's campaign ends in bloody siege of Akhulgo, where Shamil makes a desperate stand. The Russians finally capture the rock fortress, but suffer 3,000 casualties; Shamil himself escapes.

Egyptians rout Turkish army at the battle of Nezib.

In the west Caucasus, Circassian, Ubykh and Adighe chiefs unite in a series of attacks on Russian forts on the Black Sea coast, many of which they succeed in destroying. In the east Caucasus Shamil and his lieutenant Hadji Murad gain complete control of the mountains by the end of 1840, leaving the Russians with an exposed line of undermanned camps. Grabbé loses 64 officers and 1,756 men between 1839 and 1842, with a further 372 officers and 6,204 men wounded or missing.

Four Power agreement on Egyptian crisis signed in London by Britain, Russia, Austria, Prussia; Mohammed Ali, supported by France, refuses terms. But faced with revolt in Syria he agrees to accept hereditary rule of Egypt, thereby giving up any ambitions of establishing an Arab empire.

xxxvii

DATE	AUTHOR'S LIFE	LITERARY CONTEXT
1840 *cont*	Krayevsky publishes a collected edition of his poems (October). Other poems this year include 'Cossack Lullaby' and 'The Captive Knight'.	
1841	On leave in St Petersburg. Writes 'The Dispute', a lament for the lost freedom of the people of the Caucasus. 'Last Testament' appears in *Notes of the Fatherland* (February) together with an appraisal of his work by Belinsky. Other poems include 'Homeland', 'Princess of the Sea' and 'Tamara'. A second edition of *A Hero of Our Time* also published, and an eighth and final version of *The Demon* prepared. Neither pardon nor decoration for gallantry forthcoming from the Tsar, Lermontov returns to the Caucasus via Moscow (April), writing his farewell, 'Goodbye, Unwashed Russia'. Pleading ill-health, he defies orders and instead of joining his regiment goes to Pyatigorsk, where he leads a busy social life and continues to write poetry ('The Prophet', 'Alone I set forth upon the road'). Challenged by an old schoolfriend and former fellow-officer cadet, N. S. Martynov, after a trivial quarrel. The duel takes place on 15 July; Lermontov is shot through the heart at the first fire.	Cooper: *The Deerslayer*. Dickens: *The Old Curiosity Shop*. Carlyle: *On Heroes, Hero-worship and the Heroic in History*. Musset: *Le Souvenir*.

CHRONOLOGY

Beginning of Slavophile versus Westerner debate among Russian intellectuals. Westerners advocate progress by assimimilating European rationalism and civic freedom. Slavophiles assert spiritual and moral superiority of Russia to the West and argue that future development should be based upon the traditions of the Orthodox Church and the peasant commmune or *mir*.

Straits Convention between Turkey and the five European Powers; the Sultan declares the Straits to be closed to all foreign warships in time of peace (Russia loses special rights obtained in Treaty of Unkiar Skelessi).

Peel becomes prime minister in Britain.

TRANSLATOR'S FOREWORD

I

IN 1841, a few months before his death (in a pistol duel with a fellow officer at the foot of Mount Mashuk in the Caucasus), Mikhail Lermontov (1814–41) composed a prophetic poem:

> In noon's heat, in a dale of Dagestan,
> With lead inside my breast, stirless I lay;
> The deep wound still smoked on; my blood
> Kept trickling drop by drop away.
>
> On the dale's sand alone I lay. The cliffs
> Crowded around in ledges steep,
> And the sun scorched their tawny tops
> And scorched me – but I slept death's sleep.
>
> And in a dream I saw an evening feast
> That in my native land with bright lights shone;
> Among young women crowned with flowers,
> A merry talk concerning me went on.
>
> But in the merry talk not joining,
> One of them sat there lost in thought,
> And in a melancholy dream
> Her young soul was immersed – God knows by what.
>
> And of a dale in Dagestan she dreamt;
> In that dale lay the corpse of one she knew;
> Within his breast a smoking wound showed black,
> And blood ran in a stream that colder grew.

This remarkable composition (which, in the original, is in iambic pentameter throughout, with alternate feminine and masculine rhymes) might be entitled 'The Triple Dream'.

There is an initial dreamer (Lermontov, or more exactly,

I

his poetical impersonator) who dreams that he lies dying in a valley of Eastern Caucasus. This is Dream One, dreamt by Dreamer One.

The fatally wounded man (Dreamer Two) dreams in his turn of a young woman sitting at a feast in St Petersburg or Moscow. This is Dream Two within Dream One.

The young woman sitting at the feast sees in her mind Dreamer Two (who dies in the course of the poem) in the surroundings of remote Dagestan. This is Dream Three within Dream Two within Dream One – which describes a spiral by bringing us back to the first stanza.

The whorls of these five strophes have a certain structural affinity with the interlacings of the five stories that make up Lermontov's novel, *A Hero of Our Time* (*Geroy nashego vremeni*).

In the first two stories, 'Bela' and 'Maksim Maksimych', Lermontov or, more exactly, his fictional impersonator, an inquisitive traveller, relates a journey he made along the Military Georgian Road (*Voenno-gruzinskaya doroga*) in the Caucasus around 1837. This is Narrator One.

On the way north from Tiflis he meets an old campaigner, Maksim Maksimych. They travel together for a while and Maksim Maksimych tells Narrator One about a certain Grigory Pechorin who, five years before, in the Chechnya Region, north of Dagestan, kidnapped a Circassian girl. Maksim Maksimych is Narrator Two, and the story is 'Bela'.

At a second meeting on the road (in 'Maksim Maksimych'), Narrator One and Narrator Two come across Pechorin in the flesh. Henceforth, Pechorin, whose journal Narrator One publishes, becomes Narrator Three, for it is from his journal that the remaining three stories are posthumously drawn.

It will be marked by the good reader that the structural trick consists in bringing Pechorin gradually nearer and nearer until he takes over; but by the time he takes over he is dead. In the first story, Pechorin is twice removed from the reader since his personality is described through Maksim Maksimych, whose words are transmitted to us by

Narrator One. In the second story the personality of Narrator Two no longer stands between Pechorin and Narrator One, who, at last, sees the hero for himself. Maksim Maksimych, is, in fact, pathetically eager to produce the real Pechorin on top of the subject of his yarn. And, finally, in the last three stories, both Narrator One and Narrator Two step aside, and the reader meets Pechorin, Narrator Three, face to face.

This involute structure is responsible for blurring somewhat the time sequence of the novel. The five stories grow, revolve, reveal, and mask their contours, turn away and reappear in a new attitude or light like five mountain peaks attending a traveller along the meanders of a Caucasian canyon road. The traveller is Lermontov, not Pechorin. The five tales are placed in the novel according to the order in which the events become known to Narrator One; but their chronological sequence is different, going something like this:

1. Around 1830 an officer, Grigory Pechorin (Narrator Three), on his way from St Petersburg to the Caucasus, whither he is being sent on some military errand to a detachment on active duty, happens to be stranded at the village of Taman (a port facing the NE coast of the Crimea). An adventure he has there forms the subject of 'Taman', the third story in the book.

2. After some time spent on active duty in skirmishes with the mountain tribes, Pechorin, on 10 May 1832, arrives for a rest at a Caucasian spa, Pyatigorsk. At Pyatigorsk and at Kislovodsk, a neighbouring resort, he participates in a series of dramatic events that lead to his killing a fellow officer in a duel on 17 June. These events are related by him in the fourth story, 'Princess Mary'.

3. On 19 June, the military authorities have Pechorin dispatched to a fort in the Chechnya Region, Northeast Caucasus, where he arrives only in autumn (after an unexplained delay). There he meets the junior captain Maksim Maksimych. This is related to Narrator One by Narrator Two in the first story, 'Bela'.

4. In December of the same year (1832) Pechorin leaves

3

the fort for a fortnight which he spends in a Cossack settlement north of the Terek River, and there has the adventure described by him in the fifth (last) story, 'The Fatalist'.

5. In the spring of 1833, he kidnaps a Circassian girl who is assassinated by a bandit four and a half months later. In December 1833, Pechorin leaves for Georgia and some time later goes home to St Petersburg. This is related in 'Bela'.

6. Some four years later, in the autumn of 1837, Narrator One and Narrator Two, on their way north, stop at the town of Vladikavkaz and there run into Pechorin who, in the meantime, has returned to the Caucasus, and is now on his way south, to Persia. This is related by Narrator One in 'Maksim Maksimych', the second story in the book.

7. In 1838 or 1839, on his way back from Persia, Pechorin dies under circumstances possibly related to a prediction made to him that he would die in consequence of an unfortunate marriage. Narrator One now publishes the dead man's journal, obtained from Narrator Two. Pechorin's death is mentioned by Narrator One in his editorial Foreword (1841) to Pechorin's Journal containing 'Taman', 'Princess Mary', and 'The Fatalist'.

Thus the order of the five stories, in relation to Pechorin, is: 'Taman', 'Princess Mary', 'The Fatalist', 'Bela', and 'Maksim Maksimych'.

It is unlikely that Lermontov foresaw the plot of 'Princess Mary' while he was writing 'Bela'. The details of Pechorin's arrival at the Kamenny Brod Fort, as given in 'Bela' by Maksim Maksimych, do not quite tally with the details given by Pechorin himself in 'Princess Mary'.

The inconsistencies in the five stories are numerous and glaring, but the narrative surges on with such speed and force; such manly and romantic beauty pervades it; and the general purpose of Lermontov breathes such fierce integrity, that the reader does not stop to wonder why the mermaid in 'Taman' assumed that Pechorin could not swim, or why the Captain of Dragoons thought that Pechorin's seconds would not want to supervise the loading of the pistols. The plight of Pechorin, who is forced, after all, to face Grushnitsky's pistol, would be rather ridiculous, had we not understood that our hero relied not on chance but on fate. This is made quite clear in the last and best story, 'The Fatalist', where the crucial passage also turns on a pistol being or not being loaded, and where a kind of duel by proxy is fought between Pechorin and Vulich, with Fate, instead of the smirking dragoon, supervising the lethal arrangements.

A special feature of the structure of our book is the monstrous but perfectly organic part that eavesdropping plays in it. Now Eavesdropping is only one form of a more general device which can be classified under the heading of Coincidence, to which belongs, for instance, the Coincidental Meeting – another variety. It is pretty clear that when a novelist desires to combine the traditional tale of romantic adventure (amorous intrigue, jealousy, revenge, etc.) with a narrative in the first person, and has no desire to invent new techniques, he is somewhat limited in the choice of devices.

The eighteenth-century epistolary form of novel (with the heroine writing to her girl friend, and the hero writing to his old schoolmate, followed by at least ten other combinations) was so stale by Lermontov's time that he could hardly have used it; and since, on the other hand, our author was more eager to have his story move than to vary, elaborate and conceal the methods of its propulsion, he employed the convenient device of having his Maksim Maksimych and Pechorin overhear, spy upon, and witness any such scene as was needed for the elucidation or the promotion of the plot. Indeed, the author's use of this device is so consistent throughout the book that it ceases to strike the reader as a marvellous vagary of chance and becomes, as it were, the barely noticeable routine of fate.

In 'Bela', there are three cases of eavesdropping: from behind a fence, Narrator Two overhears a boy trying to coax a robber into selling him a horse; and later on, the same Narrator overhears, first from under a window, and then from behind a door, two crucial conversations between Pechorin and Bela.

In 'Taman', from behind a jutting rock, Narrator Three overhears a conversation between a girl and a blind lad, which informs everybody concerned, including the reader, of the smuggling business; and the same eavesdropper, from another point of vantage, a cliff above the shore, overhears the final conversation between the smugglers.

In 'Princess Mary', Narrator Three eavesdrops as many as eight times, in consequence of which he is always in the know. From behind the corner of a covered walk, he sees Mary retrieving the mug dropped by disabled Grushnitsky; from behind a tall shrub, he overhears a sentimental dialogue between the two; from behind a stout lady, he overhears the talk that leads to an attempt, on the part of the dragoons, to have Mary insulted by a pre-Dostoevskian drunk; from an unspecified distance, he stealthily watches Mary yawning at Grushnitsky's jokes; from the midst of a ballroom crowd, he catches her ironic retorts to Grushnitsky's romantic entreaties; from outside 'an improperly closed shutter', he sees and hears the dragoon plotting with Grushnitsky to fake a duel with him, Pechorin; through a window curtain which is 'not completely drawn', he observes Mary pensively sitting on her bed; in a restaurant, from behind a door that leads to the corner room, where Grushnitsky and his friends are assembled, Pechorin hears himself accused of visiting Mary at night; and finally, and most conveniently, Dr Werner, Pechorin's second, overhears a conversation between the dragoon and Grushnitsky, which leads Werner and Pechorin to conclude that only one pistol will be loaded. This accumulation of knowledge on the part of the hero causes the reader to await, with frantic interest, the inevitable scene when Pechorin will crush Grushnitsky with the disclosure of this knowledge.

2

This is the first English translation of Lermontov's novel. The book has been paraphrased into English several times,[1] but never translated before. The experienced hack may find it quite easy to turn Lermontov's Russian into slick English clichés by means of judicious omission, amplification, and levigation; and he will tone down everything that might seem unfamiliar to the meek and imbecile reader visualized by his publisher. But the honest translator is faced with a different task.

In the first place, we must dismiss, once and for all the conventional notion that a translation 'should read smoothly', and 'should not sound like a translation' (to quote the would-be compliments, addressed to vague versions, by genteel reviewers who never have and never will read the original texts). In point of fact, any translation that does *not* sound like a translation is bound to be inexact upon inspection; while, on the other hand, the only virtue of a good translation is faithfulness and completeness. Whether it reads smoothly or not depends on the model, not on the mimic.

In attempting to translate Lermontov, I have gladly sacrificed to the requirements of exactness a number of important things – good taste, neat diction, and even grammar (when some characteristic solecism occurs in the Russian text). The English reader should be aware that Lermontov's prose style in Russian is inelegant; it is dry and drab; it is the tool of an energetic, incredibly gifted, bitterly honest, but definitely inexperienced young man. His Russian is, at times, almost as crude as Stendhal's French; his similes and metaphors are utterly commonplace; his hackneyed epithets are only redeemed by occasionally being incorrectly used. Repetition of words in descriptive sentences irritates the purist. And all this, the translator should faithfully render, no matter how much he may be tempted to fill out the lapse and delete the redundancy.

When Lermontov started to write, Russian prose had already evolved that predilection for certain terms that became typical of the Russian novel. Every translator becomes aware, in the course of his task, that, apart from idiomatic locutions, the 'From' language has a certain number of constantly iterated words which, though readily translatable, occur in the 'Into' language far less frequently and less colloquially. Through long use, these words have become mere pegs or signs, the meeting places of mental associations, the reunions of related notions. They are tokens of sense, rather than particularizations of sense. Of the hundred or so peg words familiar to any student of Russian literature, the following may be listed as being especial favourites with Lermontov:

zadúmat'sya	To become pensive; to lapse into thought; to be lost in thought.
podoití	To approach; to go up to.
prinyát' vid	To assume an air (serious, gay, etc.). Fr. *prendre un air*.
molchát'	To be silent. Fr. *se taire*.
mel'kát'	To flick; to flicker; to dart; to be glimpsed.
neiz'yasnímyi	Ineffable (a Gallicism).
gíbkii	Supple; flexible. Too often said of human bodies.
mráchnyi	Gloomy.
prístal'no	Intently; fixedly, steadily; steadfastly (said of looking, gazing, peering, etc.).
nevól'no	Involuntarily. Fr. *malgré soi*.
on nevól'no zadúmalsya	He could not help growing thoughtful.
vdrug	Suddenly.
uzhé	Already; by now.

It is the translator's duty to have, as far as possible, these words reoccur in English as often, and as irritatingly, as they do in the Russian text; I say, as far as possible, because in some cases the word has two or more shades of meaning depending on the context. 'A slight pause', or 'a moment of silence', for instance, may render the recurrent *minuta molchan'ya* better than 'a minute of silence' would.

Another thing that has to be kept in mind is that in one language great care is taken by novelists to tabulate certain facial expressions, gestures, or motions that writers in another language will take for granted and mention seldom, or not at all. The nineteenth-century Russian writer's indifference to exact shades of visual colour leads to an acceptance of rather droll epithets condoned by literary usage (a surprising thing in the case of Lermontov, who was not only a painter in the literal sense, but saw colours and was able to name them); thus in the course of *A Hero* the faces of various people turn purple, red, rosy, orange, yellow, green and blue.[2] A romantic epithet of Gallic origin that occurs four times in the course of the novel is *tusklaya blednost'*, *paleur mate*, dull (or lustreless) pallor. In 'Taman', the delinquent girl's face is covered with 'a dull pallor, betraying inner agitation'. In 'Princess Mary', this phenomenon occurs three times: a dull pallor is spread over Mary's face when she accuses Pechorin of disrespect; a dull pallor is spread over Pechorin's face revealing 'the traces of painful insomnia'; and just before the duel, a dull pallor is spread over Grushnitsky's cheeks as his conscience struggles with his pride.

Besides such code sentences as 'her lips grew pale', 'he flushed', 'her hand trembled slightly', and so forth, emotions are signalled by certain abrupt and violent gestures. In 'Bela', Pechorin hits the table with his fist to punctuate with a bang his words 'she won't belong to anybody but me'. Two pages further, it is his forehead he strikes with his fist (a gesture deemed Oriental by some commentators) upon realizing he has bungled the seduction and driven Bela to tears. In his turn, Grushnitsky strikes the table with his fist when convinced by Pechorin's remarks that Mary is merely a flirt. And the Captain of Dragoons does the same when demanding attention. There is also a great deal of the 'seizing his arm', 'taking him by the arm', and 'pulling by the sleeve' business throughout the novel.

9

'Stamping on the ground' is another emotional signal much in favour with Lermontov, and, in Russian literature of the time, this was new. Maksim Maksimych, in 'Bela', stamps his foot in self-accusation. Grushnitsky, in 'Princess Mary', stamps his in petulance; and the Captain of Dragoons stamps his in disgust.

3

It is unnecessary to discuss here Pechorin's character. The good reader will easily understand it by studying the book; but so much nonsense has been written about Pechorin, by those who adopt a sociological approach to literature, that a few warning words must be said.

We should not take, as seriously as most Russian commentators, Lermontov's statement in his Introduction (a stylized bit of make-believe in its own right) that Pechorin's portrait is 'composed of all the vices of our generation'. Actually, the bored and bizarre hero is a product of several generations, some of them non-Russian; he is the fictional descendant of a number of fictional self-analysts, beginning with Saint-Preux (the lover of Julie d'Etange in Rousseau's *Julie ou la nouvelle Héloïse*, 1761) and Werther (the admirer of Charlotte S— in Goethe's *Die Leiden des jungen Werthers*, 1774, known to Russians mainly in French versions such as that by Sévelinges, 1804), going through Chateaubriand's *René* (1802), Constant's *Adolphe* (1815), and the heroes of Byron's long poems (especially *The Giaour*, 1813, and *The Corsair*, 1814, known to Russians in Pichot's French prose versions, from 1820 on), and ending with Pushkin's *Eugene Onegin* (1825–32) and with various more ephemeral products of the French novelists of the first half of the century (Nodier, Balzac, etc.). Pechorin's association with a given time and a given place tends to lend a new flavour to the transplanted fruit, but it is doubtful whether much is added to an appreciation of this flavour by generalizing about the exacerbation of thought produced in independent minds by the tyranny of Nicholas I's reign (1825–56).

The point to be marked in a study of *A Hero of Our Time* is that, though of tremendous and at times somewhat morbid interest to the sociologist, the 'time' is of less interest to the student of literature than the 'hero'. In the latter, young Lermontov managed to create a fictional person whose romantic dash to cynicism, tiger-like suppleness and eagle eye, hot blood and cool head, tenderness and taciturnity, elegance and brutality, delicacy of perception and harsh passion to dominate, ruthlessness and awareness of it, are of lasting appeal to readers of all countries and centuries – especially to young readers; for it would seem that the veneration elderly critics have for *A Hero* is rather a glorified recollection of youthful readings in the summer twilight, and of ardent self-identification, than the direct result of a mature consciousness of art.

Of the other characters in the book there is, likewise, little to say. The most endearing one is obviously the old Captain Maksim Maksimych, stolid, gruff, naïvely poetical, matter-of-fact, simple-hearted, and completely neurotic. His hysterical behaviour at the abortive meeting with his old friend Pechorin is one of the passages most dear to human interest readers. Of the several villains in the book, Kazbich and his florid speech (as rendered by Maksim Maksimych) are an obvious product of literary orientalia, while the American reader may be excused for substituting the Indians of Fenimore Cooper for Lermontov's Circassians. In the worst story of the book, 'Taman' (deemed by some Russian critics the greatest, for reasons incomprehensible to me), Yanko is saved from utter banality when we notice that the connection between him and the blind lad is a pleasing echo of the scene between hero and hero-worshipper in 'Maksim Maksimych'.

Another kind of interplay occurs in 'Princess Mary'. If Pechorin is a romantic shadow of Lermontov, Grushnitsky, as Russian critics have already noted, is a grotesque shadow of Pechorin, and the lowest level of imitation is supplied by Pechorin's valet. Grushnitsky's evil genius, the Captain of Dragoons, is little more than a stock character of comedy, and the continuous references to the hugger-mugger he indulges in are rather painful. No less painful is the skipping and singing of the wild girl in 'Taman'. Lermontov was singularly inept in his descriptions of women. Mary is the generalized young thing of novelettes, with no attempt at individualization except perhaps her 'velvety' eyes, which however are forgotten in the course of the story. Vera is a mere phantom, with a phantom birthmark on her cheek; Bela, an Oriental beauty on the lid of a box of Turkish delight.

What, then, makes the everlasting charm of this book? Why is it so interesting to read and reread? Certainly not for its style – although, curiously enough, Russian schoolteachers used to see in it the perfection of Russian prose. This is a ridiculous opinion, voiced (according to a memoirist) by Chekhov, and can only be held if and when a moral quality or a social virtue is confused with literary art, or when an ascetic critic regards the rich and ornate with such suspicion that, in contrast, the awkward and frequently commonplace style of Lermontov seems delightfully chaste and simple. But genuine art is neither chaste nor simple, and it is sufficient to glance at the prodigiously elaborate and magically artistic style of Tolstoy (who, by some, is considered to be a literary descendant of Lermontov) to realize the depressing flaws of Lermontov's prose.

But if we regard him as a storyteller, and if we remember that Russian prose was still in her teens, and the man still in his middle twenties when he wrote, then we do marvel indeed at the superb energy of the tale and at the remarkable rhythm into which the paragraphs, rather than the sentences, fall. It is the agglomeration of otherwise insignificant words that come to life. When we start to break the sentence or the verse line into its quantitative elements the banalities we perceive are often shocking, the shortcomings not seldom comic; but, in the long run, it is the compound effect that counts, and this final effect can be traced down in Lermontov to the beautiful timing of all the parts and particles of the novel. Its author was careful to dissociate himself from his hero; but, for the emotional type of reader, much of the novel's poignancy and fascination resides in the fact that Lermontov's own tragic fate is somehow superimposed upon that of Pechorin, just as the Dagestan dream acquires an additional strain of pathos when the reader realizes that the poet's dream came true.

A HERO OF OUR TIME

THE AUTHOR'S INTRODUCTION

IN every book the preface is the first and also the last thing. It serves either to explain the purpose of the work or to justify it and answer criticism. But the readers are generally not concerned with moral purposes or with attacks in reviews, and in result, they do not read prefaces. It is a pity that this should be so, particularly in our country. Our public is still so young and naïve that it fails to understand a fable unless it finds a lesson at its end. It misses a humorous point and does not feel irony; it simply is badly brought up. It has not yet learned that in decent company as in a decent book open abuse cannot occur; that modern education has evolved a much sharper weapon – which, though almost invisible, is nevertheless lethal and which, under the guise of flattery, deals an inescapable and accurate blow. Our public resembles a provincial who, upon overhearing the conversation of two diplomats belonging to two warring Courts, is convinced that each envoy is betraying his government in the interests of a most tender mutual friendship.

The present book has only recently suffered from the unfortunate faith that certain readers and even certain reviewers have in the literal meaning of words. Some were dreadfully offended, quite in earnest, that such an immoral person as the Hero of Our Time should be set as a model to them; others very subtly remarked that the author had drawn his own portrait and the portraits of his acquaintances . . . What an old and paltry jest! But apparently Russia is created in such a way that everything in it changes for the better, except this sort of nonsense. With us the most fantastic of all fairy tales would hardly escape the reproach of being meant as some personal insult.

A Hero of Our Time, gentlemen, is indeed a portrait, but not of a single individual; it is a portrait composed of

15

all the vices of our generation in the fullness of their development. You will tell me again that a man cannot be as bad as all that; and I shall tell you that since you have believed in the possibility of so many tragic and romantic villains having existed, why can you not believe in the reality of Pechorin? If you have admired fictions far more frightful and hideous, why does this character, even as fiction, find no quarter with you? Is it not, perchance, because there is more truth in this character than you would desire there to be?

You will say that morality gains nothing from this. I beg your pardon. People have been fed enough sweetmeats; it has given them indigestion: they need some bitter medicine, some caustic truths. However, do not think after this that the author of this book ever had the proud dream of becoming a reformer of mankind's vices. The Lord preserve him from such benightedness! He merely found it amusing to draw modern man such as he understood him, such as he met him – too often, unfortunately, for him and you. Suffice it that the disease has been pointed out; goodness knows how to cure it.

BELA

I WAS travelling post from Tiflis.[4] All the luggage in my small springless carriage[5] consisted of one valise stuffed half-full of notes on my travels in Georgia.[6] The greater part of them, luckily for you, has been lost; while the valise with its other contents, luckily for me, remains safe.

The sun had already begun to hide behind the snowy range when I drove into the Koishaur Valley. My Ossetian driver urged the horses on unceasingly, in order that we might get to the top of Mount Koishaur before nightfall, and sang songs at the top of his voice. What a delightful place, that valley! On all sides rise inaccessible mountains, reddish cliffs, hung over with great ivy and crowned with clumps of plane trees; tawny precipices streaked with washes, and, far above, the golden fringe of the snows; below, Aragva River, infolding another, nameless, river which noisily bursts forth from a black gorge full of gloom, stretches out in a silver thread and glistens like the scaling of a snake.

Having arrived at the foot of Mount Koishaur, we stopped near a native inn. Here a score or so of Georgians and mountain tribesmen were crowding noisily about; close by, a camel caravan had encamped for the night. I had to hire oxen to drag my carriage up that confounded mountain, because it was already autumn and there was ice on the roads; and the ascent was nearly one mile and a half long.

There was nothing to do: I hired six oxen and several Ossetians. One of them heaved my valise up on his shoulders, the others began to help the oxen along, almost exclusively by means of cries.

Behind my carriage, a team of four oxen was pulling another carriage with perfect ease, despite its being loaded up to the top. This circumstance surprised me. Behind it

17

walked its owner puffing at a small Kabardan pipe mounted with silver. He wore an officer's surtout, without epaulets, and a Circassian shaggy cap. He seemed about fifty years old; his tanned complexion indicated that his face had long been acquainted with the Trans-Caucasian sun, and his prematurely greyed moustache did not harmonize with his firm gait and his vigorous appearance. I walked over to him and made a bow. He silently acknowledged my bow and exhaled a huge puff of tobacco smoke.

'We seem to be fellow-travellers?'

In silence, he bowed again.

'I presume you are going to Stavropol?'

'Yes, sir, that's right. With government property.'

'Tell me, please, why is it that four oxen draw your heavy carriage with ease while my empty one can barely be moved by means of six brutes with the help of these Ossetians?'

He smiled slyly and glanced significantly at me.

'You've probably not been long in the Caucasus?'

'About a year,' I replied.

He smiled a second time.

'Well – why?'

'It's this way, sir: these Asiatics are terrible rascals! You think they are trying to help with that shouting? But the devil knows what it is they are shouting. The oxen – they understand; you may hitch a score of them but as soon as those drivers start to shout in their own way, the oxen will not budge ... Dreadful rogues! But what can you do to them? They love to squeeze money out of travellers ... They have been spoiled, the robbers! You'll see, they'll get you to tip them, too. I know them well, they can't take me in!'

'And have you been stationed here long?'

'I was already serving here in General Aleksei Ermolov's[7] time,' he replied with a certain loftiness. 'When he took over the Border Command, I was a second lieutenant,' he added, 'and, under him, was twice promoted for action against the mountain tribes.'

'And now you are – ?'

'Now I am attached to the third battalion of the line. And you, may I ask?'

I told him.

With this, the conversation ended, and we continued to walk side by side in silence. At the summit of the mountain, we found snow. The sun had set, and night followed day without any interval, as is usual in the south; however, owing to the sheen of the snows, we could easily make out the road, which still went uphill, although no longer so steeply. I ordered my valise to be put into the carriage, the oxen to be replaced by horses, and turned back for a last glance down at the valley; but a dense mist that had surged in waves from the gorges completely covered it, and not a single sound reached our hearing from there. The Ossetians clustered around me noisily, and clamoured for tips, but the junior captain[8] berated them so sternly that they at once dispersed.

'What a crew!' he said: 'They can't even say "bread" in Russian, but they've managed to learn "officer, give me a tip." In my opinion, even the Tartars are better: at least, they don't drink.'

We were still about a mile from the station. All was quiet around, so quiet that you could follow a mosquito's flight by its hum. On our left, a deep gorge yawned black; beyond it and in front of us the dark-blue mountain tops, furrowed with wrinkles, covered with layers of snow, were silhouetted against the pale horizon, which still retained the last reflection of the sunset. Stars were beginning to twinkle in the dark sky, and, strange to say, they seemed to me to be much higher than at home, in the north. On either side of the road, bare, black rocks jutted out; here and there, from beneath the snow there emerged shrubs; but not a single dry leaf stirred, and it was a joy to hear, amid the dead sleep of nature, the snorting of the three tired posters and the irregular jangling of the Russian shaft bell.

'It will be fine tomorrow!' I said. The junior captain did not answer a word, and pointed out to me with his finger a high mountain rising directly in front of us.

'What is it?' I asked.
'Mount Gud.'[9]
'Well, what about it?'
'Look how it smokes.'

And indeed, Mount Gud was smoking; along its flanks there crept tight wisps of clouds, while on its summit there lay a black cloud, so black that it looked like a blot on the dark sky.

We could already distinguish the post station, as well as the roofs of the Caucasian huts surrounding it; and cheery lights flickered before us, when there came a gust of damp cold wind, the gorge reverberated, and a fine rain began to fall. I barely had time to throw my felt cloak over my shoulders, when it began to snow heavily. I looked with reverence at the junior captain.

'We'll have to stop here for the night,' he said with vexation. 'In a blizzard like this you can't drive over the mountains. Tell me,' he asked the coachman, 'have there been any avalanches on *Krestovaya Gora* [Mountain of the Cross]?'

'There haven't, sir,' answered the Ossetian driver, 'but there's lots and lots waiting to come down.'

In the absence of a room for travellers at the post station, we were assigned night quarters in a smoky native hut. I invited my companion to have a glass of tea with me since I travelled with a cast iron tea kettle – my sole comfort on my journeys through the Caucasus.

The hut was built with one wall against a cliff; three slippery wet steps led to its door. I groped my way in and ran smack into a cow (with these people a cattle shed replaces a vestibule). I did not know which way to turn: here, sheep were bleating, there, a dog was growling. Fortunately, a dim light gleamed on one side and helped me to another opening in the guise of a doorway. There, a rather entertaining picture was disclosed. The spacious hut whose roof rested on two smoke-blackened posts, was full of people. In the centre, there crackled a small fire built on the ground, and the smoke, forced back by the wind from the hole in the roof, spread all around in such a thick pall that, for a long time, I could not see around me: by the fire sat two old women, a multitude of children, and one lean Georgian, all of them in rags. There was nothing we could do, except settle down by the fire and light our pipes; and soon the tea kettle began to emit a friendly simmer.

'What wretched people,' I said to the junior captain, indicating our grimy hosts, who were silently gazing at us in a sort of stupor.

'An extremely foolish people,' he replied. 'Can you imagine, they don't know how to do anything and are incapable of any education! Our Kabardans or our Chechens, though they may be robbers and paupers, are at least reckless daredevils; but these people aren't even interested in weapons: you won't see a decent dagger on a single one of them. These are real Ossetians for you!'

'And have you been long in the Chechen region?'

'Yes, I was stationed there for about ten years with my company in a fort near *Kamenny Brod* [Stone Ford].[10] Know the place?'

'I've heard of it.'

'Well, my good sir, we did get tired of those cut-throats. Nowadays, thank goodness, things have quieted down, but the way it used to be – you just walked a hundred paces beyond the rampart, and there was bound to be some shaggy devil sitting and watching you: one second off guard, and it would happen: either a lariat would be around your neck or there would be a bullet in the back of your head. But what brave fellows! . . .'

'You've surely had a lot of adventures,' I said, prompted by curiosity.

'How could it be otherwise? Of course I had . . .'

At this point, he began to pull at the left end of his moustache, hung his head, and was lost in thought. I was dying to get some kind of yarn out of him – a desire peculiar to all people who travel and take notes. Meanwhile, tea was ready; I dug out of my valise two small travelling glasses, filled them and set one of them in front of him. He took a gulp and said, as though to himself: 'Yes, indeed!' This exclamation gave me great hopes. I knew that veterans of Caucasian wars like to have a talk and tell a tale; they so seldom have a chance to do so: the man might be stationed for some five years in a remote place with his company, and, during the whole five years, nobody would say 'Hello' to him (because the sergeant says 'Good morning, sir'). And there would be quite a number of things to chat about: around you there is a wild people, provoking one's curiosity, there is danger every day, extraordinary incidents happen; and no wonder there is occasion to regret that so few of us take notes.

'Would you not like to add some rum?' I said to my interlocutor. 'I have white rum from Tiflis; it is a cold night.'

'No, thanks a lot, but I do not drink.'

'How come?'

'Well, it's like this. I made a vow to myself. When I was still a second lieutenant we all got a little high one time, and during the night there was an alarm; so we came out lit up in front of the soldiers, and did we get it from Aleksei Petrovich when he found out: goodness, how furious he was! He very nearly had us court-martialled. And, indeed, here, you go a whole year without seeing a soul, and if vodka is then added, you are a lost man!'

When I heard that, I almost lost hope!

'Take the Circassians, for instance,' he went on. 'As soon as they get drunk on buza,[11] at a wedding, or at a funeral, the knife-play begins. I barely escaped once with my life, and at the house of a neutral prince[12] at that.'

'How did that happen?'

'Well . . .' (He filled his pipe, inhaled the smoke, and began his tale.)[13] 'Well, you see, I was stationed then, with my company, in a fort beyond the Terek – it will soon be five years since that happened. One autumn day, a convoy came with supplies; with it there arrived an officer, a young fellow of twenty-five or so. He reported to me in full uniform and announced that he had orders to remain at my fort. He was so thin, with such fair skin, the uniform he wore was so new, that I guessed at once that he had been but a short time in the Caucasus with our forces.

'You've probably been transferred here from Russia?'[14] I asked him. 'That's right, sir,' he answered. I clasped his hand and said: 'Delighted, delighted. You will find it a little dull – but we'll get along on a friendly footing, the two of us. So please call me simply Maksim Maksimych, and please – there is no need for a full uniform. A cap will do whenever you come to see me.' Quarters were given him, and he took up residence in the fort.

'And what was his name?' I asked Maksim Maksimych.

'He was named . . . Grigory Aleksandrovich Pechorin. A charming fellow he was, I can assure you, but a little odd. He might spend, for instance, the whole day hunting in the rain, in the cold; everybody would get chilled through and exhausted, but not he; and some other time he'd be sitting in his room, and just a gust of wind would come, and there he would be, insisting that he had caught cold; or if the shutter banged, he'd start and grow pale; yet I had seen him take on a wild boar all by himself; there were times when you could not get a word out of him for hours, but on the other hand when he happened to start telling stories you'd split your sides with laughter . . . Yes, sir, there were many odd things about him; must have been a rich fellow, too: how many different expensive trinkets he had!'

'Did he stay long with you?' I asked again.

'About a year. But a memorable year it was for me, indeed; he caused me no end of trouble, though this, certainly, is not what I remember him by. You know, there really exist certain people to whom it is assigned, at their birth, to have all sorts of extraordinary things happen to them.'

'Extraordinary things?' I exclaimed with an air of curiosity, while I poured him some more tea.

'Well, let me tell you. About four miles from the fort, there lived a neutral prince. His young son, a boy of fifteen or so, took to riding over to our place: every day he would come for one thing or another. We had really spoiled him, Pechorin[15] and I. And what a daredevil he was, game for anything – picking up a cap at full gallop or shooting a rifle. There was one thing bad about him: he had an awful weakness for money. Once, in jest, Pechorin promised him a gold piece if he would steal for him the best goat from his father's herd. And what do you think? The very next night, there he came, dragging the goat by the horns. And sometimes, we would start teasing him, and then his eyes would get all bloodshot, and his hand would at once fly to his dagger. 'Hey, Azamat, you won't keep your head long on your shoulders,' I would say to him, '*yaman* [bad] it will be with your head!'

'One day the old prince himself came to invite us to a wedding: he was marrying off his eldest daughter, and we were *kunaks* [16] with him; there was, therefore, no way to refuse, even though he was a Tatar. So we went. At his village, a lot of dogs met us with loud barking. The women hid at the sight of us. Those whose faces we were able to make out were far from being beauties. 'I had a far better opinion of Circassian women,' said Pechorin to me. 'Just wait!' I replied with a smile. I had something up my sleeve.

'A lot of people had already gathered at the prince's house. With those Asiatics,[17] you know, it is the custom to invite one and all to their weddings. We were received with all possible honours and shown into the *kunak* room. However, I did not forget to note where they had put our horses – just in case, you know.'

'How do they celebrate a wedding?' I asked the junior captain.

'Oh, the usual way. At first, the mullah reads them something out of the Koran; then, presents are given to the young couple and all their relatives; they eat, they drink buza; then the trick-riding begins, and there is always some ragamuffin, greasy with dirt, on a wretched lame pony, who fools and clowns, much to the amusement of the good company; and then after dark, what we would call a ball begins in the *kunak* room. Some miserable little old man twangs his three-stringed . . . I forget the local word for it . . .[18] anyway, something like our balalaika. The girls and the young men form two rows opposite each other, clap their hands and sing. Then one girl and one man step out into the middle and begin chanting verses to each other, anything they happen to think of, and the others pick up the refrain in chorus. Pechorin and I were sitting in the place of honour, and up to him came our host's young daughter, a girl of about sixteen, and sang to him . . . how shall I say? . . . a kind of compliment.'

'And what was it she sang to him, do you remember?'

'Yes, I believe it was like this: 'Svelte', it went, 'are our young warriors, and their caftans are trimmed with silver, but the young Russian officer is svelter than they, and his coat is braided with gold. He stands like a poplar among them, but it is not fated that he should grow and blossom in our garden.' Pechorin stood up, bowed to her, touched his hand to his forehead and then to his heart, and asked me to answer her. I know their language well, and translated his answer.

'When she had moved away from us, I whispered to Pechorin: "Well, what do you think of her?" '

' "Charming," he answered. "What is her name?" "Her name is Bela," I replied.

'And indeed, she was beautiful: tall, slender, with black eyes which resembled those of a mountain gazelle and practically peered into your soul. Lost in thought, Pechorin did not take his eyes off her, and quite often she would steal a glance at him from under her brows. But Pechorin was not the only one to admire the pretty young princess: from a corner of the room, there looked at her another pair of eyes, immobile and fiery. I looked closer, and recognized my old acquaintance, Kazbich. He was, do you know, neither exactly neutral, nor exactly hostile. He was suspected of many things, though he had never been involved in any mischief. At times, he would bring sheep[19] to our fort and sell them cheap, but he would never haggle: whatever his asking price was, you had to pay it – you could cut his throat and still he would not come down. It was rumoured of him that he liked to prowl on the Russian side of the Kuban River[20] with *abreks*.[21] And to tell the truth, his countenance was that of a regular robber: he was small, wiry, broad-shouldered . . . And how nimble he was;

it was the nimbleness of a devil! His *beshmet*[22] was always in tatters, all patched up, but his weapons were chased with silver. And his horse was the talk of the whole Kabardan region – indeed, you could not think of anything more handsome than that horse. No wonder, every horseman envied him; and there had been more than one attempt to steal it, but none succeeded. It is as if I were looking at that horse now: pitch black, legs like taut strings, and eyes no less beautiful than Bela's; and what strength! – you could ride him thirty miles; and how well he was trained – ran after his master like a dog; even knew his voice! As a matter of fact, Kazbich would never tie him. Just the right horse for a bandit!

'That night Kazbich was gloomier than ever, and I noticed that under his *beshmet* he wore a coat of mail. "It is not without reason that he has that coat of mail on," I reflected. "He must be planning something."[23]

'It got stuffy indoors, and I went outside to get a breath of fresh air. Night was already descending upon the mountains, and a mist had begun to float in the gorges. It occurred to me to look into the shelter where our horses stood, in order to check if they had any feed, and then again it never hurts to be careful; the more so as my horse was a fine one, and many a Kabardan had ogled it tenderly as he muttered to himself: "yakshi tkhe, chek yakshi [good horse, very good]!"

'As I was picking my way along the fence, I suddenly heard voices; one voice I recognized immediately: it belonged to that scamp, Azamat, the son of our host; the other spoke more seldom and more softly. "What can they be conferring about?" I thought. "Might it be about my pony?" So I squatted by the fence and began listening, trying not to miss a single word. At times the sounds of the songs and the clamour of voices, carrying from the house, would drown the conversation that interested me.

' "That's a fine horse you have," Azamat was saying. "If I were master in the house and had a herd of three hundred mares, I'd give half of them for your courser, Kazbich!"

' "Aha – Kazbich," I said to myself, and recalled the coat of mail.

' "Yes," answered Kazbich after a pause. "In the whole of Kabarda you won't find one like it. One time – this happened beyond the Terek – I rode with the *abreks* to seize Russian horse herds; we had bad luck, and scattered, each his own way. Four Cossacks were tearing after me; already I could hear the cries of the Giaours behind me, and in front of me, there was a dense forest. I leaned forward in the saddle, entrusted myself to Allah, and for the first time in my life insulted my horse with a blow of the lash. Like a bird he dived among the branches; sharp thorns tore my clothes, dry elm twigs struck my face. My horse jumped over tree stumps, tore the brush apart with his chest. It would have been better for me to abandon him at the forest edge and disappear in the woods on foot, but I could not bear to part from him – and the prophet rewarded me. Several bullets whined above my head; I could already hear the dismounted Cossacks running in pursuit . . . Suddenly, I saw a deep ravine before me; my courser hesitated, and then jumped. His hind hooves slipped back from the far edge, and he hung by his front legs. I abandoned the reins and tumbled into the ravine; this saved my steed and he scrambled up. The Cossacks saw all this, but not one of them went down to look for me: they must have thought that I had killed myself, and I heard them rush off to capture my horse. My heart bled; I began crawling through the thick grass along the ravine, then took a look: the forest had come to an end; several Cossacks rode out of it into a clearing, and there came my Karagyoz[24] galloping right upon them; they all took off after him, yelling; for a long, long time[25] they pursued him, and one, in particular, very nearly got a lasso over his head a couple of times; I trembled, lowered my eyes, and began to pray. A few seconds later, I raised them again, and saw my Karagyoz flying with streaming tail, as free as the wind, and the Giaours strung out far behind him in the steppe on their worn-out horses. By Allah! It is the truth, the truest truth. I stayed in my ravine late into the night.

Suddenly – imagine, Azamat! – in the dark I heard a horse running back and forth, along the lip of the ravine, snorting, neighing, and beating the ground with his hooves; I recognized the voice of my Karagyoz: it was he, my comrade! . . . Since then we have never parted.'

'And I could hear Kazbich patting the smooth neck of his steed and calling him various pet names.

' "If I had a herd of a *thousand* mares," said Azamat, "I'd give them all to you in exchange for your Karagyoz."

' "*Yok* [no], I'm not interested," Kazbich answered with indifference.

' "Listen, Kazbich," said Azamat coaxingly. "You're a good man, you're a brave warrior. Now, my father is afraid of the Russians and won't let me join the mountain bands; give me your horse, and I'll do anything you want, I'll steal for you my father's best rifle or sword, anything you might desire – and his sword is a real *Gurda* one; just apply its edge to your hand, and it will bite into the flesh of its own accord; even a coat of mail like yours won't help."

'Kazbich was silent.

' "The first time I saw your horse," Azamat went on, "when he pranced under you, and jumped, dilating his nostrils, and flint sparks sprayed from under his hooves, something strange happened inside my soul, and since then everything became dull to me: I looked at my father's best coursers with contempt, I was ashamed to be seen on them, and heartache possessed me; and, with aching heart, I would spend whole days sitting on the top of a cliff, and every moment there would appear to me, in thought, that black steed of yours, with his graceful gait, and his smooth spine as straight as an arrow; his lively eyes looked into my eyes, as though he wanted to utter words. I'll die, Kazbich, if you don't sell him to me!" said Azamat in a trembling voice.

'I thought I heard him start crying: and you must know that Azamat was a most stubborn boy, and there was no way you could knock a tear out of him, even when he was younger.

'In reply to his tears there sounded something like laughter.

' "Listen," said Azamat, in a firm voice. "You will see I'm ready to dare anything. Do you want me to steal my sister for you? How she can dance! How she can sing! And the gold embroidery she does is a wonder! The Turkish padishah himself never had such a wife . . . Do you want me to do it? Wait for me tomorrow night, over there, in the gorge where the torrent runs; I'll walk by with her, on the way to the next village – and she is yours. Don't tell me that Bela is not worth your courser."

'Kazbich was silent for a long, long time; finally, instead of an answer, he intoned, in a low voice, an ancient song:[26]

> "We have many beautiful girls in our villages,
> Stars are ablaze in the dark of their eyes
> Sweet is to love them – an enviable lot;
> Bold freedom, however, is merrier still.
> Gold can purchase you a foursome of wives,
> But a spirited steed is a priceless possession:
> He will not be outstripped by the wind in the steppes,
> He will never betray, he will never deceive."

'In vain did Azamat entreat him to agree, in vain did he weep, and fawn on him, and make oaths. At last, Kazbich interrupted him impatiently:

' "Go away, mad boy! *You* ride my steed? Before you've ridden three steps, he'll throw you and you'll crack the back of your head on the stones."

' "Throw me?" screamed Azamat in a rage, and the iron of a child's dagger rang against chain-armour. A strong arm pushed him away, and he hit the fence so hard that it shook. "Now we shall have some sport!" I thought, dashed into the stable, bridled our horses and led them out into the back yard. Two minutes later, there was a terrible uproar indoors. Here's what had happened: Azamat had burst in, his *beshmet* torn, saying that Kazbich had wanted to cut his throat. Everybody dashed out, grabbed their rifles – and the sport began! There was shouting, noise, rifle shots; but Kazbich was already on his horse and was wheeling in the midst of the crowd along the street, like a devil, swinging his sword in defence. "It is no fun to pay with a hangover for the feast of others," said I to Pechorin, catching him by the arm. "Hadn't we better clear out at once?"

' "Oh, wait a minute, let's see the end."

' "You may be sure that the end will be bad: it is always so with these Asiatics: they get tight on buza, and the knife-play starts!" We mounted and galloped off home.'

'And what about Kazbich?' I asked the junior captain eagerly.

'What would you expect to happen to that sort of fellow?' he answered, as he finished his glass of tea. 'He gave them the slip, naturally!'

'Unhurt?' I asked.

'Goodness only knows!' These bandits are indestructible. I've had occasion to see them in action, sir; for example, he may be as full of holes as a sieve, and still brandish his sword.'

After a short silence, the junior captain stamped his foot on the ground and continued:

'There's one thing I'll never forgive myself: when we got back to the fort, the devil moved me to relate to Pechorin all I had overheard while crouching behind that fence; he chuckled – such a sly fellow! – he had thought up something.'

'And what was it? Do tell me, please.'[27]

'Well, there is nothing to be done! Since I have started this story, I'll have to go on with it.

'In about four days, Azamat rode over to our fort. As usual, he visited Pechorin, who always fed him sweetmeats. I was present. The conversation turned to horses, and Pechorin began to praise Kazbich's mount: it was so spirited, so handsome, a regular gazelle – well, to hear him, there was not another like it in the whole world.

'The little Moslem's eyes sparkled, but Pechorin seemed not to notice; I would start speaking of something else, but before you knew, he had switched the talk back to Kazbich's horse., This business would go on every time Azamat came over. About three weeks later, I began to notice that

Azamat was getting pale and pining away, as it happens from love in novels, sir. I marvelled.

'Well, you see, I discovered the whole thing later: Pechorin had driven him to such a point with his teasing that he was close to jumping into the water. So once he said to him: "I can see, Azamat, that you've taken a mighty liking to that horse; yet you've got no more chance of seeing it than your own nape! Well, tell me, what would you give the person who made you a present of it?"

' "Anything he wanted," answered Azamat.

' "In that case I'll obtain it for you – but under one condition . . . Swear that you'll fulfil it. . . ."

' "I swear . . . But you must swear too!"

' "Good! I swear that you will own that steed; but in return you must give me your sister, Bela. Karagyoz will be the *kalym* [bride money]. I hope that you find the bargain profitable."

'Azamat was silent.

' "You're not interested? Well, as you wish! I thought you were a man, but you're still a child; it is too early for you to ride a horse."

'Azamat flushed. "What about my father?" he said.

' "Doesn't he ever go away?"

' "True . . ."

' "Do you consent?"

' "I consent," whispered Azamat, as pale as death. "When is it to be?"

' "The very next time Kazbich comes here; he promised to drive ten rams over; the rest is my business. I count on you, Azamat!"

'And so they clinched the deal – a rotten one, to say the truth! I said so to Pechorin later, but he only answered that a wild Circassian girl should consider herself lucky to have such a nice husband as he, because, according to their way of thinking, he was, after all, a husband, while Kazbich was a bandit who deserved to be punished. Judge for yourself, what could I say against that? But at the time I knew nothing of their plot. Well, one day, Kazbich arrived and asked if we did not need sheep or honey. I told him

31

to bring some next day. "Azamat!" said Pechorin, "Tomorrow, Karagyoz will be in my hands; if Bela is not here tonight, you'll never see that steed . . .'

' "All right!" said Azamat, and galloped off to the village. In the evening, Pechorin armed himself and rode out of the fort. How they managed the business, I do not know; only they both got back at night, and the sentry saw that Azamat had a woman lying across his saddle, her hands and feet tied, and a yashmak wrapped around her head.'

'What about the horses?' I asked the junior captain.

'Presently, presently. Early the next morning, Kazbich arrived, driving ten rams for sale. After tying his horse to the fence,[28] he came to see me; I treated him to some tea, since, robber though he was, he was still a *kunak* of mine.

'We began to chat about this and that . . . All at once, I saw Kazbich give a start, his face changed . . . and he made for the window; but the window, unfortunately, faced the back yard. "What's the matter with you?" I asked.

' "My horse! . . . my horse," he said, trembling all over.

'Sure enough, I heard hoofbeats. "Must be a Cossack riding by."

' "No! *Urus-yaman, yaman* [A bad, bad Russian]!" he roared, and dashed headlong out of the room, like a wild panther. In two bounds, he was in the courtyard; at the fortress gate, the sentry, with his rifle, barred Kazbich's path. He leapt over the rifle and dashed off down the road . . . Dust was whirling in the distance – it was Azamat galloping on the gallant Karagyoz. Kazbich, as he ran, pulled his rifle out of its canvas case and fired. For a moment, he stood motionless, until he was certain that he had missed; then he uttered a shrill scream, struck his rifle against a stone, smashing the weapon to bits, fell on the ground and began to sob like a child . . . Presently people from the fort gathered around him, but he did not notice anyone; they stood around for awhile, exchanged views, and went back: I had the money for the sheep placed next to him; he never touched it, but remained lying on his face, as if he were dead. Would you believe it: he lay like that until late at night, and the whole night through.[29] Then next morning, he came to the fort and asked to be told who the thief was. The sentry, who had seen Azamat untie the horse and gallop away on it, did not deem it necessary to conceal the truth. At the mention of that name, Kazbich's eyes flashed, and he set off for the village where Azamat's father lived.'

'And what did the father do?'

'Ah, that's just it, Kazbich did not find him, he was away somewhere, for six days or so; how else could Azamat have succeeded in carrying off his sister?

'When the father got back, there was neither son nor daughter. The slyboots! He realized perfectly well he would lose his life if he got caught. So he vanished, there and then; must have joined some gang of *abreks* and laid down his reckless head on the Russian side of the Terek[30] or of the Kuban; serves him right, too!

'I must confess that I also got my share of trouble. As soon as I discovered that the Circassian girl was at Pechorin's quarters, I put on my epaulets and my sword, and went to him.

'He lay on his bed in the front room, with one hand under his head; in the other, he held a pipe that had gone out; the door leading to the second room was locked, and the key was not in the keyhole. All this I noticed, at once . . . I began to clear my throat and tap the threshold with my heel, but he pretended not to hear.

' "Ensign!"[31] I said, as sternly as I could, "don't you see that I am here?"

' "Oh, hello, Maksim Maksimych! Want a pipe?" he answered, without getting up.

' "I beg your pardon, I am not Maksim Maksimych; I'm junior captain to you."

' "Makes no difference. How about some tea? If you only knew what a worry torments me!"

' "I know everything," I answered, walking up to the bed.

' "So much the better, I am not in a mood to relate."

' "Ensign, you have committed an offence for which I, too, may be held responsible . . ."

33

' "Oh, come! Where's the harm? We've long shared everything, haven't we?"

' "It's no time for joking. Your sword, if you please!"

' "Mitka,[32] my sword!"

'Mitka brought the sword. Having fulfilled my duty, I sat down beside him on the bed and said: "Look here, Grigory Aleksandrovich, you must admit that it was not a nice thing to do."

' "What wasn't?"

' "Why, your carrying off Bela . . . Ah, that blackguard Azamat! . . . Come on, own up," I said to him.

' "Suppose I like her?"

'Well, what could one say to that? . . . I was nonplussed. However, after a silence, I told him that if the father demanded her back, it would be necessary to return her.

' "Not at all necessary."

' "But if he finds out she is here?"

' "How will he find out?"

'I was again nonplussed. "Look here, Maksim Maksimych," said Pechorin, raising himself, "you're a kind man, aren't you? Now, if we give his daughter back to that savage, he'll either slit her throat or sell her. What's done is done, let's not go out of our way to make things worse than they are; let me keep Bela, and you keep my sword . . ."

' "You can at least show her to me," I said.

' "She's behind that door, but I myself have tried in vain to see her today; keeps sitting in a corner, wrapped up in her veil, neither speaks nor looks at one; shy as a wild gazelle. I've hired the wife of our innkeeper: she can speak Tatar and will take care of Bela and accustom her to the idea that she is mine, for she won't belong to anybody but me," he added, hitting the table with his fist. I agreed to this too . . . What would you have me do? There are some people with whom you just must agree."

'And what happened?' I asked Maksim Maksimych. 'Did he actually tame her, or did she pine away in captivity from homesickness?'

'Oh come, why should she be homesick? From the fort one could see the same mountains as from her village –

and that's all these savages need. Besides, Pechorin would make her some present every day; during the first days, she would silently and proudly push away the gifts, which would then go to the innkeeper's wife and excite her eloquence. Ah, gifts! What won't a woman do for a bit of coloured rag ... Let's not digress, however ... For a long time, Pechorin wasted his efforts on her; meanwhile, he was learning Tatar,[33] and she was beginning to understand Russian. Little by little she got used to looking at him, at first from under her brows, askance, and she would be sad, and softly hum her songs, so that at times I would get sad myself, as I listened to her from the adjoining room. Never shall I forget one scene: I was going past her window and glanced in; Bela was sitting on the stove ledge with her head bent low, and Pechorin was standing before her. "Listen to me, my peri," he was saying. "You know very well that, sooner or later, you must be mine – why then do you keep tormenting me? You are not in love with some Chechen, are you? If you are, I'll let you go home immediately." She gave a hardly perceptible start and shook her head. "Or is it", he went on, that I am completely hateful to you?" She sighed. "Or does your faith forbid you to fall in love with me?" She grew pale and remained silent. "Believe me, Allah is the same for all races, and if he allows me to love you, why should he forbid you to return my feelings?" She looked intently into his face, as if struck with this new idea; her eyes expressed distrust and the desire to make sure. What eyes they were! They simply glowed like two coals.

' "Listen, my dear and good Bela!" continued Pechorin. "You see how I love you; I'm ready to give anything to cheer you up; I want you to be happy, and if you start brooding again, I shall die. Tell me, will you be more cheerful?" She lapsed into thought, never taking her black eyes off him, then she smiled sweetly and nodded her head in sign of assent. He took her hand and began persuading her to kiss him; she weakly defended herself, and only repeated in broken Russian: "Please, please, don't, don't." He insisted, she started trembling and began to cry. "I am your captive," she said, "your slave; of course, you can compel me," – and there were more tears.

'Pechorin struck his forehead with his fist and rushed into the next room. I went there; he was gloomily pacing to and fro, with his arms folded on his chest. "Well, old man?" I said to him. "A demon, not a woman!" he answered. "Only I give you my word of honour that she will be mine . . ." I shook my head. "Would you like to bet?" he said. "In a week's time!" "Agreed!" We shook hands on it and parted.

'The first thing he did next day was to dispatch an express messenger to Kizlyar[34] to make various purchases; quantities of various Persian fabrics, too many to enumerate, were brought back.

' "What do you think, Maksim Maksimych," he said to me as he showed me the presents, "could an Asiatic belle withstand such an array?" "You don't know these Circassian girls,"[35] I replied, "It is not at all the same thing as the Georgian girls or the Trans-Caucassian Tatar girls . . .[36] not at all the same thing. These have their own rules, they are brought up differently." Pechorin smiled and began to whistle a march.

'And it turned out I was right; the presents produced only half the desired effect: she became sweeter, more trusting – but that was all, so he decided to try a final resource. One morning, he ordered his horse to be saddled, put on Circassian dress, armed himself and went to her. "Bela!" he said, "You know how I love you. I dared to carry you off, thinking that when you got to know me, you would love me; I have made a mistake; farewell! Remain in complete possession of everything I own; if you like, go back to your father – you are free. I am guilty before you, and must punish myself. Farewell, I am going – where? How should I know? Perchance, I shall not be long running after a bullet or a sword blow: remember me then, and forgive me." He turned away and extended his hand in farewell. She did not take his hand, she was silent. But as I stood behind the door, I could distinguish her face through the chink, and I felt sorry . . . such a deathly pallor

36

had spread over that sweet little face! Hearing no answer, Pechorin took a few steps toward the door; he was trembling – and shall I tell you? I think he was really capable of carrying out what he had spoken of in jest. That was the kind of man he was, the Lord knows! But barely had he touched the door, than she jumped up, burst into sobs and threw herself on his neck. Would you believe it? As I stood behind the door, I, too, began to cry; I mean, you know, it was not really crying, it was just – oh, silliness!'

The junior captain paused.

'Yes, I must admit,' he said after a while, pulling at his moustache. 'It vexed me to think that no woman ever loved me like that.'

'And did their happiness last long?' I asked.

'Yes, she confessed to us that ever since the day she first saw Pechorin, he often appeared to her in dreams, and that no man had ever made such an impression on her before. Yes, they were happy!'

'How dull!' I exclaimed involuntarily. Indeed, I had expected a tragic denouement, and, all of a sudden, my hopes had been deceived so unexpectedly! 'Is it possible', I went on, 'that the father did not suspect you had her in the fortress?'

'As a matter of fact, he did suspect, I think. A few days later we learned that the old man had been killed. Here is how it happened. . . .'

My attention was aroused again.

'I should tell you that Kazbich imagined that Azamat had stolen his horse with the father's consent – this is, at least, what I conjecture. Well, there he was one day, waiting by the road, a couple of miles beyond the village; the old man was riding home after a vain search for his daughter; his retainers had fallen behind – it was dusk – he was riding pensively at a walk, when suddenly Kazbich, like a cat, darted out of a bush, jumped on to his horse behind him, with a thrust of his dagger threw him to the ground, grabbed the reins, and was gone. Some of the retainers saw all this from a knoll; they dashed off after him, but could not catch up with him.'

'He made up for the loss of his horse and avenged himself,' I said, to elicit an opinion from my interlocutor.

'Of course, according to their standards,' said the junior captain, 'he was completely in the right.'

I could not help being struck by the capacity of the Russian to adapt himself to the customs of that people among which he happens to be living. I do not know whether this trait of the mind deserves blame or praise, but it attests to his incredible flexibility and the presence of that lucid common sense that pardons evil wherever it recognises its necessity or the impossibility of its abolishment.

Meanwhile, we had finished our tea; the horses, long since harnessed, had got chilled in the snow; the moon was paling in the west and was ready to immerse herself in her black clouds suspended on the distant peaks like the shreds of a torn curtain. We left the hut. Contrary to my fellow-traveller's prediction, the weather had cleared, and promised us a serene morning; the dances of stars[37] were interlinked in wondrous patterns above the distant horizon, and went out, one by one, while the palish reflection of dawn flooded the dark-violet vault, gradually illumining the steep slopes of the mountains, covered with virgin snow. Right and left, gloomy and mysterious abysses yawned black, and thither glided the mists, whirling and winding like snakes, down the furrows of nearby cliffs, as if aware and afraid of the approach of day.

All was silent in heaven and on earth, as it is in the heart of man at the moment of his morning prayer; only once in a while, a cool wind would come rippling from the east, raising a little the rime-covered manes of the horses. We set out; five skinny nags dragged our carriages with difficulty along the road winding up Mount Gud. We followed on foot, chocking the wheels with stones whenever the horses became exhausted; the road seemed to lead up into the sky because, as far as the eye could see, it kept ascending and, finally, it lost itself in the cloud which, since the previous evening, had been resting on the summit of Mount Gud, like a vulture awaiting its prey; the snow crunched underfoot; the air was becoming so rare that it was painful to breathe; the blood kept rushing to our heads every moment, but despite all this, a delightful kind of feeling spread along all my veins, and I felt somehow elated at being so far above the world – a childish feeling, no doubt, but, on getting away from social conventions and coming closer to nature, we cannot help becoming children: all the things that have been acquired are shed by the soul, and it becomes again as it was once, and as it is surely to be again some day. He who, like me, has had occasion to wander over wild mountains and scrutinize, for a long time, their fantastic shapes, and avidly swallow the vivifying air pervading their gorges, will certainly understand my desire to render, to relate, to paint those magical images. Finally, we got to the top of Mount Gud, stopped, and looked around us: upon it hung the grey cloud whose cold breath threatened us with a gathering storm; but everything was so limpid and golden-bright in the east that we, that is to say the junior captain and I, completely forgot that cloud. Yes, the junior captain too: in simple hearts, the sense of the beauty and grandeur of nature is a hundred times stronger and more vivid than it is in us, enthusiastic tellers of tales, oral or written.[38]

'You are accustomed, I suppose, to these magnificent views?' I said to him.

'Yes, sir, one can become accustomed even to the whistle of bullets, that is to say become accustomed to concealing an involuntary throbbing of the heart.'

'I have heard that, on the contrary, some old warriors find that music even pleasant?'

'Of course, it is pleasant, if you like; but again, only because one's heart beats faster. Look,' he added, pointing eastward, 'what country!'

And indeed, I doubt if I shall ever see such a panorama anywhere again: below us, lay the Koishaur Valley, crossed by the Aragva and by another river, as by two silver threads; a pale, bluish haze glided over it, heading for the neighbouring canyons, away from the warm rays of morning; right and left, the crests of mountains, each higher than the next, intersected and stretched out, covered with snow or shrubs; in the distance, more mountains, but no two cliffs were alike; and all these snows burned with a ruddy glow, so merrily, so brightly, that it made one wonder why one should not stay here forever; the sun peeped from behind a dark-blue mountain which only a practised eye could have distinguished from a storm-cloud; but above the sun there was a blood-red band, to which my companion paid particular attention. 'I told you', he exclaimed, 'that we'd have some nasty weather tonight; we've got to hurry, or else it may well catch us on the Mountain of the Cross. Get going!' he shouted to the drivers.

Chains were placed under the wheels as a substitute for brakes, so as to keep them from gathering momentum; the horses were held by the bridle, and we began to descend; on the right was the cliff, on the left, such a precipice that a whole hamlet of Ossetians dwelling at its bottom looked like a swallow's nest; I shuddered to think that often here, in the dead of night, along this road, where there is not room enough for two carriages to pass each other, some courier drives a dozen times a year, without getting out of his jolting vehicle. One of our coachmen was a Russian peasant from the Province of Yaroslavl', the other an Ossetian. The Ossetian led his shaft horse by the bridle with all possible precautions, having unhitched the outside horses beforehand; but our easygoing Russ did not even bother to get off his box seat! When I observed to him that he might, at least, take this trouble on account of my valise, which I had no desire whatever to retrieve from that abyss, he answered me: 'Why, sir! With God's help, we'll make it no worse than they: after all, this isn't my first time.' And he was right, we might well not have made it; but then again we did, and if all people reasoned more, they would be convinced that life is not worth worrying about so much. . . .

But perhaps you would like to know the ending of Bela's story? In the first place, it is not a novella I am writing, but travelling notes; consequently, I cannot make the junior captain tell the story before he actually began telling it.

Therefore, wait a while, or, if you wish, turn several pages; however, I do not advise you to do this since traversing Krestovaya-Gora, Mountain of the Cross (or, as the scholarly Gambia miscalls it, *le Mont St Christophe*[39]) is something worth your curiosity. So there we were going down Mount Gud into Chertova Valley... What a romantic name! You derive Chertova from *chort* [devil] and visualize, at once, the aerie of the Evil Spirit among forbidding cliffs, but this is not the case at all; the name of the valley comes from the word *cherta* [border] and not *chort*, for here once lay the boundary of Georgia. This valley was now packed with snowdrifts which called to mind, rather vividly, Saratov, Tambov, and other *good old places* [40] in our fatherland.

'Here we are at the Mountain of the Cross!' said the junior captain when we had driven down into Border Valley, and he indicated a hill covered by a shroud of snow; on its summit, a cross of stone showed black, and past it there ran a barely perceptible road which is travelled only when the lower one, running around the hill, is blocked by snow: our drivers announced that there had not been any snowslides, as yet, and, to spare their horses, took us by the lower road. At the turn, we met half a dozen Ossetians; they offered us their services and, taking hold of the wheels, with much shouting, set about dragging and supporting our carriages. And indeed, the road was dangerous: on the right, there hung, over our heads, masses of snow, ready, it seemed, at the first gust of wind, to come tumbling into the gorge; the narrow road was partly covered by snow which, at some places, gave way underfoot, while in others, it had turned into ice from the action of the sun's rays and night frosts, so that we had trouble making our way on foot; the horses kept falling: on our left, yawned a deep gulch, where a torrent rolled, now hiding under the icy crust, now leaping foamily over the black boulders. In two hours we could hardly get around Mt Cross – a little more than a mile in two hours! Meanwhile, the clouds had settled, it began to hail and to snow heavily; the wind, bursting into the gorges, roared, whistled like Nightingale the Robber,[41] and soon the stone cross disappeared in the mist, which was rolling in from the east, in billows each thicker and more compact than the one before. Incidentally, there exists a bizarre, but generally accepted, legend about that cross, of which it is said that it was set there by the Emperor Peter I, when he drove through the Caucasus.[42] But, in the first place, Peter went only as far as Dagestan, and in the second, an inscription on the cross, in large letters, says that it was set by order of General Ermolov, and namely, in 1824. But the legend, despite that inscription, has become so deeply rooted, that one really does not know what to believe, especially since we are not accustomed to believe inscriptions.

We had still to descend some three miles over icy rocks and treacherous snow in order to reach the Kobi station. The horses were exhausted; we were chilled; the blizzard hummed louder and louder, just like one of our own in the north, only its savage melody was more sorrowful, more plaintive. 'You, too, are an exile,' I reflected. 'You wail for your wide spacious steppes! There you had room to unfurl your cold wings, while here you are stifled and cramped like an eagle that beats with cries against the bars of his iron cage.'

'This is bad!' the junior captain was saying, 'look, you can't see a thing around, only mist and snow; any moment, one can expect to fall into a chasm or get stuck in the brushwood, and further down, the Baydara River has swollen so much, I presume, that it cannot be crossed. That's Asia for you, be it people or rivers, there is absolutely no depending on them!'

The drivers were shouting and swearing as they beat the horses, which snorted and balked and refused to budge for anything in the world, despite the eloquence of the whips. 'Your Excellency,' said one of the coachmen at last, 'we'll never make Kobi today: won't you have us turn off to the left while we still can? Over there, on the mountainside, there's a black blur, must be huts; travellers always stop there in bad weather, sir. He says he'll show the way, if you tip him,' he added, pointing to one of the Ossetians.

'I know, my friend, I know without your telling me!' said

the junior captain. 'Ah, those rascals! They'll jump at any chance to extract a tip.'

'Still, you must admit', said I, 'that, without them, we would have been worse off.'

'That's so, that's so,' he muttered. 'I'm fed up with those guides! They have a flair for lucre. As if you could not find the road without them!'

So we turned off to the left, and, somehow, after a good deal of fuss, reached a meagre shelter, consisting of two huts put together out of slabs and boulders and surrounded by a wall of the same material. The ragged proprietors received us cordially. I learned afterwards that the government pays them and feeds them on condition that they receive travellers overtaken by the storm. 'It is all for the better,' I said, settling down by the fire. 'Now you can finish telling me your story about Bela: I am sure that that was not the end of it.'

'And why are you so sure?' answered the junior captain with a wink and a sly smile.

'Because that's not the way things happen: what began in an unusual way must end likewise.'

'Well, you have guessed. . . .'

'I'm very glad.'

'It's all right for you to be glad, but it makes me really sad to recall it. She was a nice little girl, that Bela! Eventually I got so used to her, she might have been my daughter; and she was fond of me, too. I should tell you that I don't have a family; it's already been twelve years or so since I have had news of my father and mother, and I never thought of providing myself with a wife. And now, don't you know, somehow it would not seem becoming; so I was happy that I had found someone to spoil. She used to sing songs for us, or dance the *lezginka* . . . And how she danced! I have seen our young ladies in provincial cities, and once, sir, I visited the Club of the Nobility, in Moscow;[43] some twenty years ago – only none of them would stand a chance against her! It was a different thing altogether! Pechorin would dress her up like a little doll, he would pamper her and dote on her, and her beauty improved marvellously under

43

our care! Her face and hands lost their tan, colour came into her cheeks . . . And how gay she was! She would constantly make fun of me, the saucy little thing, God forgive her!'

'And what happened when you told her about her father's death?'

'We kept it from her for a long time, until she got used to her situation; and when we did tell her, she cried for a couple of days, and then forgot.

'For about four months, things could not have gone better. Pechorin, as I think I've already told you, was passionately fond of hunting: at times he would feel an uncontrollable urge to go into the woods after boar or wild goats, but now he would not even step outside the rampart of the fort. Soon, however, I began to notice that he would become pensive again, would pace his room with his hands clasped behind his back. Then one day, without telling anybody, he was off to shoot, was gone the whole morning – this happened once, and it happened again, and became more and more frequent. "That's bad," I thought, "no doubt, they must have had a tiff."

'One morning, I went to see them – I can still visualize it vividly: Bela was sitting on the bed, in a black silk *beshmet*, and the little thing looked so pale and sad, that I was frightened!

' "And where is Pechorin?" I asked.

' "Out hunting."

' "Did he go today?"

She was silent, as though she found it difficult to articulate. "No, he's been away since yesterday," she said at last, with a heavy sigh.

' "I hope nothing happened to him?"

' "Yesterday, I thought and thought all day," she answered through her tears, "I imagined various accidents: it would now seem to me that he had been wounded by a wild boar, and now, that a Chechen had carried him off to the mountains. And today I'm beginning to think that he does not love me."

44

' "Really, my dear, you couldn't have thought up anything worse!"

'She started to cry, then proudly lifted her head, wiped her tears and went on:

' "If he does not love me, who prevents him from sending me home? I don't force him. But if things go on like this, I'll go away myself: I'm not his slave, I am the daughter of a prince!"

'I began to reason with her. "Listen, Bela, after all, he can't be expected to stay here, as if sewn to your skirt; he is a young man, he likes to chase game; he'll roam for a while, and then come back, but if you are going to mope, you'll bore him all the sooner."

' "You're right, you're right!" she answered. "I'll be gay." And with a peal of laughter, she seized her tambourine, and began to sing, dance, and skip around me; but this, too, did not last; she fell on the bed again and covered her face with her hands.

'What was I to do with her? After all, do you know, I've never had occasion to deal with women. I thought and thought how I could comfort her, and could not think of anything; for some time we both remained silent . . . A most unpleasant predicament, sir!

'Finally I said to her: "How about a stroll on the rampart? The weather is fine!" This was in September.[44] And indeed, the day was wonderful, bright and not hot; you could see all the mountains as if served on a plate. We went and walked, back and forth, on the rampart, in silence; finally, she sat down on the turf, and I sat down beside her. Really, it makes me laugh to think about it: I kept running after her as if I were some kind of nurse.

'Our fort stood on high ground, and the view from the rampart was beautiful: on one side, an extensive meadow,[45] furrowed by several ravines, ended in a forest which stretched all the way up to the mountain ridge; here and there, native hamlets smoked upon it, and herds of horses ranged; on the other side, there ran a shallow river, margined by the dense brush, which covered the flinty heights, linked up with the main Caucasian range. We sat in a corner of the bastion, and thus could see everything in either direction. This is what I saw: somebody rode out of the forest on a grey horse, he came nearer and nearer, and finally, stopped on the far side of the river, some two hundred and fifty yards from us, and began wheeling his horse around like a madman. What could it mean? "Take a look, Bela," I said, "you've got young eyes, who is that fancy horseman? Whom has he come to entertain?"

'She looked, and cried: "It's Kazbich!"

' "Ah, the rascal! Has he come to make fun of us?" I looked more closely. Yes, it was Kazbich, with his swarthy face, his tatters, and dirty as usual. "That is my father's horse," said Bela, grasping me by the arm; she shook like a leaf, and her eyes flashed. "Oho!" I thought to myself, "in you, too, my dear girl, the robber blood is not silent!"

' "Come over here," I said to the sentry. "Check your rifle, and knock that fellow out of his saddle for me – you'll get a silver rouble." "Yes, sir, only he won't stay put . . ." "Order him to," I said, laughing. "Hey, chum," shouted the sentry waving to him, "wait a bit; why do you spin like a top?"

'Kazbich actually did stop and listened; he thought, no doubt, that we were opening negotiations with him. Negotiations, indeed! My grenadier took aim . . . fired . . . and missed. The instant the powder flashed in the pan, Kazbich pushed his horse, and it leaped to one side.[46] He rose in the stirrups, cried something in his own tongue, made a threatening gesture with his riding whip – and disappeared.

' "You ought to be ashamed of yourself," I said to the sentry.

' "He's gone off to die, sir," he answered. "You can't kill those damned people outright."

'A quarter of an hour later, Pechorin returned from the hunt. Bela threw herself on his neck, and there was not a word of complaint, nor was there a single reproach for his long absence.

'By now, even I was cross with him. "For goodness sake!" I said, "just a moment ago, Kazbich was right over there, on the other side of the river, and we fired at him:

nothing easier for you than to run into him. Those mountain folks are vengeful; do you think he has not guessed
that you had a hand in helping Azamat? Moreover, I'll bet
you anything that he recognized Bela today. I know that, a
year ago, he was mightily attracted to her – he told me so
himself – and if he could have hoped to get together a
decent amount of bride money, he would certainly have
asked her in marriage." Pechorin looked thoughtful. "Yes,"
he answered, "we have to be more careful . . . Bela, from
now on, you must not go walking on the rampart any more."

'That evening, I had a long talk with him. I was vexed
that he had changed toward that poor little girl; besides
spending half the day hunting, his treatment of her had
become cold, he would seldom caress her, and she began
to wilt noticeably; her little face became thinner, her big
eyes lost their lustre. You would ask her: "What are you
sighing about, Bela? Are you sad?" "No." "Is there anything you'd like?" "No." "Do you miss your family?" "I
have no family." Sometimes, for days on end, you could
not get anything but "yes" or "no" out of her.

'Well, this was what I started talking to him about. "Now
look here, Maksim Maksimych," he answered, "I have an
unfortunate disposition: whether it is my upbringing that
made me thus or whether God created me so, I don't
know: I only know that if I am a cause of unhappiness for
others, I am no less unhappy myself. Naturally, that is poor
comfort for them, nevertheless, this is a fact. In my early
youth, from the minute I emerged from under my family's
supervision, I began madly to enjoy every pleasure that
money could buy, and, naturally, those pleasures became
repulsive to me. Then I ventured out into the *grand monde*,
and, soon, I became likewise fed up with society: I have
been in love with fashionable belles, and have been loved,
but their love only irritated my imagination and vanity,
while my heart remained empty . . . I began to read, to
study – I got just as sick of studies – I saw that neither
fame nor happiness depended on them in the least, since
the happiest people are dunces, while fame is a question
of luck, and in order to obtain it, you only have to be

nimble. Then I began to be bored . . . Soon after, I was transferred to the Caucasus: this was the happiest time of my life. I hoped that boredom did not exist amid Chechen bullets.

In vain! After one month, I got so used to their buzzing and to the nearness of death, that, really, I paid more attention to the mosquitoes, and I was even more bored than before, because I had almost lost my last hope.[47] When I saw Bela in my home, when for the first time I held her in my lap and kissed her black curls, I – fool that I was – imagined she was an angel sent me by compassionate fate . . . I was wrong again. The love of a wild girl was little better than that of a lady of rank; the ignorance and the naïveté of one pall on you as much as the coquetry of the other. I still like her, I suppose; I am grateful to her for several rather sweet moments; I am ready to die for her – only I find her company dull. Whether I am a fool or a villain, I don't know; but of one thing I'm sure, that I also deserve pity, even more perhaps than she. My soul has been impaired by the fashionable world, I have a restless fancy, an insatiable heart; whatever I get is not enough; I become used as easily to sorrow as to delight, and my life becomes more empty day by day; there is only one remedy left for me: to travel. As soon as I can, I shall set out – but, not for Europe, God preserve! I shall go to America, to Arabia, to India – perchance I may die somewhere, on the way! At least, I am sure that this last consolation will not soon be exhausted with the help of storms and bad roads." He went on like this for a long time, and his words became engraved in my memory because it was the first time that I had heard such things from a man of twenty-five, and I hope to God it may also be the last. . . .'

'What a strange thing! Would you be so kind as to tell me,' the junior captain continued, addressing me, 'you've lived, it seems, in the capital, haven't you, and not too long ago: Is it true that all the young men there are like that?'

I replied that there were many people who talked like that; that probably there were some who were telling the truth; that, on the other hand, disillusionment, like all fashions, having begun in the upper strata of society, had descended to the lower, which were now wearing it out, and that nowadays those people who were really bored the most tried to conceal this misfortune as though it were a vice.

The junior captain did not understand these subtle distinctions. He shook his head and smiled slyly.

'It was the French, was it, who introduced the fashion of being bored?'

'No, the English.'

'Ah, that's how it is!' he answered. 'Well, they have always been inveterate drunkards!'

I could not help recalling one Moscow lady who maintained that Byron was nothing more than a drunkard. But then, the junior captain's remark was more pardonable: in order to abstain from liquor, he naturally tried to convince himself that all misfortunes in the world come from drinking.

Meanwhile he continued his narrative as follows:

'Kazbich did not show up again. But, somehow, I don't know why, I could not drive the thought out of my head that there had been some reason for his coming and that he was cooking up some trouble.

'Well, one day, Pechorin began persuading me to go boar-hunting with him; for a long time I kept refusing: after all, a wild boar was no novelty to me; nevertheless he did succeed in dragging me off with him. We took half a dozen soldiers with us and left early in the morning. Until ten o'clock we poked around in the rushes and in the woods, but found not one brute. "Hey, how about turning back?" I said. "What's the point in persisting? It is obviously our unlucky day!" But Pechorin, despite the heat and fatigue, did not want to return without a kill. That's the kind of man he was: whatever he set his heart on he had to have, you could see he had been spoiled by his mamma when he was young. At last, at noontime, we tracked down that damned boar. Bang, bang! went our guns, but it was not to be, the boar escaped into the rushes. It was that

49

kind of unlucky day! Well, we rested for a little while and set out for home.

'We rode side by side, in silence, our reins slack, we were almost at the fort, only the brush was now hiding it from us. Suddenly a shot rang out. We glanced at each other, the same suspicion struck us both. We galloped headlong in the direction of the shot. We saw soldiers crowding on the rampart and pointing toward the field, and there a horseman was flying at full speed, holding something white across his saddle. Pechorin let out a yell no worse than that of any Chechen. His rifle came out of its case, and off he went; I followed. Fortunately, because of our unsuccessful hunt, our horses were not worn out, they strained forward from under the saddles, and at last I recognized Kazbich, only I could not distinguish what it was that he held in front of him. At this point I came abreast of Pechorin and cried to him "It's Kazbich!" He glanced at me, nodded his head and whipped his horse.

'Well, at last we got within rifle range of him; whether Kazbich's horse was worn out or was worse than our mounts, I don't know; only, in spite of all his efforts, it was not making a great deal of progress. I think that at this moment he must have remembered his Karagyoz.

'I looked and saw Pechorin take aim at full gallop. "Don't fire!" I cried to him. "Save your shot, we'll catch up with him anyway." But those youngsters, they always lose their heads at the wrong time. The shot rang out and the bullet broke the hind leg of Kazbich's horse: carried on by impetus, it took another ten bounds or so, then stumbled and fell to its knees. Kazbich jumped off, and then we saw that he was holding in his arms a woman wrapped up in a yashmak. It was Bela, poor Bela! He shouted something at us in his own tongue, and raised his dagger over her. No time could be lost; I fired in my turn, at random; the bullet must have hit him in the shoulder because he suddenly lowered his arm. When the smoke had cleared, the wounded horse lay on the ground, and beside it lay Bela, while Kazbich, having abandoned his rifle, was scrambling like a cat up the scrub on the cliff. I would have liked to bring him down, but I had no charge ready. We jumped off our horses and rushed toward Bela. Poor little thing, she was lying motionless, and blood poured out of her wound in streams. What a villain! He could at least have hit her in the heart – then after all, it would have been over with one blow, but in the back, the most treacherous stab! She was unconscious. We tore up the veil and bound up the wound as tight as we could. In vain did Pechorin kiss her cold lips – nothing could restore her to consciousness.

'Pechorin mounted his horse; I lifted her off the ground and seated her on his saddle as best I could; he put his arm around her, and we rode back. After a few minutes of silence, Pechorin said to me: "Look here, Maksim Maksimych, we'll never get her home alive this way." "That's true," I said, and we set our horses going at full speed. A crowd of people was waiting for us at the gate of the fort. Carefully we carried the wounded girl to Pechorin's quarters and sent for the doctor. Although he was drunk, he came, examined the wound, and announced that she could not live more than one day; only he was wrong. . . .'

'She recovered?' I asked the junior captain, grasping him by the arm and involuntarily feeling glad.

'No,' he answered, 'the doctor's mistake was that she lingered two days.'

'But explain to me how on earth Kazbich managed to carry her off?'

'Well, this is how it happened: despite Pechorin's prohibition, she had gone out of the fort to the river. It was, don't you know, a very hot day; she sat down on a stone and dipped her feet in the water. Here Kazbich stealthily approached, scrabbled her up, clapped his hand over her mouth and dragged her off into the bushes. Once there, he jumped on to his horse, and off he went. Meanwhile, she had had time to scream, the sentries were alerted, they fired but missed, and at the next moment, we rode up.'

'But why did Kazbich want to take her away?'

'Well, you see, it is a known fact that these Circassians are a bunch of thieves. They cannot help filching anything that is within reach; they may not need the thing, and yet they will steal it. They simply can't be held responsible for that! And besides, he had had a liking for her, for a long time.'

'And Bela died?'

'She died; but she suffered for quite a while, and we suffered a good bit with her. Around ten at night she came to; we were sitting by her bed; as soon as she opened her eyes, she began calling for Pechorin. "I'm right here beside you, my *janechka* (that is, as we would say, 'darling')," he answered, taking her by the hand. "I'm going to die," she said.

'We began trying to comfort her; we told her that the doctor had promised to cure her without fail. She shook her head and turned away to the wall; she did not want to die!

'In the night she became delirious; her forehead was burning; a shiver of fever ran now and then over her entire body. She spoke in incoherent accents about her father, about her brother; she wanted to go to the mountains, to her home. Then she would also talk of Pechorin, give him various pet names, or else reproach him for having stopped loving his *janechka*.

'He listened to her in silence, with his head in his hands; but not once did I notice a single tear on his eyelashes: whether he actually could not cry, or whether he was controlling himself, I don't know. As for me, I'd never seen anything more pitiful.

'Toward morning her delirium ceased; for an hour or so she lay motionless and pale, and in such a state of weakness that one could hardly notice if she were breathing or not; then she felt better, and began to speak, and what do you think she spoke about? An idea like that could only have occurred to a dying person! She began to grieve that she was not a Christian, and that in the next world her soul would not meet Pechorin's soul, and that some other woman would be his sweetheart in heaven. The thought occurred to me to have her baptized before her death; this I suggested to her. She looked at me hesitantly, and for a long time could not say a word; at last she replied that she would die in the same faith in which she was born. Thus passed a whole day. How she changed in the course of that day! Her pale cheeks sank in, her eyes became so very, very large, her lips burned. She felt an inner heat as if red-hot iron lay in her breast.

'Another night came; we never closed our eyes, nor moved from her bed. She suffered dreadfully, she moaned, and whenever the pain began to subside, she endeavoured to convince Pechorin that she was better, tried to persuade him to get some sleep, kissed his hand and kept holding it in her hands. Toward morning she began to feel the restlessness before death, and started to toss; she dislodged the bandage, and the blood flowed again. When the wound was rebandaged, she quieted down for a minute and began asking Pechorin to kiss her. He knelt beside the bed, raised her head up a little from the pillow and pressed his lips to her lips which were growing cold; she firmly wound her trembling arms round his neck, as though in this kiss she had wanted to transmit her soul to him ... Ah, she did well to die! What, indeed, would have become of her if Pechorin abandoned her? And this is what would have happened, sooner or later. ...

'For half the next day, she was calm, silent and submissive, no matter how much our army doctor tormented her with poultices and potions. "For goodness' sake," I told him, "haven't you said yourself that she was sure to die, why then all those medications of yours?" "Still it's better this way, Maksim Maksimych," he answered, "so as to have a clear conscience." A clear conscience, indeed!

'In the afternoon she began to be tortured by thirst. We opened the windows, but outside it was even hotter than in the room; we put ice by the bed, but nothing helped. I knew that this unbearable thirst was a sign that the end was near, and this I told Pechorin.

"Water, water! ..." she said hoarsely, raising herself on the bed.

'He turned as white as a sheet, grabbed a glass, filled it and brought it to her. I covered my eyes with my hands

53

and began to say a prayer – I don't remember which one. Yes, sir, I've seen a lot of people die in hospitals and on the battlefield, but it was not at all like this, not at all! And another thing, I admit, saddened me: before her death she did not remember me once, and yet, it seems, I had loved her like a father. Well, God will forgive her! . . . And in truth who am I to be remembered by anybody before death?

'Immediately after that draught of water, she felt better, and three minutes later she expired. We held a mirror up to her lips – it remained unclouded! I led Pechorin out of the room and we went on to the rampart; for a long while we walked up and down, side by side, without saying a word, our hands behind our backs; his face did not express anything unusual, and this annoyed me; in his place, I would have died of grief. Finally he sat down on the ground in the shade and began to trace something in the sand with a bit of stick. I wanted to comfort him, mainly for the sake of propriety, don't you know, and started to speak; he lifted his head and laughed. A chill ran over my skin at this laughter. I went off to order the coffin.

'I must admit, I busied myself with this partly for the sake of distraction. I possessed a piece of heavy silk, and with this I lined the coffin and adorned it with Circassian silver braid which Pechorin had bought for her, anyway.

'Early the next day we buried her behind the fort, by the river, near the place where she had sat for the last time; around her little grave, bushes of white acacia and elder have spread since then. I wanted to set up a cross, but somehow, don't you know, it did not seem right; after all, she was not a Christian.'

'And what happened to Pechorin?' I asked.

'Pechorin was ill for a long time, and he lost weight, poor fellow, but never again did we talk about Bela: I saw that it would have been unpleasant for him, so why talk about it? Some three months later, he was assigned to the E. regiment, and he left for Georgia. We have not met since then . . . Yes, now that I think of it, someone was telling me recently that he had returned to Russia, but there was nothing about it in divisional orders. But then news is late in reaching the likes of us.'

Here he launched upon a long dissertation about how unpleasant it was to get news a year late – he was probably trying to drown sad memories.

I neither interrupted him, nor listened.

After an hour it became possible to continue our journey; the blizzard had subsided, the sky had cleared, and we set out. On the way I could not help starting to talk again about Pechorin and Bela.

'And have you heard what became of Kazbich?' I asked.

'Kazbich? Well, I really don't know ... I've heard that on the right flank of the Shapsugs[48] there is a Kazbich, a daredevil who wears a red *beshmet* and rides back and forth at a walk under our gunfire, and bows most politely when a bullet buzzes near him; but it could hardly be the same man!'

At Kobi, Maksim Maksimych and I parted; I continued with post horses, while he, because of his heavy load, could not follow me. We did not expect ever to meet again, and yet we did meet, and if you like, I'll tell you about it; it's quite a story ... You must admit, though, that Maksim Maksimych is a man worthy of respect, isn't he? If you admit that, I shall be fully rewarded for my story, which perhaps has been too long.

MAKSIM MAKSIMYCH

AFTER parting with Maksim Maksimych, I drove swiftly through Terek Gorge[49] and Daryal Gorge, lunched at Kazbek, had tea at Lars, and reached Vladikavkaz in time for supper. I shall spare you a description of the mountains – exclamations that do not express anything, pictures that do not represent anything, especially for those who have not been there themselves, and statistical notes that decidedly nobody would want to read.

I stopped at an inn where all travellers stop, but where, nonetheless, you cannot find anybody to roast a pheasant or cook some cabbage soup, since the three war invalids who have been put in charge of the place are so stupid or so drunk that no good whatever can be got out of them.

I was informed that I would have to spend three more days there: the military detail, the *okaziya*, from Ekaterinograd had not yet arrived and, consequentially, could not start back. What an aggravating detail! ... But a bad pun is no consolation to a Russian. It occurred to me then that I might find some diversion in writing down Maksim Maksimych's tale about Bela. Little did I think that it would become the first link of a long chain of stories: you will observe how sometimes an insignificant event has dire consequences! ... By the way, you may not know what an *okaziya* is. It means a protective detail consisting of half a company of infantry and a cannon with which convoys travel through the Kabarda region, from Vladikavkaz to Ekaterinograd.

The first day I spent most dully; on the next, early in the morning, a carriage drove into the yard. Why, Maksim Maksimych! We met like two old friends. I offered him the use of my room; he made no pretence of ceremony, he even clapped me on the shoulder and twisted his mouth into the semblance of a smile. Such a queer chap!

Maksim Maksimych was deeply versed in the culinary
art; he made a wonderful job of roasting a pheasant, and
had the happy thought of basting it with a cucumber mari-
nade; I must admit that had it not been for him, I would
have been confined to dry rations. A bottle of Kakhetian
wine helped us to forget the modest number of courses
(there was but one of them) and, upon lighting our pipes,
we settled down – I, by the window, he, by the burning
stove, for the day was damp and cold. We were silent.
What was there to talk about? He had already told me
everything about himself that was entertaining, while I had
nothing to tell. I sat looking out of the window. Through
the trees a multitude of squat little houses showed here
and there, scattered along the bank of the Terek River,
which hereabouts keeps running wider and wider; further
away blue mountains loomed like a crenulated wall, and
from behind them peered forth Mount Kazbek in its white
cardinalic mitre.[50] I was taking leave of them mentally; I
had begun to feel sorry about it.

We sat like this for a long time. The sun had hidden
behind the cold peaks, and a whitish mist had begun to
spread in the valleys, when from without came the jingle
of a harness bell and the shouts of coachmen. A few carts
with grimy Armenians entered the yard of the inn, followed
by an empty travelling calash: there was a foreign touch
about its easy ride, comfortable arrangement and smart
appearance. Behind it walked a man with a big moustache,
clad in a Hungarian jacket, fairly well dressed for a valet;
his calling could not be mistaken once you observed the
swaggering way he shook the ashes out of his pipe and
shouted at the driver. He was obviously the spoiled servant
of an easygoing master – a kind of Russian Figaro.[51] 'Say,
my good man,' I cried to him from the window, 'has the
convoy arrived or what?' He looked at me in a rather
insolent manner, adjusted his neckcloth, and turned away;
the Armenian who walked beside him answered for him,
with a smile, that the convoy had, indeed, arrived and
would go back on the morrow. 'Thank goodness,' said
Maksim Maksimych, who by that time had come up to

the window. 'What a marvellous carriage!' he added. 'Must be some functionary going to an inquest in Tiflis. Seems he's not yet acquainted with our little mountain roads! Well, the joke is on you, friend, they're not the familiar brand; they'll loosen the screws even in an English carriage!' 'But who might it be anyway? Let's go and find out . . .' We stepped out into the passage. At the end of the passage, a door stood open into a side room. Into it, the valet and the driver were lugging suitcases.

'I say, friend,' the junior captain asked him, 'whose is this marvellous carriage, hey? A splendid carriage!' The man, without turning, muttered something under his breath, while he unfastened a suitcase. Maksim Maksimych became angry; he touched the uncivil fellow on the shoulder and said: 'It's you I'm talking to, my good fellow. . . .'

'Whose carriage? My master's. . . .'

'And what's your master's name?'

'Pechorin.'

'How's that? How's that? Pechorin? . . . Good Lord! . . . And might he have served in the Caucasus?' exclaimed Maksim Maksimych, jerking me by the sleeve. Joy sparkled in his eyes.

'He did, I believe. I have not been with him long.'

'That's it! That's it! Grigory Aleksandrovich? Is that his first name and patronymic? Your master and I used to be pals,' he added, dealing the valet a friendly blow on the shoulders which made the man totter.

'Beg pardon, sir, you are getting in my way,' said the latter, with a frown.

'You've odd manners, my friend! . . . Do you realize that your master and I have been boon companions, that we roomed together? . . . But where is he himself?'

The servant declared that Pechorin had remained for supper and for the night at Colonel N–'s.

'And will he not drop in here tonight? Or else, my friend, will you not go to see him for something or other? If you do, then tell him that Maksim Maksimych is here – just that – he'll know. I'll tip you eighty kopeks.'

The valet made a scornful grimace on hearing such a modest promise, but assured Maksim Maksimych that he would carry out his errand.

'And won't he come right away at a run!' said Maksim Maksimych to me with a triumphant look. 'I'll go wait for him outside the gate ... What a pity I am not acquainted with Colonel N–.'

Maksim Maksimych seated himself on a bench outside the gate, and I went to my room. I confess that I, too, looked forward rather eagerly for this Pechorin person to appear; and although the idea of him I made myself from the captain's narrative was not particularly flattering, still certain features of his character seemed to me remarkable. An hour later, one of the veterans brought in a simmering samovar and a teapot. 'Maksim Maksimych,' I called from the window, 'won't you have some tea?'

'Thanks, I don't want any particularly.'

'Oh, do have some! Look, it's getting late and chilly.'

'I'm all right, thanks.'

'Well, please yourself!' I started to have tea by myself; ten minutes later, the old fellow came in.

'I say, you're right, it is better to have a spot of tea. You see, I kept waiting. His man went to him a long time ago, but evidently something has detained him.'

Hurriedly he gulped down one cup, declined a second, and went out to the gate looking somewhat worried. It was clear that the old man was hurt by Pechorin's neglect, the more so as he had been telling me recently about their friendship, and only an hour before, had been sure that Pechorin would come at a run the moment he heard Maksim Maksimych's name.

It was late and dark when I opened the window again and started to call Maksim Maksimych, saying that it was time to go to bed; he muttered something between his teeth; I repeated the invitation: he did not answer.

I lay down on the couch, wrapped myself in my military overcoat, left the candle burning on the stove ledge and soon dozed off. I would have had a quiet night, if, at a very late hour, Maksim Maksimych had not roused me by entering the room. He threw his pipe on the table, he began to walk about, he stirred the embers in the stove, finally he lay down, but for a long time he kept coughing, spitting, turning from side to side.

'Are bedbugs biting you?' I queried.

'Yes, bedbugs,' he answered with a heavy sigh.

Next morning I woke up early, but Maksim Maksimych had forestalled me. I found him sitting on the bench outside the gate. 'I must see the commandant,' he said, 'so please, if Pechorin comes, send for me.'

I promised. He hurried away as if his limbs had regained their youthful strength and suppleness.

The morning was fresh, but fine. Golden clouds had accumulated on the mountains like an additional, airy range. A wide square spread before the gate; beyond it, a market-place was seething with people, it being Sunday; barefooted Ossetian lads, carrying on their shoulders sacks[52] of honey combs, swarmed around me; I chased them away. I could not be bothered by them. I was beginning to share the restlessness of my good captain.

Ten minutes had hardly elapsed when, at the other end of the square, there appeared the person we were expecting. He was accompanied by Colonel N– who, after seeing him to the inn, took his leave and turned back in the direction of the fort. I immediately sent one of the veterans to fetch Maksim Maksimych.

Pechorin's valet came out to meet his master, reported that the horses were about to be harnessed, presented to him a box of cigars, and, upon receiving several instructions, went away to take care of things. His master, having lit a cigar, yawned once or twice, and sat down on the bench beyond the gate. I must now draw his portrait for you.

He was of medium height,[53] a slim waist and broad shoulders testified to a sturdy constitution which was suited to bear all the hardships of a roving life and the changes of climate, and was undefeated either by the dissolution of city life or by the tempests of the soul; his dusty velvet jacket was fastened only by the two lower buttons and

allowed one to see the dazzling clean linen which bespeaks
the habits of a gentleman; his soiled gloves appeared to be
made to order, so well did they fit his small aristocratic
hands, and when he took off one glove I was surprised to
see how thin his pale fingers were. His gait was loose and
indolent, but I observed that he did not swing his arms –
a sure sign of a certain reticence of nature. However, these
are but my private notes based on my own observations,
and by no means do I expect you to believe in them blindly.

When he settled upon the bench, his straight figure
flexed in such a way that you would think there was not a
single bone in his spine; the attitude of his whole body
expressed a kind of nervous debility; he sat there as a thirty-
year-old coquette of Balzac's would sit after a fatiguing ball,
in her armchair stuffed with down.[54] After a first glance at
his face, I would not have given him more than twenty-
three years, though later I was ready to give him thirty.
There was something childish about his smile. His skin
had a kind of feminine tenderness of texture; his fair hair,
wavy by nature, framed, so picturesquely, his pale, noble
brow, upon which only prolonged observation could make
out the traces of intersecting wrinkles, which probably
became much more clearly marked in moments of wrath
or spiritual restlessness. In contrast to the light shade of
his hair, his moustache and eyebrows were black – a sign
of breeding in man, as are a black mane and a black tail
in a white horse. To complete his portrait, let me say that
he had a slightly bobbed nose, dazzlingly white teeth, and
brown eyes – I must add a few words about those eyes of
his.

In the first place, they never laughed when he was laughing! Have you observed this bizarre trait in some people?
It is either the sign of a wicked nature or of a deep and
constant melancholy. From behind half-lowered lashes,
they shone with a kind of phosphorescent glitter, if I can
put it thus. It was not the reflection of the soul's glow or
of an effervescent imagination; this was a gleam akin to the
gleam of smooth steel, dazzling but cold; his glance, while
not lingering, was penetrating and oppressive, it left the

disagreeable impression of an indiscreet question and might have appeared insolent had it not been indifferently serene. Perhaps all these observations came to my mind only because I knew some details of his life, and perhaps upon someone else his looks might have produced an entirely different impression; but since you will hear of him from no one but me, you must needs be satisfied with this portrayal. I shall say, in conclusion, that on the whole, he was rather handsome and had one of those original faces which especially appeal to women of fashion.

The horses had been already hitched; now and then, the shaftbow bell would tinkle, and twice already the valet had come to Pechorin to report that all was ready, but still Maksim Maksimych had not turned up. Fortunately, Pechorin was immersed in meditation as he looked at the blue crenulations of the Caucasian range, and apparently was in no haste to set out on his journey. I went up to him. 'If you care to wait a little longer,' I said, 'you will have the pleasure of seeing an old comrade of yours.

'Oh, that's right!' he answered quickly. 'They told me so last night; but where is he?' I turned toward the square and saw Maksim Maksimych running as fast as he could. A few moments later, he was near us; he could hardly breathe; sweat was trickling down his face; wet shags of grey hair, escaping from under his cap, had glued themselves to his forehead; his knees were shaking, he was about to fall on Pechorin's neck, but the latter, rather coolly, though with a friendly smile, stretched out his hand. For a second the captain stood transfixed, but then avidly seized that hand in both of his; he still was not able to speak.

'How glad I am, dear Maksim Maksimych! Well, how are you?' said Pechorin.

'And thou? . . . [55] And you?' stammered the old man with tears in his eyes. 'All those years . . . all those days . . . but where are you off to?'

'I am going to Persia, and then further on. . . .'

'Not right now? . . . Oh, but wait, my dearest friend! . . .

We aren't going to part right now, are we? We have not seen each other such a long time.'

'I have to go right now, Maksim Maksimych,' was the answer.

'Oh good Lord! What is all this hurry? I'd like to tell you so much, ask so much . . . Well, how are you? retired? how's everything? what have you been doing with yourself?'

'I have been bored!' answered Pechorin with a smile.

'Remember our days at the fort? Fine country for hunting! You used to be a passionate sportsman . . . And remember Bela?'[56]

Pechorin paled slightly and turned away.[57]

'Oh yes, I remember,' he said, almost at once feigning to yawn.

Maksim Maksimych began to implore him to remain a couple of hours longer. 'We'll have a capital dinner,' he said, 'I have a brace of pheasants, and the Kakhetian wine is excellent here – naturally, not what they have in Georgia, but still first-rate. We shall talk . . . You will tell me of your life in Petersburg, won't you?'

'Really, I have nothing to tell, my dear Maksim Maksimych . . . And now I must say good-bye, time for me to leave, I am in a hurry. Thanks for not forgetting me,' he added, taking him by the hand.

The old man frowned. He was sad and cross, though he tried to conceal it. 'Forgotten!' he growled. 'I, for one, haven't forgotten anything. Well, do as you please. This is not the way I thought we would meet again. . . .'

'Oh, come, come,' said Pechorin with a friendly embrace. 'Am I not the same as of old? What's to be done? To each his own road. God alone knows if we shall have another chance to see each other . . .' Speaking thus, he was already sitting in his carriage, and the coachman had already begun to gather up the reins.

'Wait, wait,' suddenly shouted Maksim Maksimych, clutching at the door of the carriage. 'It almost escaped my mind. You left some of your papers with me, Grigory Aleksandrovich. I lug them along with me – thought I might find you in Georgia – and see now where the Lord has us see each other. What shall I do with them?'

'Whatever you like,' answered Pechorin 'Good-bye.'

'So you are off to Persia? . . . and when will you be back?' Maksim Maksimych shouted after him.

The carriage was already far, but Pechorin made a sign with his hand which might have been interpreted as most likely never! and besides what for? . . .

The jingling of the shaft bell and the clatter of the wheels on the flinty road had long ceased to be heard, but the poor old fellow still stood in the same place, deep in thought.

'Yes,' he said at last, trying to assume an indifferent air, although a tear of vexation would still sparkle from time to time on his lashes, 'of course, we used to be friends, but what is friendship in our times? What can I mean to him? I have neither wealth nor rank, nor am I at all his mate in age. Look what a dandy he has become after revisiting Petersburg. What a calash! How much luggage! And such a haughty valet!' These words were uttered with an ironic smile. 'Tell me,' he continued, turning to me, 'now, what do you think of it? What devil now is sweeping him off to Persia? Absurd, by Jove, it's absurd! Matter of fact, I knew all along that he was a volatile fellow on whom one could not rely. Still, it's a pity that he will come to a bad end . . . could not be otherwise! It's something I have always said, there's no good in him who forgets his old friends!' At this he turned away to conceal his agitation and began to walk in the yard around his carriage, pretending to examine its wheels, while his eyes, every moment, filled with tears.

'Maksim Maksimych,' I said, going up to him, 'what are those papers that Pechorin left with you?'

'Goodness knows! Some sort of memoirs.'

'And what are you going to do with them?'

'What, indeed? I'll have them made into cartridges.'

'Better give them to me.'

He looked at me with surprise, muttered something through his teeth, and began to rummage in a suitcase; presently he took out a notebook and threw it on the ground with contempt; a second, a third and up to a tenth book received the same treatment. There was something childish about his resentment; I began to feel both amused and touched.

'Here they are, all of them,' he said, 'congratulations on your find....'

'And I may do with them all I wish?'

'You may even publish them in the gazettes. What do I care? One would think I was some kind of friend or relative of his. True, we did live for a long time under one roof ... But haven't I had any number of roommates?'

I seized the papers and hastened to carry them away, fearing lest the captain might repent. Soon after, we were informed that the convoy would start in an hour. I ordered the horses to be harnessed. The captain entered the room when I had already put on my cap; it seemed he was not getting ready to go; there was something cold and constrained about his appearance.

'And you, Maksim Maksimych, aren't you coming?'

'No, sir.'

'Why not?'

'Well, I haven't yet seen the commandant; there is some government property that I have to hand over.

'But haven't you been to see him?'

'I did go, of course,' he said falteringly, 'but he was not in ... and I did not wait.'

I understood him. The poor old fellow had, perhaps for the first time in his life, abandoned official business for what in the parlance of paperdom is termed 'a private necessity' – and how he had been rewarded!

'I am very sorry,' I said, 'I am very sorry, Maksim Maksimych, that we have to part sooner than the term set.'

'How can we, unschooled old fellows, keep up with you? You are young men of fashion, you are haughty. It may be all right while one is together here under Circassian fire ... but meet you later and you're ashamed to shake hands with one of us.'

'I have done nothing to justify such reproaches, Maksim Maksimych.'

'Well, I just happened to mention it; however, I wish you all possible happiness and a merry trip.'

We parted rather drily. My good Maksim Maksimych had turned into a stubborn and grumpy junior captain! And why? Just because Pechorin, out of absent-mindedness or for some other reason, proffered his hand while Maksim Maksimych wanted to throw himself on Pechorin's neck! It is sad to see a youth lose his fondest hopes and dreams, when the rosy tulle through which he had looked upon the acts and feelings of men is torn aside before him, even though there is hope that he will replace his old delusions by new ones, no less fleeting but also no less sweet. But by what can one replace them at Maksim Maksimych's age? No wonder that the heart hardens and the soul folds up.

I drove off alone.

INTRODUCTION TO
PECHORIN'S JOURNAL

I LEARNED not long ago that Pechorin had died on his way back from Persia.[58] This news gladdened me very much, it gave me the right to publish these notes, and I took advantage of the opportunity to sign another man's work with my own name. God grant that readers do not castigate me for such an innocent forgery.

I now must explain somehow the reasons that prompted me to deliver to the public the innermost secrets of a man whom I had never known. It might have been all right had I been his friend – the perfidious indiscreetness of a true friend is intelligible to anyone – but I saw him only once in my life, on the highway, and consequently cannot harbour for him that ineffable detestation which, concealed under the mask of friendship, only awaits death or misfortune to befall the beloved object in order to break out over his head in a hail of reproach, advice, gibes, and lamentations.

While reading over these notes, I became convinced of the sincerity of this man who so mercilessly exhibited his own failings and vices. The history of a human soul, be it even the meanest soul, can hardly be less curious or less instructive than the history of an entire nation – especially when it is the result of self-observation on the part of a mature mind, and when it is written without the ambitious desire to provoke sympathy or amazement. Rousseau's *Confessions*[59] have already the defect of his having read them to his friends.

Thus, solely the desire to be useful compelled me to print excerpts from a journal that came accidentally into my possession. Although I altered all proper names, those people of whom it tells will probably recognize themselves, and possibly they will find some justification in regard to actions for which, until now, they blamed a man who, henceforth, has nothing in common with our world – we nearly always excuse what we can understand.

I have included in this book only that which refers to Pechorin's sojourn in the Caucasus. There still remains in my possession a fat notebook wherein he narrates all his life. Some day it, too, will be presented to the judgment of the world, but for the present there are important reasons why I dare not assume such a responsibility.

Perhaps some readers will want to know my opinion of Pechorin's character. My answer is the title of this book. 'But this is wicked irony!' they will say.

I wonder.

TAMAN

TAMAN is the worst little town of all the seacoast towns in Russia. I almost died of hunger there and, moreover, an attempt was made to drown me. I arrived late one night with post horses, in a small springless carriage. The driver stopped his tired troika at the gate of the only stone house in Taman, at the town entrance. The sentinel, a Black Sea Cossack,[60] startled in his sleep by the jingle of the harness-bell, yelled out in a wild voice 'Who goes there?' A sergeant and a corporal appeared. I explained to them that I was an officer going on official business to join a detachment on active duty, and demanded governmental quarters. The corporal took me over the town. Every hut we drove up to proved taken. The weather was cold; I had not slept for three nights, I was worn out, and was beginning to get angry. 'Take me somewhere, you rascal!' I cried. 'Let it be the devil's, but lead me to the place.' 'There is one more *fatéra* [quarters],' replied the corporal, scratching the back of his head, 'but your honour won't like it, it's an evil place!' I did not understand the exact sense of that word and ordered the man to go ahead. After wandering for a long time along dirty alleys where, on both sides, I could see nothing but decrepit fences, we drove up to a shanty on the very edge of the sea.

The full moon shone on the rush roof and the white-washed walls of my new abode; in the yard, within an enclosure of cobbles, there stood, all awry, a second hut, smaller and more ancient than the first. Almost at its very walls, the shore fell abruptly toward the sea, and below, with an incessant murmur, the dark-blue waves splashed. The moon mildly surveyed the element, both restless and submissive to her, and by her light, I could distinguish, far from the shore, two ships, whose motionless black rigging was outlined, gossamer-like, against the pale horizon.

'There are ships in the harbour,' I said to myself. 'Tomorrow I'll set out for Gelendzhik.'[61]

I had in my service, as orderly, a Cossack from a line regiment. I told him to take out my valise and to dismiss the coachman. Then I began calling the landlord. Silence. I knocked. Silence again. Funny situation. Finally a boy of fourteen or so crept out of the hallway.[62]

'Where is the landlord?' 'No landlord.' 'How's that? None at all?' 'None.' 'And what about a landlady?' 'Gone to the settlement.' 'Then who'll open the door for me?' I asked, and gave it a kick. The door opened of itself, a whiff of dampness came from within. I lit a sulphur match and brought it close to the lad's very nose; it illumined two white eyes. He was blind, totally blind from birth. He stood motionless before me and I began to examine his features.

I confess I have a strong prejudice against those who are blind, one-eyed, deaf, mute, legless, armless, hunchbacked, and so forth. I have observed that there always exists some strange relationship between the appearance of a man and his soul, as if with the loss of a limb, the soul lost one of its senses.

And so I began to examine the blind lad's face, but what can one read in a face that lacks eyes? For a long time, I kept looking at him with involuntary pity, when all of a sudden a hardly perceptible smile ran over his thin lips, and for some reason it made on me a most unpleasant impression. There was born in my mind the suspicion that this blind lad was not as blind as it seemed; in vain did I try to persuade myself that those white eyes could not be faked – and what would have been the purpose? But I could not help wondering. I am often inclined to prejudice.

'Are you the landlady's son?' I asked him at last. 'No.' 'Who are you then?' 'An orphan, a cripple.' 'And does the landlady have any children?' 'No. There was a daughter, but she's run off across the sea with a Tatar.' 'What Tatar?' 'The evil one knows! Some Tatar from the Crimea, a boatman, from Kerch.'

I entered the shanty; two benches and a table, plus a huge trunk by the stove, made up all its furniture. Not one ikon hung on the wall – a bad sign! The sea breeze kept blowing through the broken windowpane. I took out of my suitcase a bit of wax candle and, having lit it, began to unpack my things. I placed in one corner of the room my sword and rifle, laid my pistols on the table, spread my felt cloak on one bench, my Cossack spread his on the other: ten minutes later, he began to snore, but I could not fall asleep, the white-eyed lad kept hovering before me in the dark.

About an hour passed in this way. The moon shone in the window and one beam played on the earthen floor of the shanty. Suddenly, upon the bright band that crossed the floor, a shadow flicked by. I raised myself and glanced through the window; once again someone ran past and vanished, God knows where. I could not suppose that this creature had run down the steep slope of the shore; however, there was no other place for it to have gone. I got up, put on my *beshmet*, buckled my dagger on, and as softly as possible stepped out of the shanty: the blind lad appeared before me. I huddled beside the fence, and he went by me with a firm but cautious step. He carried a bundle under his arm; turning toward the harbour, he began to go down the narrow steep path. 'On that day the dumb shall cry out and the blind shall see,'[63] I thought, as I followed him at a distance which allowed me not to lose sight of him.

Meanwhile, the moon had begun to clothe herself in clouds and above the sea a mist had risen; through it, a lantern glimmered on the stern of the nearer ship. Close to the beach, there gleamed the foam of the breakers[64] which threatened to flood it any minute. Descending with difficulty, I groped my way down the precipitous slope, and this is what I saw: the blind lad stopped for a moment, then turned to the right at the bottom of the slope; he walked so close to the water, that it looked as if any moment a wave might seize him and carry him away; but evidently this was not the first time he took this walk, judging by the assuredness with which he stepped from stone to stone and avoided holes. Finally, he stopped as if listening to something, sat down on the ground and laid down the bundle beside him. I followed his movements as I stood concealed behind a projecting part of the rocky coast. After a few minutes, a white figure came in sight, from the opposite direction. It advanced toward the blind lad and sat down beside him. From time to time, the wind brought me snatches of their conversation.

'Well, blind one?' said a woman's voice. 'The storm is heavy; Yanko will not come.' 'Yanko does not fear the storm,' the other replied. 'The mist is getting thicker,' the woman's voice retorted with a note of sadness.

'A mist is best for slipping past the patrol ships,' was the answer. 'And what if he drowns?' 'Well, what of it? You'll go to church Sunday without a new ribbon.'

There followed a silence; one thing, however, had struck me: to me, the blind lad had spoken in the Ukrainian dialect, now he expressed himself in perfect Russian.

'You see, I was right,' spoke the blind lad again, clapping his hands together. 'Yanko is not afraid either of the sea or the winds or the mist or the coast guards. Listen! That is not water splashing – one cannot deceive me – it's his long oars!'

The woman jumped up and began to peer into the distance, with an air of anxiety.

'You're dreaming, blind one,' she said, 'I don't see anything.'

I confess that no matter how I strained to make out, in the distance, anything resembling a boat, my efforts were in vain. Some ten minutes elapsed; then, amid the mountains of the waves, a black dot appeared; it grew now bigger, now smaller. Slowly rising upon the wave crests, and rapidly coming down them, a boat was nearing the shore. He must be a valiant navigator, indeed, to venture on such a night to cross the straits, a distance of fifteen miles; and it must be an important reason that induced him to do so! These were my thoughts as, with an involuntary throbbing of the heart, I looked at the wretched boat; but she kept diving like a duck and then, with a wing-like upsweep of oars, would spring out of the abyss amid a burst of foam;

72

and now, I thought, her impetus will dash her against the shore and she will be smashed to bits; but cleverly she turned sideways and bounded, unharmed, into a cove. A man of medium height, in a Tatar cap of sheepskin, came ashore. He waved his hand, and all three began to drag something out of the boat; the load was so great that, to this day, I cannot understand how she had not sunk. Each having shouldered a bundle, they started to walk away along the coast, and I soon lost sight of them. I had to go back to my lodgings; but, I confess, all these strange things worried me, and I had a hard time awaiting the morning.

My Cossack was much surprised when, upon waking, he saw me all dressed; I did not, however, tell him the reason. After admiring, for a while, from the window, the blue sky strewn with torn cloudlets, and the distant shore of the Crimea which extended in a lilac line and ended in a rock on the summit of which a lighthouse loomed white, I made my way to Phanagoria Fort[65] to find out from the commandant the hour of my departure for Gelendzhik.

But, alas, the commandant could tell me nothing definite. The ships that lay in the harbour were either patrol ships or merchantmen that had not even begun to load. 'Maybe within three or four days the mailboat will come,' said the commandant, 'and then we shall see.' I returned home, gloomy and cross. In the doorway my Cossack met me with a frightened face.

'It's a bad business, sir,' he said to me.

'Yes, my friend, the Lord knows when we shall get out of here!' At this he became even more perturbed and, bending toward me, said in a whisper:

'It's an evil place![66] Today, I met a Black Sea sergeant; he's a friend of mine who was in our detachment, last year. The moment I told him where we were quartered, he said to me: "Brother, it's an evil place, those are bad people!" And, true enough, what kind of a blindman is this? Goes alone everywhere, to the market, to get bread, to get water ... seems all are used to it around here....'

'Well, at least, did the landlady show up?'

'When you were out today, there came an old woman, and her daughter.'

'What daughter? She has no daughter.'

'The Lord knows who she is then if she is not her daughter. Anyway, the old woman is in her hut now.'

I entered the smaller hut. The stove had been thoroughly heated, and in it, a dinner was cooking, fairly luxurious for paupers. To all my questions, the old woman replied that she was deaf, could not hear me. What was I to do with her? I turned to the blind lad who sat before the stove, feeding the fire with brushwood. 'Well now, you blind little devil,' I said, taking him by the ear, 'out with it . . . where did you go prowling last night with that bundle . . . hey?' All at once my blind lad began to weep, to shriek, to moan. 'Where did I go? Nowhere at all . . . With a bundle? What bundle?' This time the old woman did hear, and began to grumble: 'What things people will make up! And about a poor cripple, too! Why are you after him? What has he done to you?' I got tired of this and left, firmly resolved to obtain the key to this riddle.

I wrapped myself in my felt cloak and, seating myself on a stone beside the fence, fell to looking idly afar. In front of me, there spread the sea, stirred up by last night's storm, and its monotonous sound, akin to the murmur of a city settling down to sleep, reminded me of past years, and carried my thoughts northward, toward our cold capital. I was troubled by memories and lost myself in them. Thus passed an hour, perhaps even more. Suddenly, something resembling a song struck my hearing. It was, indeed, a song, and the limpid young voice was that of a woman – but where did it come from? I listened; the tune was bizarre, now slow and sad, now fast and lively. I turned – there was no one around; again I listened – the sounds seemed to fall from the sky. I raised my eyes; on the roof of my hut stood a girl in a striped dress, her hair hanging loose, a regular water nymph. Shading her eyes from the rays of the sun with the palm of her hand, she fixedly peered afar, now laughing and reasoning with herself, now singing her song.

74

I memorized that song, word for word:

> Over the free franchise
> of the green sea
> good ships keep going,
> white-sailed.
>
> Among those good ships
> is my own small boat,
> a boat unrigged,
> two-oared.
>
> Let a storm run riot:
> the old ships
> will lift their wings
> and scatter over the sea.
>
> To the sea I shall bow
> very low:
> "You, bad sea, do not touch
> my small boat.
>
> My small boat carries
> costly things;
> it is guided through the dark night
> by a bold daredevil."

Involuntarily, the thought struck me that last night I had heard the same voice: I was lost in meditation for a moment, and when I looked again at the roof, the girl was no longer there. All at once, she ran past me, singing some other snatch and then, snapping her fingers, ran into the old woman's hut, upon which a dispute arose between them. The old woman was furious, the girl laughed loudly. Presently, I saw my undine[67] skip out again. On coming up level with me, she stopped and looked fixedly into my eyes as if she were surprised at my presence; then she turned away casually and slowly walked toward the harbour.

This was not the end: all day long she hovered about my dwelling; her singing and skipping did not cease for one minute. What an odd creature she was! Her face showed no signs of insanity; on the contrary, her eyes rested upon me with brisk perspicacity. Those eyes, it seemed, were endowed with some kind of magnetic power, and every time they looked, they seemed to be waiting for a question. But barely did I begin to speak, than she would run away, with a crafty smile.

Really, I had never seen such a woman! She was far from beautiful, but I have my preconceptions in regard to beauty, too. She revealed a good deal of breeding . . . and breeding in women, as in horses, is a great thing: *les Jeunes-France*[68] are responsible for this discovery. It (that is, breeding, not Young France) is most visible in the gait, in the hands and feet; the nose is especially significant. In Russia, a straight nose is rarer than a small foot. My songstress did not appear to be more than eighteen. The extraordinary suppleness of her figure, a special inclination of the head, peculiar to her alone, her long auburn hair, a kind of golden sheen on the slightly sun-tanned skin of her neck and shoulders, and, especially, her straight nose – all this was enchanting to me. Although I detected in her oblique glances something wild and suspicious, and although there was an odd vagueness about her smile, still such is the force of preconception; her straight nose drove me crazy. I imagined I had discovered Goethe's Mignon[69] – that extravagant product of his German imagination – and indeed, there was a lot in common between them: the same rapid transitions from intense restlessness to complete immobility, the same enigmatic accents, the same capers and strange songs.

Toward nightfall I accosted her by the door, and started the following conversation with her:

'Tell me, my pretty girl,' I said, 'what were you doing today on the roof?'

'Oh, just tried to see whence the wind was blowing.'

'What is that to you?'

'Whence the wind comes, happiness comes, too.'

'So you were inviting happiness with your song?'

'Where there are songs, there is happiness.'

'And what if you chance to sing sorrow in?'

'What of it? Where it will not get better, it will get worse, and then again, it is not far from bad to good.'

76

'And who taught you that song?'

'Nobody taught me, I sing when I feel like singing; he who is meant to hear it, will hear, and he who is not, will not understand.'

'And what's your name, my songstress?'

'The one who christened me knows.'

'And who christened you?'

'How should I know?'

'What reticence! Yet look, there is something I've found out about you.' (Her face did not change, her lips did not move, as if I were not speaking of her.) 'I've found out that you went down to the shore last night.' At this point I very solemnly related to her all I had seen, expecting she would be taken aback. Not in the least! She burst into roars of laughter. 'You've seen much, but you know little,' she said. 'And whatever you do know, you'd better keep under lock.'

'And what if, for instance, I took it into my head to inform the commandant?'

At this point, I assumed a very serious, even severe, expression. Suddenly, off she hopped, broke into song and vanished like some little bird that has been flushed out of the shrubbery. My last words had been entirely out of place: at the time, I did not realize all their importance, but later had a chance to regret them.

It had just got dark; I ordered the Cossack to heat the tea kettle, bivouac-fashion, lit a candle and sat down at the table, quietly puffing at my travelling pipe. By the time I was finishing my second glass of tea, the door creaked, suddenly, and I heard, behind me, the light rustle of a dress and the sound of steps: I started and turned around – it was she, my undine. Softly, silently, she sat down, facing me across the table, and fixed me with her eyes, and I do not know why, but her look seemed to me wondrously tender;[70] it reminded me of those gazes which, in past years, so despotically toyed with my life. She seemed to be waiting for a question, but I remained silent, filled with an ineffable confusion. A dull pallor, betraying inner agitation, covered her face, her hand strayed over the table aimlessly, and I noticed a slight tremor in it; now her bosom would rise high, and now she would seem to be holding her breath. This comedy was beginning to bore me, and I was prepared to break the silence in a most prosaic way – that is, to offer her a glass of tea – when she suddenly jumped up, twined her arms around my neck, and a moist, burning kiss[71] sounded upon my lips. Everything turned dark before my eyes, my head swam, I crushed her in my embrace with all the force of youthful passion, but she, like a snake, glided between my arms, whispering in my ear: 'Tonight, when everybody is asleep, come on to the shore,' and, like an arrow, sped out of the room. In the hallway, she overturned the kettle and a candle which stood on the floor. 'That she-devil!' cried the Cossack, who had made himself comfortable on some straw and had been looking forward to warming himself with the remainder of the tea. Only then, did I come to my senses.

Some two hours later, when everything had quieted down in the harbour, I roused my Cossack. 'If I fire my pistol,' I told him, 'come down to the shore, as fast as you can.' His eyes bulged and he answered automatically: 'At your orders, sir.' I stuck a pistol in my belt and went out. She was waiting for me at the edge of the declivity; her garment was more than light, a flimsy kerchief girded her supple figure.[72]

'Follow me!' she said, taking me by the hand, and we started to walk down. I wonder that I did not break my neck: once below, we turned right and went along the same road along which I had tracked the blind lad on the previous night. The moon had not yet risen, and only two little stars, like two guiding beacons, sparkled in the dark-blue vault. Heavy waves rolled rhythmically and evenly one after the other, hardly raising the lone boat that was moored to the shore. 'Let's get into the boat,' said my companion. I hesitated – I am no amateur of sentimental promenades on the sea – but this was not the moment to retreat. She jumped into the boat, I followed, and had barely recovered my senses when I noticed that we were adrift. 'What does this mean?' I said crossly. 'It means,' she said, making me sit on a bench, and winding her arms around my waist, 'it means that I love you.' Her cheek pressed mine and I felt, on my face, her flaming breath. Suddenly, something fell into the water, with a noisy splash; my hand flew to my belt – my pistol was gone. Ah, what a terrible suspicion stole into my soul! The blood rushed to my head; I looked around – we were a hundred yards from the shore, and I could not swim! I tried to push her away, but she clung to my clothes like a cat, and suddenly a powerful push almost precipitated me overboard. The boat rocked, but I regained my balance, and a desperate struggle started between us; my rage gave me strength, but I soon realized that, in agility, I was inferior to my adversary. 'What do you want?' I cried, squeezing her small hands hard. Her fingers crunched, but she did not cry out; her serpent nature withstood this torture.

'You saw,' she replied, 'you will tell!' And with a super-human effort she brought me crashing down against the side of the boat; we both hung over from the waist up; her hair touched the water; it was a decisive moment. I braced my knee against the bottom of the boat; with one hand I seized her by the hair, with the other got hold of her throat; she released my clothes, and I instantly shoved her into the waves.

By that time it was rather dark: once or twice, I glimpsed her head amid the foam, and then I saw nothing more. . . .

At the bottom of the boat, I found one half of an old oar, and, after protracted efforts, somehow managed to reach the landing place. As I made my way along the shore toward my hut, I could not help peering in the direction where, on the eve, the blind lad had waited for the nocturnal navigator. The moon was already riding the sky, and it seemed to me that someone in white sat on the shore: egged on by curiosity, I stole close up and lay in the grass on the brink of the steep shore. Sticking out my head a little, I could clearly see from the cliff all that took place below, and was not much surprised, but felt almost glad, to recognize my mermaid. She was wringing the wet foam out of her long hair; her wet shift outlined her supple figure and raised breasts. In the distance, there soon appeared a boat; quickly it approached; out of it, as on the night before, there stepped a man in a Tatar cap, but with his hair cut in the Cossack fashion, and a large knife sticking out of his leather belt. 'Yanko,' she said, 'all is lost!' After this, their conversation continued, but in such low tones that I could not make out a word of it. 'And where is the blind one?' Yanko said at last raising his voice. 'I sent him on an errand,' was the answer. A few minutes later the blind lad appeared hauling, on his back, a sack which they put into the boat.

'Listen, blind one,' said Yanko, 'you watch that place ... know what I mean? ... there are some rich wares there ... Tell (I did not catch the name) not to count on my services any longer. Things have gone wrong, he will not see me again; it is dangerous now. I'll go to look for work at some other place, but he will never again find such a bold fellow. Also tell him that if he had paid me better for my labours, then Yanko would not have left him: as for me I'll always find an open road wherever the wind blows and the sea sounds!' After a silence, Yanko continued: 'She'll go with me, she can't stay here. And tell the old woman that I guess it is time for her to die, she's lived too long, one ought to know when to quit. As to us, she won't see us again.'

'And what about me?' said the blind lad in a piteous voice.

'What use are you to me?' was the answer.

Meanwhile, my undine had jumped into the boat and signalled with her hand to her companion; he put something in the blind lad's hand, saying: 'Here, get yourself some gingerbread.' 'Is that all?' said the blind lad. 'Well, here's some more,' – and a fallen coin rang against a stone. The blind lad did not pick it up. Yanko got into the boat; the wind blew offshore; they hoisted a small sail and sped away. For a long time, the white sail glanced in the moonlight amid the dark waves; the blind lad kept sitting on the shore, and presently I heard something resembling a sob, and indeed, the blind little fellow was crying. He cried for a long long time ... I felt sad. What business did fate have to land me into the peaceful midst of *honest smugglers?* Like a stone thrown into the smooth water of a spring, I had disturbed their peace, and like a stone, had very nearly gone to the bottom myself!

I returned to my lodgings. In the hallway, the burned-down candle sputtered in a wooden plate, and my Cossack, despite my orders, lay sound asleep, holding his rifle in both hands. I left him in peace, took the candle and went into the interior of the hut. Alas! My travelling box, my sword chased with silver, my Dagestan dagger – a present from a pal – all had disappeared. It was then that I realized the nature of the things that the confounded blind lad had been hauling. Upon rousing the Cossack with a rather uncivil push, I scolded him and vented my anger a little, but there was nothing to be done! Really, would it not be absurd to complain to the authorities that I had been robbed by a blind boy, and had almost been drowned by an eighteen-year-old girl? Fortunately, next morning it proved possible to continue my journey, and I left Taman. What became of the old woman and of the poor blind lad I do not know. And besides, what do I care about human joys and sorrows – I, a military man on the move, and holder, moreover, of a road-pass issued to those on official business!

PRINCESS MARY

11 May[73]

YESTERDAY, I arrived in Pyatigorsk[74] and rented lodgings on the outskirts of the town, at its highest point, at the foot of Mount Mashuk: when there is a thunderstorm, the clouds will descend down to my roof. At five this morning, when I opened the window, my room was filled with the perfume of flowers growing in the modest front garden. The branches of cherry trees in bloom look into my window, and the wind occasionally strews my desk with their white petals. The view on three sides is marvellous: to the west, the five-peaked Besh Tau looms blue like 'the last thundercloud of a tempest dispersed';[75] to the north, Mount Mashuk rises like a shaggy Persian fur cap and closes off all that part of the horizon; to the east, the outlook is gayer; right below me, lies the varicoloured, neat, brand-new little town, the medicinal springs babble, and so does the multilingual crowd; and, beyond the town, amphitheatrical mountains pile up, ever bluer and mistier, while on the edge of the horizon there stretches a silver range of snowy summits, beginning with Mount Kazbek, and ending with the bicephalous Mount Elbruz.[76] It is gay to live in such country! A kind of joyful feeling permeates all my veins. The air is pure and fresh, like the kiss of a child, the sun is bright, the sky is blue – what more, it seems, could one wish? Who, here, needs passions, desires, regrets? However, it is time. I shall go to the Elizabeth Spring: there, I am told, the entire spa society gathers in the morning.

. . . .[77]

Upon descending into the centre of town, I followed the boulevard where I came across several melancholy groups that were slowly going uphill. These were mostly families of landowners from the steppe provinces: this could be inferred immediately from the worn-out, old-fashioned frock coats of the husbands and the elaborate attires of the wives and daughters. Obviously they had already taken stock of all the young men at the waters for they looked at me with tender curiosity. The St Petersburg cut of my military surtout misled them, but soon, recognizing the epaulets of a mere army officer,[78] they turned away in disgust.

The wives of the local officials, the hostesses of the waters, so to speak, were more favourably disposed; they have lorgnettes, they pay less attention to uniforms, they are used to encountering in the Caucasus an ardent heart under a numbered army button, and a cultivated mind under a white army cap. These ladies are very charming, and remain charming for a long time! Every year, their admirers are replaced by new ones, and herein, perhaps, lies the secret of their indefatigable amiability. As I climbed the narrow path leading to the Elizabeth Spring, I overtook a bunch of men, some civilian, some military, who, as I afterwards learned, make up a special class of people among those hoping for the action of the waters. They drink – but not water, they walk little, they flirt only in passing, they gamble and complain of ennui. They are dandies: as they dip their wicker-encased glasses into the well of sulphurous water, they assume academic poses: the civilians wear pale-blue neckerchiefs, the military men allow ruffles to show above their coat-collars. They profess a profound contempt for provincial houses and sigh after the capitals' aristocratic salons where they are not admitted.

At last, there was the well. Near it, on the terrace, a small red-roofed structure was built to house the bath, and a little further, there was the gallery where one walked when it rained. Several wounded officers sat on a bench, their crutches drawn up, looking pale and sad. Several ladies walked briskly back and forth on the terrace awaiting the action of the waters. Among them there were two or three pretty faces. In the avenues of vines that cover the slope of Mount Mashuk, one could glimpse now and then the variegated bonnets of ladies partial to shared isolation, since I would always notice, near such a bonnet, either a military cap or one of those round civilian hats that are so ugly. On a steep cliff where the pavilion termed The Aeolian Harp is built, the lovers of scenery perched and trained a telescope on Mount Elbruz: among them were two tutors with their charges, who had come to have their scrofula treated.

I had stopped out of breath on the edge of the hill and, leaning against the corner of the bathhouse, had begun to survey the picturesque landscape, when suddenly I heard a familiar voice behind me:

'Pechorin! Have you been here long?'

I turned around: it was Grushnitsky! We embraced, I had made his acquaintance in a detachment on active duty. He had been wounded by a bullet in the leg and had left for the waters about a week before me.

Grushnitsky is a cadet. He has been in the service only one year; he wears, following a peculiar kind of foppishness, a soldier's thick coat.[79] He has a soldier's St George's Cross. He is well built, swarthy and black-haired; judging by his appearance, one might give him twenty-five years of age, although he is hardly twenty-one. He throws his head back when he speaks, and keeps twirling his moustache with his left hand since he uses his right for leaning on his crutch. His speech is rapid and ornate; he is one of those people who, for every occasion in life, have ready-made pompous phrases, whom unadorned beauty does not move, and who solemnly drape themselves in extraordinary emotions, exalted passions, and exceptional sufferings. To produce an effect is rapture to them; romantic provincial ladies go crazy over them. With age they become either peaceful landowners, or drunkards; sometimes, both. Their souls often possess many good qualities, but not an ounce of poetry. Grushnitsky's passion was[80] to declaim; he bombarded you with words as soon as the talk transcended the circle of everyday notions: I have never been able to argue with him. He does not answer your objections, he does not listen to you. The moment you stop, he launches upon a long tirade apparently having some connection with what you have said, but actually being only a continuation of his own discourse.

He is fairly witty; his epigrams are frequently amusing, but they are neither to the point nor venomous; he will never kill anyone with a single word; he does not know people and their vulnerable spots, since all his life he has been occupied with his own self. His object is to become the hero of a novel. So often has he tried to convince others that he is a being not made for this world and doomed to suffer in secret, that he has almost succeeded in convincing himself of it. That is why he wears, so proudly, that thick soldier's coat of his. I have seen through him, and that is why he dislikes me, although outwardly we are on the friendliest of terms. Grushnitsky has the reputation of an exceptionally brave man. I have seen him in action: he brandishes his sword, he yells, he rushes forward with closed eyes. Somehow, this is not Russian courage!

I don't like him either: I feel that one day we shall meet on a narrow path, and one of us will fare ill.

His coming to the Caucasus is likewise a consequence of his fanatic romanticism. I am sure that on the eve of his departure from the family country seat, he told some pretty neighbour, with a gloomy air, that he was going to the Caucasus not merely to serve there, but that he was seeking death because . . . and here, probably, he would cover his eyes with his hand and continue thus: 'No, you must not know this! Your pure soul would shudder! And what for? What am I to you? Would you understand me? . . .' and so forth.

He told me himself that the reason which impelled him to join the K. regiment would remain an eternal secret between him and heaven.

Yet during those moments when he casts off the tragic cloak, Grushnitsky is quite pleasant and amusing. I am curious to see him with women: that is when, I suppose, he really tries hard!

We met like old chums. I began to question him about life at the spa and its noteworthy people.

'Our life here is rather prosaic,' he said with a sigh. 'Those who drink the waters in the morning are insipid like all invalids, and those who drink wine in the evening are unbearable like all healthy people. Feminine society exists, but there is little comfort therein: these ladies play whist, dress badly and speak dreadful French! From Moscow this year, there is only Princess Ligovskoy with her daughter, but I am not acquainted with them. My soldier's coat is like a seal of rejection. The sympathy that it arouses is as painful as charity.'

At that moment, two ladies walked past us in the direction of the well: one was elderly, the other young and graceful. Their bonnets prevented me from getting a good look at their faces, but they were dressed according to the strict rules of the best taste: there was nothing superfluous. The younger one wore a pearl-grey dress closed at the throat, a light silk fichu twined around her supple neck; shoes, *couleur puce*, so pleasingly constricted at the ankle her spare little foot, that even one uninitiated into the mysteries of beauty would have certainly uttered an exclamation, if only of surprise. Her light yet noble gait had something virginal about it that escaped definition, but was comprehensible to the gaze. As she walked past us, there emanated from her that ineffable fragrance which breathes sometimes from a beloved woman's letter.

'That's Princess Ligovskoy,' said Grushnitsky, 'and with her is her daughter, Mary, as she calls her after the English fashion. They have been here only three days.'

'And yet you already know her name?'

'Yes, I happened to hear it,' he answered flushing. 'I confess, I do not wish to meet them. Those proud aristocrats look upon us army men as savages. And what do they care whether or not there is a mind under a numbered regimental cap and a heart under a thick army coat?'[81]

'Poor coat,' I said with a smile. 'And who is the gentleman going up to them and so helpfully offering them tumblers?'

'Oh, that's the Moscow dandy Raevich. He is a gamester: it can be seen at once by the huge, golden watch
chain that winds across his sky-blue waistcoat. And what
a thick walking stick – like Robinson Crusoe's; and his
beard and haircut *à la moujik*[82] are also characteristic.'

'You are embittered against the whole of humanity?'

'And there is a good reason for that.'

'Oh, really?'

At this point the ladies moved away from the well and
came level with us. Grushnitsky had time to assume a
dramatic attitude with the help of his crutch, and loudly
answered me in French:

*'Mon cher, je hais les hommes pour ne pas les mépriser, car
autrement la vie serait une farce trop dégoûtante.'*[83]

The pretty young princess turned her head and
bestowed a long curious glance upon the orator. The
expression of this glance was very indefinite, but it was not
derisive, a fact on which I inwardly congratulated him with
all my heart.

'This Princess Mary is extremely pretty,' I said to him.
'She has such velvety eyes – yes, velvety is the word for
them. I advise you to appropriate this term when you speak
of her eyes: the upper and lower lashes are so long, that
the pupils do not reflect the rays of the sun. I like this kind
of lustreless eyes: they are so soft, they seem to stroke you.
However, this seems to be the only nice thing about her
face. And her teeth, are they white? This is very important!
Pity she did not smile at your pompous phrase.'

'You talk of a pretty woman as of an English horse,' said
Grushnitsky with indignation.

'Mon cher,' I answered trying to copy his manner, *'je
méprise les femmes pour ne pas les aimer, car autrement la vie
serait un mélodrame trop ridicule.'*

I turned and walked away from him. For about half an
hour, I strolled along the viny avenues, the limestone
lodges, and the bushes hanging between them. It was getting hot, and I decided to hurry home. When passing the
sulphurous spring, I stopped at the covered walk to draw
a deep breath in its shade, and this provided me with the

opportunity to witness a rather curious scene. This is how the actors were placed. The elderly princess and the Moscow dandy sat on a bench in the covered walk, and both seemed to be engrossed in serious conversation. The young princess, probably having finished her last glass of water, strolled pensively near the well. Grushnitsky stood right beside it; there was no one else on the terrace.

I drew closer and hid behind a corner of the walk. At this moment, Grushnitsky dropped his glass upon the sand and tried hard to bend down in order to pick it up. His injured leg hampered him. Poor fellow! How he exerted himself while leaning on his crutch, but all in vain. His expressive face reflected real pain.

Princess Mary saw it all even better than I. Lighter than a little bird, she skipped up to him, bent down, picked up the glass, and handed it to him with a movement full of inexpressible charm. Then she blushed dreadfully, glanced back at the covered walk, but having convinced herself that her mamma had seen nothing, appeared at once to regain her composure. When Grushnitsky opened his mouth to thank her she was already far away. A minute later, she left the gallery with her mother and the dandy, but as she passed by Grushnitsky she assumed a most formal and dignified air, she did not even turn her head, did not even take notice of the passionate glance with which he followed her for a long time until she reached the bottom of the hill and disappeared beyond the young lindens of the boulevard. Presently, her bonnet could be glimpsed crossing the street; she hurried through the gate of one of the best houses in Pyatigorsk. Her mother walked in after her, and at the gate gave Raevich a parting nod.

Only then did the poor passionate cadet notice my presence.

'Did you see?' he said, firmly gripping me by the hand. 'A very angel!'

'Why?' I asked, with an air of the most genuine naïveté.

'Didn't you see?'

'I did: she picked up your glass. Had an attendant been around, he would have done the same thing, and with even

88

more alacrity since he would be hoping for a tip. However, one can quite understand that she felt sorry for you: you made such an awful face when you shifted your weight onto your wounded leg.'

'And you did not feel at all touched looking at her at the moment her soul shone in her face?'

'No.'

I lied, but I wanted to infuriate him. Contradiction is, with me, an innate passion; my entire life has been nothing but a chain of sad and frustrating contradictions to heart or reason. The presence of an enthusiast envelops me with midwinter frost, and I think that frequent commerce with an inert phlegmatic individual would have made of me a passionate dreamer. I further confess that a nasty but familiar sensation, at that moment, skimmed over my heart. This sensation was envy: I boldly say 'envy' because I am used to being frank with myself in everything, and it is doubtful if there can be found a young man who, upon meeting a pretty woman who has riveted his idle attention and has suddenly given obvious preference to another man equally unknown to her, it is doubtful, let me repeat, that there can be found a young man (provided, of course, that he has lived in the *grand monde* and is accustomed to indulge his vanity), who would not be unpleasantly struck by this.

In silence, Grushnitsky and I descended the hill and walked along the boulevard past the windows of the house into which our charmer had vanished. She was sitting at the window. Grushnitsky jerked me by the arm, and threw upon her one of those blurrily tender glances which have so little effect upon women. I trained my lorgnette on her and noticed that his glance made her smile, and that my insolent lorgnette angered her in no uncertain way. And how, indeed, does a Caucasian army officer dare to train his quizzing-glass on a young princess from Moscow?

This morning my doctor friend called on me: his surname is Werner, but he is Russian. Why should this be surprising? I used to know an Ivanov who was German.

Werner is a remarkable man in many respects. He is a sceptic and a materialist, like almost all medical men, but he is also a poet, and this I mean seriously. He is a poet in all his actions, and frequently in his utterings, although in all his life he never wrote two lines of verse. He has studied all the live strings of the human heart in the same way as one studies the veins of a dead body, but he has never learned how to put his knowledge to profit: thus sometimes an excellent anatomist may not know how to cure a fever. Ordinarily, Werner made unobtrusive fun of his patients, but once I saw him cry over a dying soldier. He was poor; he dreamt of becoming a millionaire but would never have taken one additional step for the sake of money. He told me once that he would rather do a favour for an enemy than for a friend, because in the latter case it would mean selling charity, whereas hatred only grows in proportion to an enemy's generosity. He had a caustic tongue: under the label of his epigram, many a kindly man acquired the reputation of a vulgarian and a fool. His competitors, envious resort doctors, once spread the rumour that he drew cartoons of his patients – the patients became infuriated – and almost all refused to be treated by him. His friends, that is to say, all the really decent people serving in the Caucasus, tried in vain to restore his fallen credit.

His appearance was[84] of the kind that, at first glance, impresses one unfavourably but attracts one later, when the eye has learned to decipher in irregular features the imprint of a dependable and lofty soul. Examples are known of women falling madly in love with such people and of not exchanging their ugly exterior for the beauty of the freshest and rosiest Endymions. Women must be given their due: they have a flair for spiritual beauty. This may be why men like Werner are so passionately fond of women.

Werner was of small stature, thin and frail like a child. One of his legs was shorter than the other, as in the case of Byron; in proportion to his body, his head seemed enormous; he cropped his hair; the bumps of his skull, thus revealed, would have amazed a phrenologist by their bizarre interplay of contradictory inclinations. His small black eyes, never at rest, tried to penetrate your mind. His dress revealed taste and tidiness; his lean, wiry, small hands sported light-yellow gloves. His frock coat, neckcloth and waistcoat were always black. The younger men dubbed him Mephistopheles. He pretended to resent this nickname, but, in point of fact, it flattered his vanity. We soon came to understand each other and became pals – for I am not capable of true friendship. One of the two friends is always the slave of the other, although, often, neither of the two admits this to himself. I can be nobody's slave, while to assume command in such cases is tiresome work because it has to be combined with deceit. I, moreover, am supplied with lackeys and money. We became pals in the following way: I first met Werner in the town of S—, among a numerous and noisy group of young men. Toward the end of the evening, the conversation took a philosophic and metaphysical turn; convictions were discussed; everyone was convinced of something or other.

'As for me, I am convinced of only one thing,' said the doctor.

'Of what?' I asked, wishing to learn the opinion of this man who up to now had been silent.

'Of the fact', he answered, 'that, sooner or later, one fine morning, I shall die.'

'I'm better off than you,' I said. 'I've one more conviction besides yours, namely that one miserable evening I had the misfortune to be born.'

Everybody found that we were talking nonsense, but, really, not one of them said anything more intelligent than that. Henceforth, we distinguished each other in the crowd. We would often see each other and discuss, together, with great seriousness, abstract matters, until we noticed that we were gulling each other. Then, after looking meaningly into each other's eyes, we began to laugh as Roman augurs[85] did, according to Cicero, and having had our fill of mirth, we would separate well-content with our evening.

I was lying on the divan, with eyes directed at the ceiling and hands clasped under my head, when Werner entered my room. He sat down in an armchair, placed his cane in a corner, yawned, and declared that it was getting hot out of doors. I answered that the flies were bothering me, and we both fell silent.

'Observe, my dear doctor,' said I, 'that without fools, the world would be a dull place . . . Consider: here we are, two intelligent people; we know beforehand that one can argue endlessly about anything, and therefore we do not argue; we know almost all the secret thoughts of each other; one word is a whole story for us; we see the kernel of our every emotion through a triple[86] shell. Sad things seem to us funny, funny things seem to us melancholy, and generally we are, to tell the truth, rather indifferent to everything except our own selves. Thus, between us there can be no exchange of feelings and thoughts: we know everything about each other that we wish to know, and we do not wish to know anything more. There remains only one solution: telling the news. So tell me some piece of news.'

Tired by my long speech, I closed my eyes and yawned.

He answered, after a moment's thought: 'Nevertheless, your drivel contains an idea.'

'Two ideas,' I answered.

'Tell me one, and I'll tell you the other.'

'All right, you start!' said I, continuing to examine the ceiling and inwardly smiling.

'You'd like to learn some details about some resort guest, and I have already an inkling as to the subject of your concern, because there have already been inquiries about you in that quarter.'

'Doctor! It is definitely impossible for us to converse: we read in each other's souls.'

'Now, the other idea . . .'

'Here is the other idea: I wanted to make you relate

something or other – in the first place, because to listen is less fatiguing; in the second place, because a listener cannot give himself away; in the third place, because one can discover another's secret; and in the fourth place, because such intelligent people as you prefer an audience to a storyteller. Now, to business! What did the old Princess Ligovskoy say to you about me?'

'You are quite sure that it was the old princess and not the young one?'

'I'm absolutely sure.'

'Why?'

'Because the young princess asked about Grushnitsky.'

'You've a great talent for putting two and two together. The young princess said she was sure that that young man in the soldier's coat had been degraded to the ranks for a duel.'

'I hope you left her under this pleasant delusion.'

'Naturally.'

'We have the beginning of a plot!'I cried in delight. 'The dénouement of this comedy will be our concern. Fate is obviously taking care of my not being bored.'

'I have a presentiment', said the doctor, 'that poor Grushnitsky is going to be your victim . . .'

'Go on with your story, doctor.'

'The old princess said that your face was familiar to her. I observed to her that no doubt she had met you in Petersburg, at some fashionable reception. I told her your name. The name was known to her. I believe your escapade caused a big sensation there. The old princess started to tell of your exploits, adding her own remarks to what was probably society gossip. Her daughter listened with curiosity. In her imagination, you became the hero of a novel in the latest fashion. I did not contradict the old lady, though I was aware she was talking nonsense.'

'My worthy friend!' said I, extending my hand to him. The doctor shook it with feeling, and continued:

'If you wish, I'll introduce you . . .'

'Mercy!' said I, raising my hands. 'Does one introduce

heroes? They never meet their beloved other than in the act of saving her from certain death.'

'And so you really intend to flirt with the young princess?'

'On the contrary, quite on the contrary! Doctor, at last I triumph: you do not understand me! This, however, saddens me, doctor,' I went on, after a moment of silence. 'I never disclose my secrets myself, but I am awfully fond of having them divined, because that way I can always repudiate them if necessary. But come, you must describe to me the mamma and the daughter. What sort of people are they?'

'Well, in the first place, the mother is a woman of forty-five,' answered Werner. 'Her digestion is excellent, but there is something wrong with her blood; there are red blotches on her cheeks. She has spent the latter half of her life in Moscow, and there, in retirement, has grown fat. She likes risqué anecdotes and sometimes, when her daughter is not in the room, says improper things herself. She announced to me that her daughter was as innocent as a dove. What do I care? I was on the point of replying that she need not worry, I would not tell anybody. The mother is being treated for rheumatism, and what the daughter's complaint is, goodness knows. I told them both to drink two glasses of oxysulphuric water daily, and take a diluted bath twice a week. The old princess, it seems, is not used to command; she has great respect for the intelligence and the knowledge of her daughter, who has read Byron in English[87] and knows algebra. It seems that in Moscow young ladies have taken to higher education, and, by Jove, it's a good thing! Our men, generally speaking, are so boorish that to coquet with them must be unbearable for any intelligent woman. The old princess is very fond of young men; the young princess looks at them with a certain contempt – a Moscow habit! In Moscow, all they enjoy is the company of forty-year-old wags.'

'And you, doctor, have you been in Moscow?'

'Yes, I had a fair amount of practice there.'

'Go on with your story.'

'Well, I seem to have told you everything . . . Oh yes! One more thing: the young princess seems fond of discussing sentiments, passions, and so forth. She spent one winter in Petersburg, and did not like it, especially the society there: probably she was given a cool reception.'

'You saw no one at their house today?'

'On the contrary, there was one adjutant, one stiff-looking guardsman, and a lady who has recently arrived, a relative of the princess by marriage, a very pretty woman but a very sick one, it seems . . . Didn't you chance to meet her at the well? She's of medium height, a blonde, with regular features, her complexion is consumptive, and she has a little black mole on her right cheek. Her face struck me by its expressiveness.'

'A little mole!' I muttered through my teeth. 'Really?'

The doctor looked at me and said solemnly, placing his hand on my heart: 'She is someone you know! . . .' My heart, indeed, was beating faster than usual.

'It is now your turn to triumph,' I said, 'but I rely on you; you will not betray me. I have not seen her yet, but I am sure that I recognize, from your depiction, a certain woman I loved in the old days. Don't tell her a word about me; should she ask, give a bad account of me.'

'As you please!' said Werner with a shrug.

When he left, a dreadful sadness constrained my heart. Was it fate that was bringing us together again in the Caucasus, or had she come here on purpose, knowing she would meet me? And how would we meet? And, anyway, was it she? Presentiments never deceive me. There is no man in the world over whom the past gains such power as it does over me. Every reminder of a past sorrow or joy painfully strikes my soul and extracts from it the same old sounds . . . I am stupidly made, I forget nothing . . . nothing!

After dinner, around six, I went out on to the boulevard: there was a crowd there; the princess sat with her daughter on a bench, surrounded by young men who vied in paying attention to them. I sat down on another bench some way off, stopped two officers of the D. regiment whom I knew, and began telling them something; apparently, it was amusing, because they began laughing like mad. Curiosity attracted to me some of those who surrounded the young princess; little by little, they all abandoned her and joined my group. I never ceased talking; my stories were clever to the point of stupidity, my raillery, directed at the freaks who passed by, was wicked to the point of frenzy. I went on entertaining my audience till sunset. Several times, the young princess and her mother passed by me, arm in arm, accompanied by a little old man with a limp; several times her glance, falling upon me, expressed vexation while striving to express indifference.

'What has he been telling you?' she inquired of one of the young men who had returned to her out of politeness. 'Surely, a very entertaining story . . . his exploits in battles?' She said this rather loudly and probably with the intention of pin-pricking me. 'Aha,' I thought, 'you are angry in earnest, my dear princess; just wait, there is more to come!'

Grushnitsky watched her like a beast of prey and never took his eyes off her: I bet that tomorrow he will beg somebody to introduce him to her mother. She will be very pleased, because she is bored.

16 May

During the last two days, my affairs have advanced tremendously. The young princess definitely hates me: people have already reported to me two or three epigrams aimed at me, fairly caustic, but at the same time very flattering. She finds it awfully strange that I, who am used to high society and am on such intimate terms with her Petersburg female cousins and aunts, do not try to make her acquaintance. Every day, we run into each other at the well or on the boulevard; I do my best to lure away her admirers, brilliant adjutants, pallid Moscovites and others – and almost always, I succeed. I have always hated to entertain guests at my house. Now, my place is full every day; people dine, sup, play cards, and, alas, my champagne triumphs over the power of her magnetic young eyes![88]

Yesterday, I saw her in Chelakhov's store: she was bargaining for a wonderful Persian rug. The young princess kept begging her mamma not to be stingy; that rug would be such an adornment for her dressing room! I offered forty roubles more and outbid her; for this I was rewarded by a glance in which glittered the most exquisite rage. About dinner time, I purposely ordered my Circassian horse to be covered with that rug and led past her windows. Werner was with them at the time, and told me that the effect of that scene was most dramatic. The young princess wants to preach a crusade against me: I have even noticed that already two adjutants in her presence greet me very drily, although they dine at my house every day.

Grushnitsky has assumed a mysterious air: he walks with his hands behind his back and does not seem to recognize anybody; his leg has suddenly got well, he hardly limps at all. He has found the occasion to enter into conversation with the old princess and to pay a compliment to her daughter. The latter is apparently none too choosy, for since then she has been acknowledging his salute with the prettiest of smiles.

'You are sure you do not wish to make the acquaintance of the Ligovskoys?' he said to me yesterday.

'Quite sure.'

'Oh come! Theirs is the pleasantest house at the spa! All the best society here . . .'

'My friend, I am dreadfully sick of the best society which is not here. And you . . . do you go there?'

'Not yet. I have talked to the young princess a couple of times, and more.[89] It is kind of embarrassing to fish for an invitation, you know, though it is done here . . . It would have been another matter, if I wore epaulets. . . .'

'Oh come! You are much more intriguing this way! You simply don't know how to take advantage of your lucky situation. In the eyes of any sentimental young lady, your soldier's coat is bound to make a hero of you, a martyr.'

Grushnitsky smiled smugly.

'What nonsense!' he said.

'I'm sure', I went on, 'that the young princess is already in love with you.'

He blushed to the ears, and puffed out his chest.[90]

O vanity! you are the lever by means of which Archimedes wished to lift the earth!

'You always joke!' he said, feigning to be cross. 'In the first place, she knows me so little as yet.'

'Women love only those whom they do not know.'

'But I have no pretension whatever to make her fond of me, I simply want to gain access to a pleasant house, and it would have been quite absurd if I had any hopes . . . Now you people, for example, are another matter; you St Petersburg lady-killers, you have only to look . . . and women melt . . . By the way, Pechorin, do you know what the young princess said about you?'

'Really? Has she already started to speak to you about me?'

'Wait – there is nothing to be glad about. The other day I entered into conversation with her at the well, by chance. Her third word was: "Who is that gentleman with that unpleasant oppressive gaze? He was with you when . . ." She blushed and did not want to name the day, remembering her charming gesture. "You don't have to mention the day," I replied to her, "it will always remain in my memory." Pechorin, my friend! I do not congratulate you; you are on her black list. And this, indeed, is regrettable because [my][91] Mary is a very charming girl!'

It should be noted that Grushnitsky is one of those people who, when speaking of a woman whom they hardly know, call her *my Mary, my Sophie,* if she had the fortune to catch their fancy.

I assumed a serious air and replied to him:

'Yes, she is not bad . . . But beware, Grushnitsky! Russian young ladies, for the most part, nourish themselves on platonic love, without admixing to it any thought of marriage: now, platonic love is the most troublesome kind. The young princess seems to be one of those women who want to be amused: if she is bored in your presence for two minutes together, you are irretrievably lost. Your silence must excite her curiosity, your talk should never entirely satisfy it; you must disturb her every minute. She will disregard convention, publicly, a dozen times for your sake, and will call it a sacrifice, and, in order to reward herself for it, she will begin to torment you, and after that she will simply say that she cannot stand you. Unless you gain some ascendancy over her, even her first kiss will not entitle you to a second: she will have her fill of flirting with you, and in two years or so she will marry a monster out of submissiveness to her mother, and will start persuading herself that she is miserable, that she loved only one man, meaning you, but that Heaven had not wished to unite her with him because he wore a soldier's coat, although under that thick grey coat there beat a passionate and noble heart . . .'

Grushnitsky hit the table with his fist and started to pace up and down the room.

I inwardly roared with laughter, and even smiled once or twice, but fortunately he did not notice.

It is clear that he is in love, for he has become even more credulous than before: there even appeared on his finger, a nielloed, silver ring of local production. It looked suspicious to me. I began to examine it, and what would you think? . . . The name *Mary* was engraved in minuscule letters on the inside, and next to it was the day of the month when she picked up the famous glass. I concealed my discovery. I do not wish to force a confession from him, I want him to choose me for a confidant himself – and it is then that I shall enjoy myself! . . .

.   .   .   .

Today I rose late; when I reached the well, there was already nobody there. It was getting hot; furry white clouds were rapidly scudding from the snowy mountains with the promise of a thunderstorm; the top of Mount Mashuk smoked like an extinguished torch; around it there coiled and slithered, like snakes, grey shreds of cloud, which had been delayed in their surge and seemed to have caught in its thorny brush. The air was pervaded with electricity. I plunged into a viny avenue that led to a grotto; I was sad.

I kept thinking of that young woman with the little birth-mark on her cheek of whom the doctor had been talking. Why was she here? And was it she? And why did I think it was she? And why was I even so sure of it? Were there not many women with little moles on their cheeks! Meditating in this fashion, I came close to the grotto. As I looked in, I saw in the cool shade of its vault, on a stone bench, a seated woman, wearing a straw hat, a black shawl wrapped around her shoulders, her head sunken on her breast: the hat screened her face. I was on the point of turning back, so as not to disturb her revery, when she looked up at me.

'Vera!' I cried involuntarily.

She started and grew pale.

'I knew that you were here,' she said.

I sat down near her and took her hand. A long-forgotten thrill ran through my veins at the sound of that dear voice: she looked into my eyes with her deep and calm eyes; they expressed distrust and something akin to reproachfulness.

'We have not seen each other for a long time,' I said.

'Yes, a long time, and we have both changed in many ways!'

'So this means that you do not love me any more? . . .'

'I am married! . . .' she said.

'Again? Several years ago, however, the same reason existed, and yet . . .'

She snatched her hand out of mine. And her cheeks flamed.

'Perhaps you love your second husband . . .'

She did not answer and turned away.

'Or is he very jealous?'

Silence.

'Well? He is young, handsome, he is, in particular, rich, no doubt, and you are afraid . . .' I glanced at her and was shocked: her face expressed profound despair, tears sparkled in her eyes.

'Tell me,' she whispered at last, 'do you find it very amusing to torture me? I ought to hate you. Ever since we have known each other, you gave me nothing but sufferings . . .' Her voice trembled; she leaned toward me to lay her head on my breast.

'Perhaps', I thought, 'this is exactly why you loved me: one forgets joys, one never forgets sorrows. . . .'

I embraced her warmly, and thus we remained for a long time. At last our lips came close together and merged in an ardent rapturous kiss; her hands were as cold as ice, her brow was burning. Between us, started one of those conversations which have no sense on paper, which cannot be repeated and which one cannot even retain in one's mind: the meaning of sounds replaces and enhances the meaning of words, as in the Italian opera.

She definitely does not wish that I meet her husband, that little old gentleman with the limp whom I glimpsed on the boulevard: she married him for the sake of her son. He is rich and suffers from rheumatism. I did not allow myself a single jibe at him: she respects him as a father – and will deceive him as a husband. What a bizarre thing, the human heart in general, and a woman's heart in particular!

Vera's husband, Semyon Vasilievich G–v, is a distant relation of Princess Ligovskoy. He lives near her: Vera often visits the old princess. I gave her my word that I would get acquainted with the Ligovskoys and court the young princess in order to divert attention from Vera. In this way, my plans have not been upset in the least, and I shall have a merry time. . .

Merry time! Yes, I have already passed that stage of the soul's life when one seeks only happiness, when the heart feels the need to love someone strongly and passionately. At present, all I wish is to be loved, and that by very few: it even seems to me that I would be content with one permanent attachment, a pitiful habit of the heart!

One thing has always struck me as strange: I never became the slave of the women I loved; on the contrary, I have always gained unconquerable power over their will and heart, with no effort at all. Why is it so? Is it because I never treasured anything too much, while they incessantly feared to let me slip out of their hands? Or is it the magnetic influence of a strong organism? Or did I simply never succeed in encountering a woman with a stubborn will of her own?

I must admit that, indeed, I never cared for women with wills of their own; it is not their department.

True, I remember now – once, only once did I love a strong-willed woman, whom I could never conquer. We parted enemies – but even so, perhaps, had our meeting occurred five years later, we would have parted differently.

Vera is ill, very ill, although she will not admit it: I fear she may have consumption, or that disease which is called *fièvre lente*,[92] a completely non-Russian disease, for which there is no name in our language.

The thunderstorm caught us in the grotto and detained us there for an extra half hour. She did not make me swear that I would be true to her, did not ask if I had loved other women since we had parted. She entrusted herself to me again with the same unconcern as before – and I will not deceive her. She is the only woman on earth whom I could not bear to deceive. I know that we shall soon part again – perhaps, forever; that each of us will go his separate way, graveward. But her memory will remain inviolable in my soul: I have always repeated this to her, and she believes me, although she says she does not.

At last, we separated: for a long time, I followed her with my gaze until her hat disappeared behind the shrubs and cliffs. My heart painfully contracted as after the first parting. Oh, how that feeling gladdened me! Could it be that youth with its beneficial storms wants to return to me again, or is it merely its farewell glance – a last gift to its memory? And yet it's absurd to think that in appearance I am still a boy: my face is pale but still fresh-complexioned, my limbs are supple and svelte, my thick hair curls, my eyes sparkle, my blood is ebullient.

When I returned home, I got on my horse and galloped out into the steppe. I love to gallop on a spirited horse through tall grass, against the wind of the wilderness; avidly do I swallow the redolent air and direct my gaze into the blue remoteness, trying to distinguish the nebulous outlines of objects that become, every minute, clearer and clearer. Whatever sorrow may burden my heart, whatever anxiety may oppress my mind, everything is dispersed in a moment: the soul feels easy, bodily fatigue vanquishes mental worry. There is no feminine gaze that I would not forget at the sight of mountains covered with curly vegetation,[93] and illumined by the southern sun, at the sight of the blue sky, or at the sound of a torrent that falls from crag to crag.

I think that the Cossacks yawning on the top of their watchtowers, upon seeing me galloping without need or goal, were for a long time tormented by this riddle, for I am sure they must have taken me for a Circassian because of my dress. Indeed, I have been told that when riding in Circassian garb, I look more like a Kabardan than many a Kabardan. And, in point of fact, as regards that noble battle garb, I am an absolute dandy: not one bit of superfluous braid; costly arms in plain setting; the fur of the cap neither too long nor too short; leggings and boots fitted with the utmost exactitude; a white *beshmet;* a dark-brown *cherke-ska.*[94] I have studied, for a long time, the mountain peoples' style of riding: there is no better way of flattering my vanity than to acknowledge my skill in riding a horse in the Caucasian fashion. I keep four horses: one for myself, three for pals, so as not to feel dull while ranging the fields alone: they take my horses with alacrity, and never ride with me. It was already six in the evening, when I remembered that it was time to dine. My horse was worn out; I came on to the road which led from Pyatigorsk to the German settlement where the spa society frequently went for picnics. The road ran winding among bushes, and descending into small ravines where noisy creeks flowed under the shelter of tall grasses; all around rose an amphitheatre of blue masses – Besh Tau, Snake Mountain, Iron Mountain and Bald Mountain. Upon descending into one of these ravines, called *balkas*[95] in the local dialect, I stopped to water my horse. At that moment, there appeared on the road a noisy and resplendent cavalcade, the ladies in black or light-blue riding habits, and the gentlemen in costumes representing a mixture of Circassian and Nizhny-Novgorodan:[96] Grush-nitsky rode in front with Princess Mary.

Ladies at Caucasian spas still believe in the possibility of Circassian attacks in broad daylight: presumably, this is why Grushnitsky had hung a sword and a brace of pistols on to his soldier's coat. He was rather absurd in this heroic attire. A tall shrub hid me from them, but through its foliage I could see everything and could guess from the expressions on their faces that the conversation was senti-mental. Finally, they drew close to the declivity; Grushnit-sky took the princess's horse by the bridle, and then I heard the end of their conversation:

'And you wish to remain for the rest of your life in the Caucasus?' the princess was saying.

'What is Russia to me?' answered her companion, 'a country where thousands of people will look on me with contempt because they are richer than I am – whereas here – this thick soldier's coat has not prevented me from making your acquaintance . . .'

'On the contrary . . .' said the princess, blushing.

Grushnitsky's face portrayed pleasure. He went on:

'My life here will flow by noisily, unnoticeably, and rapidly under the bullets of the savages, and if God would send me, every year, one radiant feminine glance, one glance similar to the one . . .'

At this point they came level with me; I struck my horse with my riding crop and rode out from behind the bush. . . .

'*Mon Dieu, un Circassien!* . . .' cried the princess in terror.

In order to dissuade her completely, I answered in French, bowing slightly:

'*Ne craignez rien, madame – je ne suis pas plus dangereux que votre cavalier.*' She was embarrassed – but why? Because of her mistake, or because my answer seemed insolent to her? I would have liked my second supposition to be the correct one. Grushnitsky cast a look of displeasure at me.

Late this evening, that is to say around eleven, I went for a stroll in the linden avenue of the boulevard. The town was asleep: only in some windows lights could be glimpsed. On three sides, there loomed the black crest of cliffs, offshoots of Mount Mashuk, on the summit of which an ominous little cloud was lying. The moon was rising in the east; afar glittered the silvery rim of snow-covered mountains. The cries of sentries alternated with the sound of the hot springs, which had been given free flow for the night. At times, the sonorous stamp of a horse was heard in the street, accompanied by the creaking of a Nogay[97] wagon and a mournful Tatar song. I sat down on a bench and became lost in thought. I felt the need of pouring out my thoughts in friendly talk – but with whom? What was Vera doing now, I wondered. I would have paid dearly to press her hand at that moment.

Suddenly I heard quick irregular steps – Grushnitsky, no doubt. So it was!

'Where do you come from?'

'From Princess Ligovskoy,' he said very importantly. 'How Mary can sing!'

'Do you know what?' I said to him, 'I bet she does not know that you are a cadet; she thinks you have been degraded to the ranks.'

'Perhaps! What do I care?' he said absently.

'Oh, I just happened to mention it.'

'Do you know, you made her dreadfully angry today? She found it an unheard-of insolence. I had a lot of trouble convincing her that you are too well brought up and that you know the *grand monde* too well to have had any intention of insulting her: she says that you have an impudent gaze and that, no doubt, you have the highest opinion of yourself.'

'She is not mistaken . . . Perhaps you would like to stand up for her?'

'I regret that I do not have that right yet . . .'

'Oh, oh!' I thought, 'I see he already has hopes.'

'Well, so much the worse for you,' Grushnitsky continued, 'it would be difficult for you to make their acquaintance now; and that's a pity! It is one of the most pleasant houses that I know of.'

I smiled inwardly.

'The most pleasant house for me is now my own,' I said yawning, and got up to go.

'But first confess, you repent?'

'What nonsense! If I choose, I shall be at the old princess's house tomorrow evening . . .'

'We shall see . . .'

'And even, to oblige you, I shall flirt with the young princess. . . .'

'Yes, if she is willing to speak to you . . .'

'I shall only wait for the moment when your conversation begins to bore her . . . Good-bye.'

'And I shall go roaming; I could never fall asleep now . . . Look, let's better go to the restaurant, there is gambling there . . . tonight I require strong sensations . . .'

'I wish you bad luck.'

I went home.

21 May

Almost a week has passed, and I still have not made the acquaintance of the Ligovskoys. I am waiting for a convenient occasion. Grushnitsky, like a shadow, follows the young princess everywhere; their conversations are endless: when will he begin to bore her at last? Her mother does not pay any attention to this because he is not an 'eligible' young man. That's the logic of mothers for you! I have observed two or three tender glances – an end must be put to it.

Yesterday, Vera appeared for the first time at the well. Since our meeting in the grotto, she has not been out of the house. We dipped our glasses simultaneously and, bending, she said to me in a whisper:

'You don't want to get acquainted with the Ligovskoys? It's the only place where we could see each other.'

A reproach! How dull! But I have deserved it . . .

Apropos, tomorrow there is a subscription dance in the ballroom of the restaurant, and I am going to dance the mazurka with the young princess.

22 May

The restaurant's ballroom was transformed into that of the Club of the Nobility. By nine o'clock, everybody had arrived. The old princess and her daughter were among the last to appear: many ladies looked at her with envy and ill will because Princess Mary dresses with taste. Those ladies who regard themselves as the aristocrats of the place concealed their envy and attached themselves to her. What can you do? Where there is feminine society, there will appear at once a higher and a lower circle. Outside the window, in a crowd of people, stood Grushnitsky,[98] pressing his face to the windowpane and never taking his eyes off his goddess: as she passed by, she gave him a hardly perceptible nod. He beamed like the sun. The dancing began with a polonaise; then the band began to play a waltz. Spurs tinkled, coat tails flew up and whirled.

I stood behind a stout lady: her head was crowned with pink plumes; the luxuriance of her dress recalled the times of farthingales, and the variegation of her rough skin, the happy era of black taffeta patches. The largest wart on her neck was concealed by the clasp of a necklace. She was saying to her dancing partner, a captain of dragoons:

'That young Princess Ligovskoy is an intolerable little thing! Fancy, she bumped into me and never apologized, but in addition turned around and looked at me through her lorgnette ... *C'est impayable!* ... And what is she so proud of? She ought to be taught a lesson ...'

'No trouble in getting that done,' answered the obliging captain, and went into the next room.

I immediately went up to the young princess and engaged her for the waltz, taking advantage of the easy local customs which allow one to dance with ladies to whom one has not been introduced.

She could hardly force herself not to smile and not to hide her triumph: she managed, however, rather soon to assume a completely indifferent and even severe air. She nonchalantly dropped her hand on my shoulder, slightly inclined her pretty head to one side and off we went. I do not know a waist more voluptuous and supple! Her fresh breath touched my face; sometimes a curl that had become separated in the whirl of the waltz from its fellows, would brush my burning cheek. I made three turns (she waltzes amazingly well). She was out of breath, her eyes were dim, her half-opened lips could hardly murmur the obligatory 'Merci, monsieur.'

After several moments of silence, I said to her, assuming a most submissive air:

'I hear, princess, that despite my being completely unknown to you, I have already had the misfortune to earn your displeasure . . . that you've found me insolent . . . Can this be true?'

'And now you would like to confirm me in this opinion?' she replied with an ironic little grimace, which incidentally was very becoming to her mobile features.

'If I had the insolence to offend you in any way, then allow me to have the still greater insolence to beg your pardon. And truly, I would wish very much to prove to you that you are mistaken about me.'

'You will find this rather difficult.'

'Why so?'

'Because you do not come to our house, and these balls will probably not take place very often.'

'This means', I thought, 'that their door is closed to me forever.'

'Do you know, princess,' I said with some vexation, 'one should never turn down a repentant criminal: out of sheer despair he may become twice as criminal as before, and then . . .'

Laughter and whispering among the people around us made me turn and interrupt my sentence. A few steps away from me stood a group of men, and among them was the Captain of Dragoons who had declared hostile intentions against the charming young princess. He was particularly satisfied with something; he rubbed his hands, he laughed and exchanged winks with his companions. Suddenly out of their midst emerged a person in a dresscoat, with a long moustache and a florid face, and directed his unsteady steps straight toward the young princess: he was drunk. Having come to a stop in front of the disconcerted princess, and clasping his hands behind his back, he fixed her with his bleary, grey eyes and uttered in a hoarse, treble voice:

'Permetay . . . oh, what's the use of that! . . . I simply engage you for the mazurka . . .'

'What do you want?' she uttered in a trembling voice, as she cast around her an imploring glance. Alas! her mother was far away, and in her vicinity she could see none of the gentlemen she knew. One adjutant, I think, witnessed it all, but hid behind the crowd so as not to be involved in a row.

'Well?' said the drunk, winking at the Captain of Dragoons, who was encouraging him with signs, 'don't you want to? Here I am again requesting the honour of engaging you *pour mazurque*[99] . . . You think, perhaps, that I am drunk? That does not matter! One is much freer that way, I can assure you.'

I saw that she was about to swoon from fear and indignation.

I went up to the drunk, took him rather firmly by the arm and looking steadily into his eyes, asked him to go away, because, I added, the princess had long ago promised to dance the mazurka with me.

'Well, nothing to be done! . . . Some other time!' he said with a laugh, and went off to join his abashed companions, who immediately led him away into the other room.

I was rewarded by a deep, wonderful glance.

The princess went up to her mother and told her everything: the latter sought me out in the crowd and thanked me. She informed me that she used to know my mother and was on friendly terms with half a dozen of my aunts.

'I do not know how it happened that we have not met before now,' she added, 'but you must admit that you alone are to blame for this; you shun everybody: I have never seen anything like it. I hope that the atmosphere of my drawing room will dissipate your spleen . . . Am I right?'

I said to her one of those phrases which everyone should have in store for such occasions.

The quadrilles dragged on for a terribly long time.

At last, the mazurka resounded from the upper balcony. The young princess and I seated ourselves.

Never once did I allude either to the tipsy man, or to my former behaviour, or to Grushnitsky. The impression that the unpleasant scene had made upon her gradually dissipated. Her pretty face bloomed, she joked very charmingly, her conversation was witty, without any pretension to wit, it was lively and free; her observations were sometimes profound. I gave her to understand, by means of a very involved sentence, that I had long been attracted to her. She inclined her young head and coloured slightly.

'You're a bizarre person!' she presently said, raising upon me her velvety eyes and laughing in a constrained way.

'I did not wish to make your acquaintance,' I continued, 'because you were surrounded by too dense a crowd of admirers, and I was afraid of getting completely lost in it.'

'Your fears were unfounded: all of them are most dull . . .'

'All! Are you sure you mean all?'

She looked at me intently, as if trying to recall something, then she slightly blushed again, and finally uttered resolutely: '*all!*'

'Including even my friend Grushnitsky?'

'Why, is he your friend?' she said, revealing some doubt.

'Yes.'

'He does not enter, of course, into the category of dull people.'

'Rather the category of unfortunate ones,' I said laughing.

'Of course! You find it funny? I wish you were in his place.'

'Well, I used to be a cadet myself and indeed it was the very best time of my life!'

'But is he a cadet? . . .' she said quickly, and then added: 'I thought that . . .'

'What is it you thought?'

'Nothing! . . . Who is that lady?'

Here the conversation took another direction, and did not return to that subject any more.

The mazurka came to an end, and we parted – until our next meeting. The ladies left. I went to have supper and ran into Werner.

'Aha!' he said, 'so that's the way you are! Didn't you intend not to make the princess's acquaintance in any other way than by saving her from certain death?'

'I did better,' I answered him, 'I saved her from fainting at a ball . . .'

'How's that? Tell me. . . .'

'No, try and guess – you, who can guess all things in the world!'

23 May

Around seven tonight, I was out strolling on the boulevard. Grushnitsky, on seeing me in the distance, came up to me: a kind of absurd exaltation shone in his eyes. He gripped my hand and said in a tragic voice:

'I thank you, Pechorin . . . You understand me?'

'No; but whatever it is, it is not worth gratitude,' I answered, having indeed no charitable action on my conscience.

'But what about last night? You can't have forgotten?. . . Mary told me everything . . .'

'Do you two have everything in common now? Even gratitude?'

'Look,' said Grushnitsky very importantly, 'please do not make fun of my love, if you wish to remain my pal . . . You see, I love her to distraction. And I think, I hope, that she loves me too . . . I have a favour to ask of you. You are going to visit them tonight: promise me to observe everything. I know you are experienced in these matters, you know women better than I do . . . Women! Women! Who will understand them? Their smiles contradict their glances, their words promise and lure, while the sound of their voices drives us away. One minute they comprehend and divine our most secret thought, and the next, they do not understand the clearest hints. Take the young princess, for instance, yesterday her eyes blazed with passion when they rested upon me, today they are dull and cold . . .'

'This, perhaps, is due to the effect of the waters,' I answered.

'You see in everything the nasty side . . . you materialist,' he added contemptuously. 'Let us switch, however, to another matter.' And pleased with this poor pun, he cheered up.

Around half past eight, we went together to the princess's house.

Walking past Vera's windows, I saw her at the window. We threw each other a fleeting glance. She entered the Ligovskoys' drawing room soon after us. The old princess introduced me to her as to a relation of hers. Tea was being served; there were many visitors; the conversation was general. I endeavoured to ingratiate myself with the old princess; I jested, I made her laugh heartily several times: the young princess also wanted to laugh more than once, but she restrained herself so as not to depart from the role she had assumed. She finds that a languorous air suits her, and perhaps she does not err, Grushnitsky was apparently very glad that my gaiety did not infect her.

After tea, we all went into the music room.

'Are you pleased with my obedience, Vera?' I said as I passed her.

She threw me a glance full of love and gratitude. I am now used to those glances, but there was a time when they made my bliss. The old princess had her daughter sit down at the piano: everyone was asking her to sing something. I kept silent and, taking advantage of the hubbub, I drew away toward a window with Vera, who wanted to tell me something very important for both of us. It turned out to be nonsense.

Meanwhile, my indifference was annoying to the young princess, as I could conjecture by a single angry, blazing glance . . . Oh, I understand wonderfully that kind of conversation, mute but expressive, brief but forcible! . . .

She started to sing: her voice is not bad, but she sings

poorly. I did not listen, however. In compensation, Grushnitsky, with his elbows on the piano, facing her, devoured her with his eyes and every minute kept saying under his breath: '*Charmant! Délicieux!*'

'Listen,' Vera was saying to me, 'I do not want you to meet my husband, but you must, without fail, please the old princess. It is easy for you; you can achieve anything you want. We shall see each other only here. . . .'[100]

'Only here? . . .'

She coloured and went on: 'You know that I am your slave; I never was able to resist you . . . and for this I shall be punished. You will cease to love me. I wish, at least, to save my reputation . . . not for my own sake: you know that very well! Oh, I beseech you, do not torment me as before with empty doubts and feigned coldness. I shall die soon, perhaps, I feel myself getting weaker every day . . . and, in spite of that, I cannot think of a future life, I think only of you . . . You men do not understand the delights of a glance, of a handshake . . . while I, I swear to you, I, when listening to your voice, I experience such deep, strange bliss that the most ardent kisses could not replace it.'

Meanwhile Princess Mary had stopped singing. A murmur of praise sounded around her. I went up to her after all the other guests and said something to her about her voice, rather casually.

She made a grimace, protruding her lower lip and curtsied in a very mocking manner.

'It is all the more flattering to me,' she said, 'since you did not listen to me at all; but then, perhaps, you do not like music?'

'On the contrary . . . particularly after dinner.'

'Grushnitsky is right in saying that you have most prosaic tastes . . . And I see that you like music in a gastronomic way.'

'You are wrong again. I am far from being a gourmet: my digestion is exceedingly bad. But music after dinner puts one to sleep, and sleep after dinner is good for one's health. Consequently, I like music from a medical point of view. In the evening, on the contrary, it irritates my nerves too much; my mood becomes either too melancholy, or too gay. Both are exhausting, when there is no positive cause to be sad or to be joyful, and, moreover, melancholy at a social gathering is absurd, while immoderate gaiety is improper . . .'

She did not hear me out, moved away, sat down next to Grushnitsky, and there started between them some kind of sentimental conversation. The young princess, it seemed, replied rather absently and irrelevantly to his wise pronouncements, though she tried to show that she listened to him with attention, for now and then he would glance at her with surprise, trying to guess the reason for the inward agitation that expressed itself now and then in her restless glance.

But I have found you out, my dear princess. Beware! You want to repay me in my own coin, to prick my vanity – you will not succeed. And if you declare war on me, I shall be merciless.

In the course of the evening, I tried several times, on purpose, to join their conversation, but she countered my remarks rather drily, and, with feigned annoyance, I finally moved away. The young princess triumphed; Grushnitsky, likewise. Have your triumph, my friends, hurry – you won't triumph long! What is to be done? I have a presentiment . . . Whenever I become acquainted with a woman, I always guess without fail, whether she will fall in love with me or not.

I spent the rest of the evening at Vera's side and talked of old times to my heart's content. What does she love me for so much – I really don't know; particularly since she is the only woman who has completely understood me with all my petty weaknesses and wicked passions. Can evil possibly be so attractive?

Grushnitsky and I left together: when we got outside, he put his arm through mine and said after a long silence:

'Well, what do you think?'

'That you are a fool,' I wanted to answer, but restrained myself, and merely shrugged my shoulders.

29 May

During all these days, I never once departed from my system. The young princess begins to like my conversation. I told her some of the strange occurrences in my life, and she begins to see in me an extraordinary person. I laugh at everything in the world, especially at feelings: this is beginning to frighten her. In my presence she does not dare to launch upon sentimental debates with Grushnitsky, and has several times already replied to his allies with a mocking smile; but every time that Grushnitsky comes up to her, I assume a humble air and leave them alone together. The first time she was glad of it or tried to make it seem so; the second time she became cross with me; the third time she became cross with Grushnitsky.

'You have very little vanity!' she said to me yesterday. 'Why do you think that I have more fun with Grushnitsky?'

I answered that I was sacrificing to a pal's happiness my own pleasure.

'And mine,' she added.

I looked at her intently and assumed a serious air. After this, I did not say another word to her all day. In the evening, she was pensive, this morning, at the well, she was more pensive still. When I went up to her, she was absently listening to Grushnitsky, who, it seems, was being rhapsodical about nature; but as soon as she saw me, she began to laugh (very much *mal à propos*), pretending not to notice me. I walked off some distance and stealthily watched her: she turned away from her interlocutor and yawned twice. Decidedly, Grushnitsky has begun to bore her. I shall not speak to her for two more days.

3 June

I often wonder, why I do so stubbornly try to gain the love of a little maiden whom I do not wish to seduce, and whom I shall never marry? Why this feminine coquetry? Vera loves me more than Princess Mary will ever love anyone: if she had seemed to me to be an unconquerable belle, then perhaps I might have been fascinated by the difficulty of the enterprise.

But it is nothing of the sort! Consequently, this is not that restless need for love that torments us in the first years of youth, and drives us from one woman to another, until we find one who cannot abide us: and here begins our constancy – that true, infinite passion, which can be mathematically expressed by means of a line falling from a given point into space: the secret of that infinity lies solely in the impossibility of reaching a goal, that is to say, reaching the end.

Why then do I take all this trouble? Because I envy Grushnitsky? Poor thing! He has not earned it at all. Or is it the outcome of that nasty but unconquerable feeling which urges us to destroy the sweet delusions of a fellow man, in order to have the petty satisfaction of saying to him, when he asks in despair, what is it he should believe:

'My friend, the same thing happened to me, and still, you see, I dine, I sup, I sleep in perfect peace, and hope to be able to die without cries and tears.'

And then again . . . there is boundless delight in the possession of a young, barely unfolded soul! It is like a flower whose best fragrance emanates to meet the first ray of the sun. It should be plucked that very minute and after inhaling one's fill of it, one should throw it away on the road: perchance, someone will pick it up! I feel in myself this insatiable avidity, which engulfs everything met on the way. I look upon the sufferings and joys of others only in relation to myself as on the food sustaining the strength of my soul. I am no longer capable myself of frenzy under the influence of passion: ambition with me has been suppressed by circumstances, but it has manifested itself in another form, since ambition is nothing else than thirst for power, and my main pleasure – which is to subjugate to my will all that surrounds me, and to excite the emotions of love, devotion, and fear in relation to me – is it not the main sign and greatest triumph of power? To be to somebody the cause of sufferings and joys, without having any positive right to it – is this not the sweetest possible nourishment for our pride? And what is happiness? Sated pride. If I considered myself to be better and more powerful than anyone in the world, I would be happy; if everybody loved me, I would find in myself infinite sources of love. Evil begets evil: the first ache gives us an idea of the pleasure of tormenting another. The idea of evil cannot enter a person's head without his wanting to apply it to reality: ideas are organic creations. Someone has said that their very birth endows them with a form, and this form is action; he in whose head more ideas have been born is more active than others. This is why a genius chained to an office desk must die or go mad, exactly as a powerfully built man, whose life is sedentary and whose behaviour is virtuous, dies of apoplexy.

The passions are nothing else but ideas in their first phase of development; they are an attribute of the youth of the heart; and he is a fool who thinks he will be agitated by them all his life. Many a calm river begins as a turbulent waterfall, yet none hurtles and foams all the way to the sea. But that calm is often the sign of great, though concealed, strength; the plenitude and depth of feelings and thoughts does not tolerate frantic surgings; the soul, while experiencing pain or pleasure, gives itself a strict account of everything and becomes convinced that so it must be; it knows that without storms, a constantly torrid sun will wither it; it becomes penetrated with its own life, it fondles and punishes itself, as if it were a beloved child. Only in this supreme state of self-knowledge can a man evaluate divine justice.

On rereading this page, I notice that I have strayed far from my subject ... But what does it matter? ... I write this journal for myself and, consequently, anything that I may toss into it will become, in time, for me, a precious memory.

. . . .

Grushnitsky came and threw himself on my neck: he had been promoted to an officer's rank. We had some champagne. Dr Werner dropped in soon after him.

'I do not congratulate you,' he said to Grushnitsky.
'Why?'

'Because a soldier's coat is very becoming to you, and
you must admit that an infantry army officer's uniform,
made in this watering place, will not give you any glamour.
You see, up to now you were an exception, while now you
will come under the general rule.'

'Talk on, talk on, doctor! You will not prevent me from
being delighted. He does not know', added Grushnitsky,
whispering into my ear: 'what hopes these epaulets give
me . . . Ah . . . epaulets, epaulets! Your little stars are guiding stars. No! I'm entirely happy now.'

'Are you coming with us for that walk to The Hollow?'
I asked him.

'I? For nothing in the world shall I show myself to the
young princess till my uniform is ready.'

'Do you wish me to announce the glad news to her?'

'No, please do not tell her . . . I want to surprise her . . .'
'By the way, tell me, how are you getting on with her?' He
lost countenance and grew pensive: he wanted to boast and
lie, but he was ashamed to do so, and yet it would have
been mortifying to admit the truth.

'What do you think, does she love you?'

'Love me? Come, Pechorin, what notions you do
have! . . . How could this happen so fast? . . . Even if she
does love me, a decent woman would not tell . . .'

'Fine! And probably, according to you, a decent man
should also keep silent about his passion?'

'Ah, my good fellow! There is a way of doing things;
there is much that is not said, but guessed . . .'

'That's true . . . However, the love that is read in the
eyes does not bind a woman to anything, whereas words . . .
Take care, Grushnitsky, she is fooling you.'

'She? . . .' he answered, raising his eyes to Heaven and
smiling complacently: 'I pity you, Pechorin!'

He left.

In the evening, a numerous party set out on foot for
The Hollow.

In the opinion of local scientists, that 'hollow' is nothing else than an extinguished crater: it is situated on a slope of Mount Mashuk, less than a mile from town. To it leads a narrow trail, among bushes and cliffs. As we went up the mountain, I offered the young princess my arm, and she never abandoned it during the entire walk.

Our conversation began with gossip: I passed in review our acquaintances, both present and absent: first, I brought out their comic traits, and then their evil ones. My bile began to stir. I started in jest and finished in frank waspishness. At first it amused her, then frightened her.

'You are a dangerous man!' she said to me. 'I would sooner find myself in a wood under a murderer's knife than be the victim of your sharp tongue ... I ask you seriously, when it occurs to you to talk badly about me, better take a knife and cut my throat: I don't think you will find it very difficult.'

'Do I look like a murderer?'

'You are worse. . . .'

I thought a moment, and then said, assuming a deeply touched air:

'Yes, such was my lot since my very childhood! Everybody read in my face the signs of bad inclinations which were not there, but they were supposed to be there – and so they came into existence. I was modest – they accused me of being crafty: I became secretive. I felt deeply good and evil – nobody caressed me, everybody offended me: I became rancorous. I was gloomy – other children were merry and talkative. I felt myself superior to them – but was considered inferior: I became envious. I was ready to love the whole world – none understood me: and I learned to hate. My colourless youth was spent in a struggle with myself and with the world. Fearing mockery, I buried my best feelings at the bottom of my heart: there they died. I spoke the truth – I was not believed: I began to deceive. When I got to know well the fashionable world and the mechanism of society, I became skilled in the science of life, and saw how others were happy without that skill, enjoying, at no cost to themselves, all those advantages which I so indefatigably pursued. And then in my breast despair was born – not that despair which is cured with the pistol's muzzle, but cold, helpless despair, concealed under amiability and a good-natured smile. I became a moral cripple. One half of my soul did not exist; it had withered away, it had evaporated, it had died. I cut it off and threw it away – while the other half stirred and lived, at the service of everybody. And this nobody noticed, because nobody knew that its dead half had ever existed; but now you have aroused its memory in me, and I have read to you its epitaph. To many people, all epitaphs, in general, seem ridiculous, but not so to me; especially when I recall what lies beneath them. However, I do not ask you to share my views; if my outburst seems to you ridiculous, please laugh: I warn you, that it will not distress me in any way.'

At that moment, I met her eyes: tears danced in them;[101] her arm, leaning on mine, trembled, her cheeks glowed; she was sorry for me! Compassion – an emotion to which all women so easily submit – had sunk its claws into her inexperienced heart. During the whole walk she was absent-minded, did not coquet with anyone – and that is a great sign!

We reached The Hollow: the ladies left their escorts, but she did not abandon my arm. The witticisms of the local dandies did not amuse her; the steepness of the precipice near which she stood did not frighten her, while the other young ladies squealed and closed their eyes.

On the way back, I did not renew our melancholy conversation, but to my trivial questions and jokes she replied briefly and absently.

'Have you ever loved?' I asked her at last.

She glanced at me intently, shook her head and again became lost in thought: it was evident that she wanted to say something, but she did not know how to begin. Her breast heaved . . . What would you – a muslin sleeve is little protection, and an electric spark ran from my wrist[102] to hers. Almost all passions start thus! and we often deceive ourselves greatly in thinking that a woman loves us for our physical or moral qualities. Of course, they prepare and incline their hearts for the reception of the sacred fire: nonetheless, it is the first contact that decides the matter.

'Don't you think I was very amiable today?' said the young princess to me, with a forced smile when we returned from the excursion.

We parted.

She is displeased with herself; she accuses herself of having treated me coldly . . . Oh, this is the first, the main triumph!

Tomorrow she will want to recompense me. I know it all by heart – that is what is so boring.

4 June

Today, I saw Vera. She has exhausted me with her jealousy. The young princess, it seems, took it into her head to confide the secrets of the heart to Vera: not a very fortunate choice, one must admit!

'I can guess to what it all tends,' Vera kept saying to me. 'Better tell me now, plainly, that you love her.'

'But if I don't?'

'Then why pursue her, disturb her, excite her imagination? Oh, I know you well! Listen, if you want me to believe you, then come next week to Kislovodsk: we are going there after tomorrow. The Ligovskoys remain here for a little while longer. Rent an apartment near by. We shall be living in the big house near the spring, on the mezzanine floor, Princess Ligovskoy will be on the first floor, and next door, there is a house belonging to the same proprietor, which is not yet occupied . . . Will you come?'

I promised, and on the same day sent a messenger to rent those lodgings.

Grushnitsky came to see me at six in the evening, and announced that his uniform would be ready on the morrow, just in time for the ball.

'At last I shall dance with her the whole evening . . . What a chance to talk!' he added.

'When is that ball?'

'Why, tomorrow! Didn't you know? A big festival. And the local authorities have undertaken to arrange it . . .'

'Let's go for a walk on the boulevard.'

'Not for anything, in this horrid coat . . .'

'What, have you ceased liking it?'

I went alone and, upon meeting Princess Mary, asked her to dance the mazurka with me. She seemed surprised and pleased.

'I thought you danced only out of necessity, as last time,' she said, smiling very prettily.

It seems she does not notice at all Grushnitsky's absence. 'Tomorrow you will be agreeably surprised,' I said to her.

'What will that be?'

'It's a secret . . . You will discover it for yourself at the ball.'

I finished the evening at the old princess's: there were no visitors except Vera and a very entertaining old gentleman. I was in high spirits, I improvised all kinds of extraordinary stories: the young princess sat opposite me and listened to my tosh with such deep, tense, even tender attention that I felt ashamed of myself. What had become of her vivacity, her coquetry, her whims, her arrogant mien, scornful smile, abstracted gaze?

Vera noticed it all: deep melancholy expressed itself on her sickly face: she sat in shadow, near the window, sunk in an ample armchair . . . I felt sorry for her.

Then I related the whole dramatic story of our acquaintanceship, of our love – naturally, concealing it under invented names.

So vividly did I picture my tenderness, my anxiety, my transports, in such an advantageous light did I present her actions, her character, that, willy-nilly, she had to forgive me my flirtation with the princess.

She got up, came over to us, became animated . . . and only at two in the morning did we remember that the doctor's order was to go to bed at eleven.

5 June

Half an hour before the ball, Grushnitsky appeared before me in the full splendour of an infantry army officer's uniform. To the third button, he had attached a bronze chainlet from which hung a double lorgnette; epaulets of incredible size were turned upward like the wings of a cupid; his boots squeaked; in his left hand, he held a pair of brown kid gloves and his cap, and with his right he kept fluffing up, every moment, his shock of hair, which was waved in small curls. Self-satisfaction and, at the same time, a certain lack of assurance were expressed in his countenance: his festive exterior, his proud gait, would have made me burst out laughing, had that been in accordance with my plans.

He threw his cap and gloves on to the table and began to pull down the skirts of his coat and to preen himself before the mirror: a huge black neckcloth that was wound over a tremendously high stiffener, the bristles of which propped up his chin, showed half an inch above his collar. He thought this was not enough: he pulled it up, till it reached his ears. This laborious task – for the collar of his uniform was very tight and uncomfortable – caused the blood to rush to his face.

'I'm told you have been flirting terribly with my princess these days?' he said rather casually, and without looking at me.

'It's not for us, oafs, to drink tea!' I answered him, repeating the favourite saying of one of the most dashing rakes of the past, of whom Pushkin once sang.[103]

'Tell me, how does the coat fit me? Oh, that confounded Jew! . . .[104] How it cuts me under the arms! . . . Have you got any perfume?'

'Good gracious, do you need any more? You simply reek of rose pomade, as it is.'

'No matter. Give it here.'

He poured out half of the vial between neck and neckcloth, onto his pocket handkerchief, and upon his sleeves.

'Are you going to dance?' he asked.

'I don't think so.'

'I'm afraid that I shall have to begin the mazurka with the princess, and I hardly know one figure of it.'

'Have you asked her for the mazurka?'

'Not yet . . .'

'Look out, you might be forestalled . . .'

'That's right!' he said, clapping a hand to his forehead. 'Good-bye . . . I'm going to wait for her at the entrance door.' He seized his cap and ran off.

Half an hour later, I also set out. The streets were dark and deserted; around the club, or tavern – whichever you choose to call it – the crowd was dense; the windows shone; the sounds of the military band were brought to me by the evening breeze. I walked slowly; I felt sad . . . 'Is it possible', I thought, 'that my only function on earth is to ruin other people's hopes? Ever since I have lived and acted, fate has always seemed to bring me in at the dénouement of other people's dramas, as if none could either die or despair without me! I am the indispensable persona in the fifth act; involuntarily, I play the miserable part of the executioner or the traitor. What could be fate's purpose in this? Might it not be that it had designated me to become the author of bourgeois tragedies and family novels, or the collaborator of some purveyor of stories for the 'Library for Reading'?[105] How should one know? How many people, in the beginning of life, think they will finish it as Alexander the Great or Lord Byron, and instead, retain for the whole of their existence, the rank of titulary counsellor?[106]

Upon coming into the ballroom, I hid in the crowd of men and began to make my observations. Grushnitsky stood next to the young princess and was saying something to her with great animation: she listened to him absent-mindedly, kept glancing this way and that, putting her fan to her lips. Her face expressed impatience, her eyes sought around for someone: I softly approached from behind, in order to overhear their conversation.

'You torment me, princess,' Grushnitsky was saying. 'You have changed tremendously since I last saw you . . .'

'You too have changed,' she answered, casting upon him a swift glance, in which he failed to discern secret mockery.

'I? I have changed? . . . Oh, never! You know that it is impossible! He who has once seen you, will carry with him, forever, your divine image.'

'Stop, please . . .'

'Why then will you not listen now to what only recently, and so often, you listened with favour?'

'Because I do not like repetition,' she answered laughing.

'Oh, I've made a bitter mistake! . . . I thought, in my folly, that at least these epaulets would give me the right to hope . . . No, it would have been better for me had I remained all my life in that miserable soldier's coat to which, maybe, I owed your attention.'

'Indeed, that coat suited you much better . . .'

At this point I came up and bowed to the young princess: she blushed slightly and said quickly:

'Am I not right, Monsieur Pechorin, that the grey soldier's coat was much more becoming to Monsieur Grushnitsky?'

'I disagree with you,' I replied. 'In this uniform, he looks even more youthful.'

Grushnitsky could not bear this blow: like all youths, he professes to be an old man; he thinks that deep traces of passions replace the imprint of years. He cast on me a furious glance, stamped his foot and walked away.

'Now confess', I said to the young princess, 'that despite his having always been very absurd, still, quite recently, you thought him interesting . . . in his grey coat?'

She dropped her eyes and did not answer.

All evening Grushnitsky pursued the young princess, either dancing with her or being her *vis-à-vis*; he devoured her with his eyes, sighed and pestered her with entreaties and reproaches. After the third quadrille, she already detested him.

'I did not expect this of you,' he said, coming up to me and taking me by the arm.

'What, exactly?'

'You are dancing the mazurka with her, aren't you?' he asked in a solemn voice. 'She confessed to me. . . .'

'Well, what of it? Is it a secret?'

'Naturally . . . I should have expected this from a frivolous girl, from a flirt . . . But I'll have my revenge!'

'Blame your soldier's coat or your officer's epaulets, but why blame her? Is it her fault that you no longer appeal to her?'

'Why then give me hopes?'

'Why then did you hope? I can understand people who desire something and strive for it; but who wants to hope?'

'You have won your bet, though not quite,' he said with a wrathful smile.

The mazurka began. Grushnitsky kept choosing nobody but the princess, the other men chose her continuously: it was obviously a conspiracy against me. So much the better.

She wants to talk to me, they prevent her – she will want it twice as much.

Once or twice, I pressed her hand: the second time, she snatched it away, without saying a word.

'I shall sleep badly tonight,' she said to me when the mazurka was over.

'It's Grushnitsky's fault.'

'Oh no!' And her face became so pensive, so sad, that I promised myself to kiss her hand, without fail, that evening.

People began to leave. As I handed the princess into her carriage, I rapidly pressed her small hand to my lips. It was dark, and no one could see it.

I re-entered the ballroom, well-content with myself.

At a long table, young men were having supper, and among them was Grushnitsky. When I came in, they all fell silent; evidently, they had been talking about me. Many are ill-disposed toward me since the last ball, especially the Captain of Dragoons, and now, it seems, an inimical gang is actually being organized against me, under the leadership of Grushnitsky. He had such a proud and courageous air.

I am very glad; I love my enemies, although not in a Christian sense: they amuse me, they quicken my pulses.

To be always on the lookout, to intercept every glance, to catch the meaning of every word, to guess intentions, to thwart plots, to pretend to be fooled, and suddenly, with one push, to upset the entire enormous and elaborate structure of cunning and scheming – that is what I call life.

During the supper Grushnitsky kept whispering and exchanging winks with the Captain of Dragoons.[107]

6 June

This morning, Vera left for Kislovodsk with her husband. I met their coach as I was on my way to Princess Ligovskoy. Vera nodded to me: there was reproach in her glance.

Whose fault is it? Why does she not want to give me the chance to see her alone? Love, like fire, goes out without fuel. Perchance jealousy will accomplish what my entreaties could not.

I stayed at the princess's an hour by the clock. Mary did not appear; she was ill. In the evening she was not on the boulevard. The newly organized gang, armed with lorgnettes, has assumed a truly threatening appearance: I am glad that the princess is ill: they might have done something insolent in regard to her. Grushnitsky's hair was all awry and he looked desperate: I think he is really distressed. His vanity, in particular, is injured; but, oddly enough, there are people who are ludicrous even in their despair!

On coming home, I noticed a lack of something. *I have not seen her! She is ill!* Can it be that I have really fallen in love? ... What nonsense!

7 June

At eleven in the morning – the hour at which the old Princess Ligovskoy is usually sweating it out in the Ermolov bathhouse – I was walking past her house. The young princess was sitting pensively at the window. When she saw me, she rose abruptly.

I entered the vestibule, none of the servants were there, and without being announced, taking advantage of the local customs, I made my way into the drawing room.

A dull pallor was spread over the princess's pretty face. She stood at the piano, leaning with one hand on the back of an armchair: that hand trembled ever so slightly. I quietly went up to her and said:

'You are angry with me?'

She raised upon me a languid, deep gaze and shook her head; her lips wanted to utter something, and could not; her eyes filled with tears; she sank into the armchair and covered her face with her hand.

'What is the matter with you?' I said, taking her hand.

'You do not respect me! . . . Oh, leave me alone!'

I made a few steps . . . She straightened herself up in her chair; her eyes glittered.

I stopped, with my hand on the door handle, and said:

'Forgive me, princess, I have acted like a madman . . . This will not happen again: I will see to it . . . Why must you know what, up to now, has been taking place in my soul?[108] You will never learn it, and so much the better for you. Adieu.'

As I went out, I believe I heard her crying.

Till evening, I roamed on foot about the outskirts of Mount Mashuk, got terribly tired and, on coming down, threw myself on my bed in utter exhaustion.

Werner dropped in.

'Is it true', he asked, 'that you are going to marry the young Princess Ligovskoy?'

'Why?'

'The whole town says so; all my patients are preoccupied with this important news: that's the kind of people patients are; they know everything!'

'Grushnitsky's tricks,' I thought to myself.

'In order to prove to you, doctor, that these rumours are false, let me inform you in secret that tomorrow I am moving to Kislovodsk.'

'And the Ligovskoys, too?'

'No; they remain here for another week.'

'So you are not marrying her?'

'Doctor, doctor! Look at me: do I resemble a fiancé, or anything of the kind?'

'I do not say it . . . But you know there are cases', he added with a cunning smile, 'in which an honourable man is obliged to marry, and there are mammas who do not at least avert such cases. Therefore, I advise you as a pal to be more careful. Here at the spa the atmosphere is most dangerous: I have seen so many fine, young men, worthy of a better lot, who have gone straight from here to the altar. Would you believe it, there has even been an attempt to have me marry! Namely, on the part of a provincial mamma whose daughter was very pale. I had had the misfortune to tell her that her daughter's face would regain its colour after marriage. Then, with tears of gratitude, she offered me her daughter's hand and their entire fortune – fifty serfs, I believe.[109] But I answered that I was incapable of marriage.'

Werner left, fully convinced that he had put me on my guard.

From his words, I note that various nasty rumours have already been spread in town about the young princess and me. Grushnitsky will have to pay for this!

10 June

I have been here, in Kislovodsk, three days already. Every day I see Vera at the well and at the promenade. In the morning, upon awakening, I sit down by the window and train my lorgnette on her balcony: she is already long since dressed and awaits the prearranged signal: we meet, as if by chance, in the garden, which descends from our houses to the well. The vivifying mountain air has brought back her colour and strength. It is not for nothing that Narzan[110] is termed 'The Fountain of Mightiness'. The local inhabitants maintain that the air of Kislovodsk disposes one romantically, that here comes the dénouement of all the love affairs that ever were started at the foot of Mount Mashuk. And, indeed, everything here breathes seclusion; everything here is mysterious – the dense canopies of linden avenues that bend over the torrent which, as it noisily and foamily falls from ledge to ledge, cuts for itself a path between the verdant mountains, and the gorges filled with gloom and silence that branch out from here in all directions; and the freshness of the aromatic air, laden with the emanations of tall southern grasses and white acacias;[111] and the constant deliciously somniferous babble of cool brooks which, meeting at the far end of the valley, join in a friendly race and, at last, fall into the Podkumok River. On this side the gorge widens and turns into a green glen; a dusty road meanders through it. Every time I look at it, I keep imagining that a close carriage comes there, and from the window of the carriage, there peers out a rosy little face. Many coaches have, by now, passed on that road, but never that one. The suburb beyond the fort has grown populous: in the restaurant, built on a bluff a few steps from my dwelling, lights begin to flicker in the evenings through a double row of poplars; noise and the clinking of glasses resound there till late at night.

Nowhere is there consumed so much Kakhetian wine and mineral water as here.

> To mix these two pursuits, a lot of men
> Are eager – I'm not one of them.[112]

Grushnitsky with his gang every day carouses at the tavern, and hardly nods to me.

He arrived only yesterday,[113] and has already managed to quarrel with three old men who wanted to take their baths before him: definitely – misfortunes develop in him a martial spirit.

11 June

They have come at last. I was sitting by the window when I heard the rattle of their coach: my heart quivered . . . What is it then? Could it be that I am in love? . . . I am so stupidly made that this could be expected from me.

I have dined at their house. The old princess looks at me very tenderly and does not leave her daughter's side . . . That's bad! On the other hand, Vera is jealous of the young princess – this is a nice state of things I have brought about! What will not a woman do in order to vex a rival? I remember one woman who fell in love with me, because I was in love with another. There is nothing more paradoxical than a woman's mind: it is difficult to convince women of anything; you have to bring them to a point where they will convince their own selves. The sequence of proofs by means of which they overcome their prejudices, is very original: to learn their dialectic, one must overturn in one's mind all the school rules of logic. Here, for instance, is the normal method:

That man loves me; but I am married: consequently, I must not love him.[114]

Now for the feminine method:

I must not love him for I am married, but he loves me – consequently . . .

Here come several dots, for reason does not say anything more, and what speaks mainly, is the tongue, the eyes, and in their wake, the heart, if the latter exists.

What if these notes should ever fall under a woman's eyes? 'Slander!' she will cry with indignation.

Ever since poets have been writing and women reading them (for which they should receive the deepest gratitude), they have been called angels so many times, that in the simplicity of their souls, they have actually believed this compliment, forgetting that the same poets dubbed Nero a demigod, for money.

It is not I who should speak of women with such spite – I, who love nothing in the world save them – I, who have always been ready to sacrifice to them peace of mind, ambition, life. But then, it is not in a fit of annoyance and offended vanity that I try to tear from them that magic veil, through which only an experienced gaze penetrates. No, all that I am saying about them is only a result of

> The mind's cold observations,
> The mournful comments of the heart.[115]

Women ought to desire that all men know them as well as I do, because I love them a hundred times better, ever since I stopped fearing them and comprehended their little weaknesses.

Apropos, the other day Werner compared women to the enchanted forest of which Tasso tells in his 'Jerusalem Liberated':[116] 'Only come near,' said Werner: 'and mercy, what horrors will come flying at you from every side: Duty, Pride, Propriety. Public Opinion, Mockery, Scorn . . . All you have to do is not look and walk straight on: little by little, the monsters disappear and before you there opens a serene and sunny meadow, in the midst of which, green myrtle blooms. On the other hand, woe to you if, at the first steps, your heart fails you and you look back!'

12 June

This evening has been rich in events. Within two miles of Kislovodsk, in a canyon through which flows the Podkumok River, there is a cliff, called The Ring. This is a gateway formed by nature, it rises from a high hill, and through it the setting sun throws its last flaming glance on the world. A large cavalcade set out thither to view the sunset through that window of stone. None of us, to say the truth, was thinking of sunsets. I was riding by the young princess's side: on our way home, the Podkumok River had to be forded. The shallowest mountain streams are dangerous, especially because their bottom is an absolute kaleidoscope: every day it changes from the pressure of the waves. Where yesterday there was a stone, today there is a hole. I took the princess's horse by the bridle and led it down into the water, which was no more than knee-deep: we started to advance slowly in an oblique direction against the current. It is well-known that when fording rapid streams, one should not look at the water, for otherwise one immediately gets dizzy. I forgot to warn Princess Mary of this.

We were already in midstream, where the current was swiftest, when she suddenly swayed in her saddle. 'I feel faint!' she said in a weak voice. I quickly bent toward her and wound my arm around her supple waist.

'Look up!' I whispered to her. 'It is nothing, only don't be afraid; I'm with you.'

She felt better; she wanted to free herself from my arm, but I wound it still tighter around her tender, soft body; my cheek almost touched her cheek; flame emanated from it.

'What are you doing to me? . . . Good God! . . .'

I paid no attention to her tremor and confusion, and my lips touched her tender cheek; she gave a start but said nothing. We were riding behind: nobody saw. When we got out on to the bank, everybody started off at a trot. The young princess held her horse in; I stayed by her. It could be seen that my silence worried her, but I swore not to say a word – out of curiosity. I wanted to see how she would extricate herself from this embarrassing situation.

'Either you despise me, or love me very much!' she said at last, in a voice in which there were tears. 'Perhaps you want to laugh at me, to trouble my soul, and then leave me . . . It would be so base, so mean, that the mere supposition . . . Oh no! Isn't it true,' she added in a tone of tender trust, 'isn't it true that there is nothing in me that would preclude respect? Your insolent action . . . I must, I must forgive it you, because I allowed it . . . Answer, do speak, I want to hear your voice . . .'

In the last words, there was such feminine impatience that I could not help smiling. Fortunately, it was beginning to get dark . . . I did not answer anything.

'You are silent?' she went on. 'Perhaps you wish me to be the first to say that I love you.'

I was silent.

'Do you wish it?' she went on, quickly turning toward me. In the determination of her gaze and voice, there was something frightening.

'What for?' I answered shrugging my shoulders.

She gave her horse a cut of the whip and set off at all speed along the narrow dangerous road. It happened so fast, that I hardly managed to overtake her, and when I did, she had already joined the rest of the party. All the way home she talked and laughed incessantly. In her movements there was something feverish; not once did she glance at me. Everybody noticed this unusual gaiety. And the old princess inwardly rejoiced, as she looked at her daughter; yet her daughter was merely having a nervous fit. She will spend a sleepless night and will weep. This thought gives me boundless delight: there are moments when I understand the vampire . .[117] And to think that I am reputed to be a jolly good fellow and try to earn that appellation!

Having dismounted, the ladies went to the old princess's. I was excited and galloped off into the mountains to dissipate the thoughts that crowded in my head. The dewy evening breathed delicious coolness. The moon was rising from behind the dark summits. Every step of my unshod horse produced a hollow echo in the silence of the gorges. At the cascade, I watered my steed, avidly inhaled, a couple of times, the fresh air of the southern night, and started back. I rode through the suburb. The lights were beginning to go out in the windows; the sentries on the rampart of the fort, and the Cossacks in outlying pickets, exchanged long-drawn calls.

In one of the houses of the suburb, which stood on the edge of a ravine, I noticed an extraordinary illumination: at times there resounded discordant talk and cries, indicating that an officers' banquet was in progress. I dismounted and stole up to the window: an improperly closed shutter allowed me to see the revellers and to make out their words. They were speaking about me.

The Captain of Dragoons, flushed with wine, struck the table with his fist, demanding attention.

'Gentlemen!' he said, 'this is really impossible! Pechorin must be taught a lesson! These fledglings from Petersburg always give themselves airs, till you hit them on the nose! He thinks that he alone has lived in the world of fashion, just because he always has clean gloves and well-polished boots.'

'And what an arrogant smile! Yet I'm sure he is a coward – yes, a coward!'

'I think so too,' said Grushnitsky. 'He likes to jest his

way out. I once said to him such things, for which another would have hacked me to pieces then and there, but Pechorin gave it all a humorous interpretation. I, naturally, did not call him out, because it was up to him. Moreover, I did not want to get entangled . . .'

'Grushnitsky is mad at him because he took away the young princess from him,' said someone.

'What a notion! As a matter of fact, I did flirt slightly with her, but gave it up at once, because I do not want to marry, and it is not in my rules to compromise a young girl.'

'Yes, I assure you that he is a first-rate coward – that is to say, Pechorin, and not Grushnitsky. Oh, Grushnitsky is a capital fellow, and moreover, he is a true friend of mine!' said the Captain of Dragoons. 'Gentlemen! Nobody here stands up for him? Nobody? All the better! Would you like to test his courage? You might find it entertaining.'

'We would like to; but how?'

'Well, listen, Grushnitsky is particularly angry with him – he gets the main part! He will pick some kind of silly quarrel with him and challenge Pechorin to a duel . . . Now wait a bit, here comes the point . . . He will challenge him to a duel – good! All this – the challenge, the preparations, the conditions – will be as solemn and terrible as possible – I shall see to that. I shall be your second, my poor friend! Good! But now, here is the hitch: we shall not put any balls into the pistols. I here answer for it that Pechorin will funk it – I shall have them face each other at six paces distance, by Jove! Do you agree, gentlemen?'

'A capital plan! We agree! Why not?' sounded from all sides.

'And you, Grushnitsky?'

In a tremor of eagerness, I awaited Grushnitsky's reply. Cold fury possessed me at the thought that, had it not been for chance, I might have become the laughing stock of those fools. If Grushnitsky had refused, I would have thrown myself upon his neck. But after a short silence, he rose from his chair, offered his hand to the captain and said very pompously: 'All right, I agree.'

It would be difficult to describe the delight of the whole honourable company.

I returned home, agitated by two different emotions. The first was sadness. 'What do they all hate me for?' I thought. 'What for? Have I offended anybody? No. Could it be that I belong to the number of those people whose appearance alone is sufficient to produce ill will?' And I felt a venomous rancour gradually filling my soul. 'Take care, Mr Grushnitsky!' I kept saying, as I paced to and fro in my room, 'I am not to be trifled with like this. You may have to pay dearly for the approval of your stupid cronies. I am not a plaything for you!'

I did not sleep all night. By morning, I was as yellow as a wild orange.

In the morning, I met the young princess at the well.

'Are you ill?' she said, looking at me intently.

'I did not sleep all night.'

'Nor did I . . . I accused you . . . perhaps, wrongly? But explain your behaviour, I may forgive you everything.'

'Everything?'

'Everything . . . Only tell me the truth . . . and hurry . . . I have thought a lot, trying to explain, to justify your conduct: perhaps, you are afraid of obstacles on the part of my family . . . It does not matter. When they hear of it . . . (her voice trembled) my entreaties will convince them . . . Or is it your own situation . . . But I want you to know that I can sacrifice anything for the one I love . . . Oh, answer quick . . . have pity . . . You do not despise me, do you?'

She grasped my hand.

The old princess was walking in front of us with Vera's husband, and did not see anything, but we might have been seen by the promenading patients, of all inquisitive people the most inquisitive gossipers, and I quickly freed my hand from her passionate grasp.

'I shall tell you the whole truth,' I replied to the princess, 'I shall neither justify myself, nor explain my actions. I do not love you.'

Her lips paled slightly.

'Leave me,' she said almost inaudibly.

I shrugged my shoulders, turned, and walked away.

14 June

I sometimes despise myself... Is this not why I despise others?... I have become incapable of noble impulses. I am afraid of appearing laughable to myself. Another man in my place would offer the young princess *son cœur et sa fortune;* but over me the word 'marry' has some kind of magic power. However much I may love a woman, if she only lets me feel that I must marry her – farewell to love! My heart turns to stone, and nothing can warm it again. I am ready to make any sacrifice except this one. I may set my life upon a card twenty times, and even my honour – but I will not sell my freedom. Why do I treasure it so? What good is it to me? What do I prepare myself for? What do I expect from the future?... Indeed, nothing whatever. It is a kind of innate fear, an ineffable presentiment. Aren't there people who have an unaccountable fear of spiders, cockroaches, mice? Shall I confess? When I was still a child, an old woman told my fortune to my mother. She predicted of me 'death from a wicked wife'. It made a deep impression upon me then: in my soul was born an insuperable aversion to marriage. Yet something tells me that her prediction will come true,[118] at least, I shall do my best to have it come true as late as possible.

15 June

Yesterday there arrived here the conjurer Apfelbaum. On the door of the restaurant, there appeared a long *affiche,* informing the esteemed public that the above-named wonderful conjurer, acrobat, chemist, and optician, would have the honour to give a superb performance at eight tonight, in the reception hall of the Club of the Nobility (in other words, the restaurant); admission two roubles fifty.

Everybody intends to go to see the wonderful conjurer: even Princess Ligovskoy, despite the fact that her daughter is ill, took a ticket for herself.

Today after dinner, I passed under Vera's windows. She was sitting on the balcony alone. A billet fell at my feet:

'Tonight, around half past nine, come to me by the main staircase. My husband has gone to Pyatigorsk and will return only tomorrow morning. My footmen and maid-servants will not be in the house: I have distributed tickets to all of them, as well as to the princess's servants. I await you. Come without fail.'

'Aha!' I thought, 'at last I am having my way after all.'

At eight, I went to see the conjurer. The spectators assembled shortly before nine: the performance began. In the back rows of chairs, I recognized the lackeys and the maids of Vera and the princess. Everybody was here. Grushnitsky sat in the front row, with his lorgnette. The conjurer turned to him every time he needed a pocket hand-kerchief, a watch, a ring, and so forth.

Grushnitsky does not greet me since some time ago, and tonight, once or twice, he glanced at me rather insolently. All this shall be remembered when the time comes to settle our accounts.

Shortly before ten I rose and left.

It was pitch dark outside. Heavy, cold clouds lay on the summits of the surrounding mountains; only now and then a dying breeze soughed in the crests of the poplars around the restaurant. There was a crowd of people outside the windows. I descended the hill and, turning into the gate-way, accelerated my pace. Suddenly it seemed to me that someone was walking behind me. I stopped and looked about me. Nothing could be distinguished in the darkness; however, I took the precaution to go around the house as if I were taking a stroll. As I passed under the windows of the young princess, I again heard steps behind me. A man wrapped up in a military cloak ran past me. This alarmed me: however, I stole up to the porch and swiftly ran up the dark stairs. The door opened, a small hand grasped my hand.

'No one saw you?' said Vera in a whisper, pressing herself to me.

'No one.'

'Now do you believe that I love you? Oh! For a long time I wavered, for a long time I was tormented . . . But you make of me all you want.'

Her heart was beating violently, her hands were as cold as ice. There began the reproaches of jealousy, plaints: she demanded of me that I confess to her all, saying she would bear, with submission, my unfaithfulness, since all she desired was my happiness. I did not quite believe this, but I calmed her with vows, promises, and so forth.

'So you are not going to marry Mary? You don't love her? And she thinks . . . do you know, she is madly in love with you, the poor thing!'

. . . .
. . . .

Around two o'clock in the morning, I opened the window and, having tied two shawls together, let myself down from the upper balcony to the lower one, holding onto a pillar.

In the young princess's room, a light was still burning. Something urged me toward that window. The curtain was not completely drawn, and I could cast a curious glance into the interior of the room. Mary was sitting on her bed, her hands folded in her lap; her abundant hair was gathered under a night cap fringed with lace; a large crimson kerchief covered her slender white shoulders; her small feet hid in variegated Persian slippers. She sat motionless, her head sunk onto her breast; before her, on a little table, a book was opened, but her eyes, motionless and full of ineffable sadness, seemed, for a hundredth time, to skim over the same page, while her thoughts were far away.

At this moment, somebody stirred behind a bush. I jumped down from the balcony on to the turf. An invisible hand seized me by the shoulder.

'Aha!' said a rough voice, 'you're caught! . . . I'll teach you to visit young princesses at night! . . .'

'Hold him tight!' cried somebody else, springing from behind a corner.

They were Grushnitsky and the Captain of Dragoons.

I struck the latter upon the head with my fist, knocked him down, and dashed into the shrubbery. All the paths of the garden which covered the sloping ground in front of our houses were known to me.

'Thieves! Help!' they cried. A gun shot rang out; a smoking wad fell almost at my feet.

A minute later, I was already in my room; I undressed and lay down. Hardly had my valet locked the door, than Grushnitsky and the captain began to knock.

'Pechorin! Are you asleep? Are you there?' the captain cried.

'I am asleep,' I answered crossly.

'Get up! . . . Thieves . . . Circassians . . .'

'I have a cold,' I answered, 'I'm afraid to catch a chill.'

They left. I should not have answered them: they would have gone on looking for me in the garden for another hour. In the meantime, the alarm became terrific. A Cossack came, at full speed, from the fort. There was a universal stir: they started to look for Circassians in every bush – and, naturally, found nothing. But many people, probably, remained firmly convinced that, had the garrison revealed more courage and promptness, at least a score of pillagers would have remained lying about.

16 June

This morning, at the well, there was nothing but talk about the night raid of the Circassians. Having drunk the prescribed number of glasses of the Narzan water, and having walked the length of the long linden avenue ten times or so, I met Vera's husband, who had just arrived from Pyatigorsk. He took my arm, and we went to the restaurant to have lunch. He was terribly anxious about his wife. 'How frightened she was last night,' he kept saying, 'and to think it should have happened precisely during my absence.' We sat down to lunch near a door which led to the corner room, where a dozen young people were assembled, including Grushnitsky. For a second time, destiny provided me with the chance to overhear a conversation, which was to decide his fate. He could not see me and, consequently, I could not suspect him of a deliberate purpose; but this only increased his guilt in my eyes.

'Could it have really been the Circassians?' someone said. 'Did anybody see them?'

'I shall tell you the whole story,' answered Grushnitsky, 'but please do not give me away. This is how it was. Last night, a man, whom I shall not name to you, came to me and told me that shortly before ten he saw someone steal into the house where the Ligovskoys live. I should mention to you that the old princess was here, and the young princess was at home. So he and I betook ourselves under their windows to waylay the lucky fellow.'

I must confess that I was alarmed, although my interlocutor was very busy with his luncheon. He might have heard things that would be disagreeable to him, if Grushnitsky had inadvertently guessed the truth; but being blinded by jealousy, the latter did not suspect it.

'Well, you see,' Grushnitsky went on, 'we set out, taking a gun with us, loaded with a blank cartridge – just to frighten him. Till two o'clock, we waited in the garden. Finally – God knows where he appeared from, certainly not from the window, because it was never opened, but presumably he came out through the glass door which is behind the pillar – finally, as I say, we saw someone come down from the balcony . . . How do you like the princess's behaviour, eh? Well, I must say, those Moscow misses are something! After that, what would you believe? We wanted to seize him, but he freed himself and, like a hare, dashed into the bushes. It was then I took a shot at him.'

A murmur of incredulity resounded around Grushnitsky. 'You do not believe me?' he continued. 'I give you my honest and honourable word that all this is the very truth, and in proof, if you wish it, I shall name the gentleman.'

'Tell us, tell us who he is!' resounded from all sides.

'Pechorin,' answered Grushnitsky.

At this moment, he raised his eyes – I was standing in the door opposite him – he flushed dreadfully. I went up to him and said slowly and distinctly:

'I regret very much that I entered after you had already

given your word of honour in support of the vilest slander. My presence would have saved you from extra knavery.'

Grushnitsky jumped up from his seat and was about to flare up.

'I beg you,' I continued, in the same tone of voice, 'I beg you to retract your words at once: you know very well that it is an invention. I do not think that a woman's indifference to your brilliant qualities merits so awful a vengeance. Think well. By affirming your opinion, you lose your right to the name of a gentleman, and you risk your life.'

Grushnitsky stood before me, with lowered eyes, in violent agitation. But the struggle between conscience and vanity did not last long. The Captain of Dragoons, who was sitting next to him, nudged him with his elbow: he started and quickly replied to me, without raising his eyes:

'Sir, when I say something, I mean it, and am ready to repeat it. I am not afraid of your threats, and am prepared for anything.'

'This last you have already proved,' I answered coldly and, taking the Captain of Dragoons by the arm, I left the room.

'What is it you want?' asked the captain.

'You are a friend of Grushnitsky and will probably be his second?'

The captain bowed with great importance.

'You have guessed,' he answered. 'I am even obliged to be his second, because the insult inflicted upon him refers also to me. I was with him last night,' he added, straightening his stooping shoulders.

'Ah! So it was you that I hit so awkwardly on the head?'

He turned yellow, turned blue; concealed malevolence was expressed in his face.

'I shall have the honour to send you my second today,' I added with a very polite bow, pretending not to pay any attention to his rage.

On the porch of the restaurant, I came across Vera's husband. Apparently, he had been waiting for me.

He grasped my hand with an emotion resembling enthusiasm.

'Noble young man,' he said with tears in his eyes, 'I heard it all. What a scoundrel! What lack of gratitude! Who will want to admit them into a decent house after that! Thank God I have no daughters! But you will be rewarded by her for whom you risk your life. You may rely on my discretion for the time being,' he went on. 'I have been young myself, and have served in the military service: I know one should not interfere in these matters. Goodbye.'

Poor thing! He rejoices he has no daughters.

I went straight to Werner, found him at home and told him everything – my relations with Vera and with the young princess, and the conversation I had overheard, from which I had learned the intention those gentlemen had of making a fool of me by forcing me to fight a duel with pistols loaded with blanks. But now the matter was going beyond a joke: they, probably, had not expected such an outcome.

The doctor agreed to be my second; I gave him some instructions concerning the terms of the duel. He was to insist on the affair remaining as secret as possible because, although I am ready to brave death any time, I am not at all disposed to ruin, forever, my future career in this world.

After this I went home. An hour later, the doctor returned from his expedition.

'There is, indeed, a plot against you,' he said. 'I found at Grushnitsky's the Captain of Dragoons and yet another gentleman, whose name I do not remember. For a moment I stopped in the vestibule to take off my rubbers. They were making a lot of noise and arguing. "For nothing in the world shall I agree," Grushnitsky was saying. "He insulted me in public: before that, things were entirely different." "What business is this of yours?" answered the captain. "I take everything upon myself. I was a second in five duels, and you may be sure I know how to arrange it. I have planned it all. Only please do not interfere. It won't do any harm to scare the fellow. But why expose oneself to danger if one can avoid it? . . ." At this moment, I entered. They were suddenly silent. Our negotiations lasted a considerable time. Finally, we decided the matter in the following way: within three miles from here there is a desolate gorge; they will drive there tomorrow at four in the morning, and we shall set out half an hour after them; you will shoot at each other at six paces – Grushnitsky himself demanded this. The one who is killed is to be put down to the Circassians. Now, here are my suspicions: they, that is to say the seconds, have apparently altered somewhat their former plan and want to load, with a bullet, only Grushnitsky's pistol. This slightly resembles murder, but in time of war, and especially Asiatic war, trickery is allowed. However, Grushnitsky seems to be a little nobler than his companions. What do you think, should we show them that we have found them out?'

'Not for anything on earth, doctor! Rest assured, I shall not fall in their trap.'

'What then do you want to do?'

'That's my secret.'

'See that you don't get caught ... Remember, the distance is six paces!'

'Doctor, I expect you tomorrow at four: the horses will be ready ... Good-bye.'

Till evening I remained at home, locked up in my room. A footman came with an invitation from the old princess – I had him told that I was ill.

. . . .

Two o'clock in the morning ... Sleep does not come ... Yet I ought to have some sleep so that my hand does not shake tomorrow. Anyway, it would be difficult to miss at six paces. Ah, Mr Grushnitsky! Your mystification will not come off ... We shall exchange parts: it is now I who will search your pale face for signs of secret fear. Why did you designate yourself those fatal six paces? You think that I shall present my forehead to you without arguing ... But we shall cast lots ... and then ... then ... what if his luck outweighs mine? What if my star at last betrays me? ... It would hardly be strange, it has so long served my whims faithfully. There is no more constancy in heaven than there is on earth.

Well, what of it? If I am to die, I'll die! The loss to the world will not be large and, anyway, I myself am sufficiently bored. I am like a man who yawns at a ball and does not drive home to sleep, only because his carriage is not yet there. But now the carriage is ready... good-bye! ...

I scan my whole past in memory and involuntarily wonder: why did I live, for what purpose was I born? ... And yet that purpose must have existed, and my destination must have been a lofty one, for I feel, in my soul, boundless strength. But I did not divine that destination, I became enticed by the lure of hollow and thankless passions. From their crucible, I emerged as hard and cold as iron, but lost forever the ardour of noble yearnings – the best blossom of life. And since then, how many times I have played the part of an axe in the hands of fate! As an executioner's tool, I would fall upon the head of doomed victims, often without malice, always without regret. My love brought happiness to none, because I never gave up anything for the sake of those whom I loved. I loved for myself, for my proper pleasure; I merely satisfied a bizarre need of my heart, avidly consuming their sentiments, their tenderness, their joys and sufferings – and never could I have my fill. Thus a man, tormented by hunger and fatigue, goes to sleep and sees before him rich viands and sparkling wines; he devours with delight the airy gifts of fancy, and he seems to feel relief; but as soon as he awakes – the vision vanishes. He is left with redoubled hunger and despair!

And, perhaps tomorrow, I shall die! ... And there will not remain, on earth, a single creature that would have understood me completely. Some deem me worse, others better than I actually am. Some will say he was a good fellow; others will say he was a scoundrel. Both this and that will be false. After this, is it worth the trouble to live? And yet one lives – out of curiosity. One keeps expecting something new... Absurd and vexatious!

It is now a month and a half already that I have been in the fort of N—. Maksim Maksimych is out hunting. I am alone, I am sitting at the window. Grey clouds have shut off the mountains to their base: through the mist, the sun looks like a yellow blur. It is cold: the wind whistles and shakes the shutters . . . How dull . . . I am going to continue my journal, which has been interrupted by so many strange events.

I read over the last page: how funny! – I expected to die: it was impossible. I had not yet drained the cup of sufferings, and I now feel that I still have many years to live.

How clearly and sharply the past has crystallized in my memory! Time has not erased one line, one shade!

I remember that, during the night before the duel, I did not sleep one minute. I could not write long: a secret restlessness had taken possession of me. For an hour or so, I paced the room, then I sat down and opened a novel by Walter Scott which lay on my table: it was *The Scottish Puritans*.[119] At first I read with an effort, but then I lost myself in it, carried away by the magic fantasy. Could it be that, in the next world, the Scottish bard is not paid for every glad minute that his book gives?

Dawn came at last. My nerves had quieted down. I looked at myself in the mirror: a dull pallor was spread over my face, which bore the traces of painful insomnia; but the eyes, although surrounded by brown shadows, glittered proudly and inflexibly. I was satisfied with myself.

After having ordered the horses to be saddled, I dressed and ran down to the bathhouse. As I immersed myself in the cold ebullience of Narzan water, I felt the forces of my body and soul return. I emerged from the bath, refreshed and braced up, as if I were about to go to a ball. Try to say after this that the soul is not dependent on the body!

Upon returning home, I found the doctor there. He wore grey riding breeches, a Caucasian overcoat and a Circassian cap. I burst out laughing at the sight of his small figure under that huge shaggy cap: his face is anything but that of a warrior, and on this occasion it looked longer than ever.

'Why are you so sad, doctor?' I said to him. 'Haven't you seen people off on their way to the next world with the greatest indifference, a hundred times before? You should imagine that I have bilious fever. I may get well, and again, I may die; both are in the natural order of things. Try to see in me a patient afflicted with an illness that is still unknown to you – and then your curiosity will be roused to the highest pitch. By watching me you can now make several important physiological observations. Isn't the expectation of violent death, after all, a genuine illness?'

This thought impressed the doctor and he cheered up.

We got to our horses. Werner clutched at the bridle with both hands, and we set off. In a twinkle we had galloped past the fort by way of the suburb, and entered the gorge along which the road wound, half-choked with tall grasses, and constantly crossed and recrossed by a loud brook, which had to be forded, to the great dismay of the doctor, for every time his horse stopped in the water.

I do not remember a bluer and fresher morning. The sun had just appeared from behind the green summits, and the merging of the first warmth of its rays with the waning coolness of the night pervaded all one's senses with a kind of delicious languor. The glad beam of the young day had not yet penetrated into the gorge; it gilded only the tops of the cliffs that hung on both sides above us. The dense-foliaged bushes, growing in the deep crevices, asperged us with a silver rain at the least breath of wind. I remember that on this occasion, more than ever before, I was in love with nature. How curiously I examined every dewdrop that trembled upon a broad vine leaf and reflected a million iridescent rays! How avidly my gaze tried to penetrate into the hazy distance! There, the road was becoming narrower, the cliffs were growing bluer and more awesome, and finally, they seemed to blend in an impenetrable wall. We rode in silence.

'Have you made your will?' Werner suddenly asked.

'No.'

'And what if you are killed?'

'My heirs will turn up of themselves.'

'Do you mean you have not got any friends to whom you would wish to send a last farewell?'

I shook my head.

'Do you mean there is not one woman in the world to whom you would want to leave something in remembrance?'

'Do you want me, doctor,' I answered him, 'to open my soul to you? ... You see, I have outlived those years when people die uttering the name of their beloved and bequeathing a tuft of pomaded or unpomaded hair to a friend. When I think of near and possible death, I am thinking of myself only: some people don't do even that. Friends who, tomorrow, will forget me or, worse, will saddle me with goodness knows what fictions; women who, while embracing another, will laugh at me so as not to make him jealous of a dead man – what do I care for them all! Out of life's storm I carried only a few ideas – and not one feeling. For a long time now, I have been living not with the heart, but with the head. I weigh and analyse my own passions and actions with stern curiosity, but without participation. Within me there are two persons: one of them lives in the full sense of the word, the other cogitates and judges him. The first will, perhaps, in an hour's time, take leave of you and the world forever, while the other ... what about the other? ... Look, doctor, do you see on that cliff on the right three black figures? These are our adversaries, I believe.'

We set off at a trot.

In the bushes at the foot of the cliff, three horses were tied. We tied our horses there too, and clambered up a narrow path to a flat ledge, where Grushnitsky was awaiting with the Captain of Dragoons and his other second, whose name and patronymic were Ivan Ignatievich. I never learned his surname.

'We have been expecting you for a long time,' the Captain of Dragoons said with an ironic smile.

I took out my watch and showed it to him.

He apologized, saying that his was fast.

For several moments there was an awkward silence: at last, the doctor broke it by addressing himself to Grushnitsky:

'It seems to me', he said, 'that both parties having shown their readiness to fight, and having thus satisfied the demands of honour, you might, gentlemen, talk matters over and close the affair amicably.'

'I'm willing,' I said.

The captain gave Grushnitsky a wink, and he, thinking that I was scared, assumed a proud air, although up to then a dull pallor had been spread over his cheeks. For the first time since we had come, he raised his eyes to look at me; but in his glance there was some kind of perturbation betraying an inner struggle.

'Explain your terms,' he said, 'and whatever I can do for you, you may be assured . . .'

'Here are my terms: this very day you will publicly retract your slander and will apologize to me.'

'Sir, I am amazed that you dare offer such things to me!'

'What else could I offer you?'

'We shall fight.'

I shrugged my shoulders.

'As you please; but consider – one of us will certainly be killed.'

'My wish is that it may be you.'

'And I'm convinced of the opposite.'

He lost countenance, coloured, then burst into forced laughter.

The captain took his arm and led him aside: for a long time, they whispered together. I had arrived in a fairly peaceable state of mind, but all this was beginning to annoy me.

The doctor came up to me.

'Listen,' he said with obvious anxiety, 'you must have forgotten about their plot? I do not know how to load a pistol, but in the present case . . . You are a strange fellow! Tell them that you are aware of their intention, and they will not dare . . . What is the sense of this? They'll bring you down like a bird.'

'Please don't worry, doctor, and wait a bit . . . I shall arrange everything in such a way that on their side there will be no advantage whatever. Let them hugger-mugger a little.'

'Gentlemen! This is becoming tiresome,' I said in a loud voice. 'If we are to fight, let us fight: you had plenty of time to talk it over yesterday.'

'We are ready,' answered the captain. 'To your places, gentlemen! Doctor, have the kindness to measure off six paces.

'To your places!' repeated Ivan Ignatievich, in a squeaky voice.

'Allow me!' I said. 'There is one further condition. Since we are going to fight to the death, we should do everything possible to keep the matter secret and to avoid our seconds being held responsible. Do you agree?'

'We completely agree.'

'Well, this is what I have thought up. Do you see at the summit of that sheer cliff on the right, a narrow bit of flat ground? There is a drop of about three hundred feet or more from there; below, there are sharp rocks. Each of us will take his stand on the very edge of the shelf, and in this way even a light wound will be fatal. This must be in keeping with your desire for you stipulated yourself, a distance of six paces. The one who is wounded will inevitably topple down and will be dashed to pieces; the doctor will take out the bullet, and then it should be very easy to ascribe this sudden death to an unfortunate leap. We shall draw lots to decide who is to shoot first. Let me inform you, in conclusion, that otherwise I will not fight.'

'Have it your way!' said the captain after glancing meaningly at Grushnitsky, who nodded in sign of consent. His face kept changing every minute. I had placed him in an awkward position. Had we fought under ordinary conditions, he might have aimed at my leg, wounded me lightly and satisfied, in this way, his thirst for revenge, without burdening his conscience too heavily. But now he had either to discharge his pistol into the air, or become a murderer, or lastly, abandon his vile plan and expose himself to equal danger with me. At this moment, I would not have wished to be in his place. He led the captain aside and began to say something to him with great heat. I saw his livid lips tremble, but the captain turned away from him with a contemptuous smile. 'You're a fool!' he said to Grushnitsky, rather loudly, 'you do not understand anything! Let us go, gentlemen!'

A narrow trail led up the precipice between the bushes; broken rocks formed the precarious steps of this natural staircase: holding on to bushes, we started to climb up. Grushnitsky was in front, behind him were his seconds, and after them came the doctor and I.

'I am amazed at you,' said the doctor, giving my hand a strong squeeze. 'Let me feel your pulse! . . . Oho! it's feverish! . . . But nothing shows in your face . . . Only your eyes shine brighter than usual.'

Suddenly, small stones noisily rolled down to our feet. What was it? Grushnitsky had stumbled. The branch which he had grasped broke and he would have slid down on his back, had not his seconds supported him.

'Take care!' I cried to him. 'Don't fall beforehand: it's a bad omen. Remember Julius Caesar!' [120]

Presently we reached the top of the jutting cliff: its flat surface was covered with fine sand, as if made especially for a duel. All around, melting in the golden mist of the morning, mountain summits teemed like an innumerable herd, and to the south Mount Elbruz raised its white mass, the last link in the chain of icy crests among which wispy clouds, which had blown from the east, were already roaming. I went to the edge of the natural platform and looked down: my head almost began to turn. Down below it was dark and cold as in the tomb; mossgrown jags of rocks, cast down by storm and time, were awaiting their prey.

The platform on which we were to fight presented an almost regular triangle. Six paces were measured off from the jutting angle and it was decided that he who would have to face first his foe's fire, should stand at the very apex, with his back to the chasm. If he were not killed, the principals were to change places.

I decided to give Grushnitsky every advantage; I wished to test him. A spark of magnanimity might awaken in his soul – and then everything would turn out for the best; but vanity and weakness of character were to triumph! . . . I wished to give myself the full right to show him no quarter, if fate spared me. Who has not concluded similar agreements with his conscience?

'Spin the coin, doctor!' said the captain.

The doctor took out of his pocket a silver coin and held it up.

'Tails!' cried Grushnitsky hurriedly, like a man who has been suddenly awakened by a friendly nudge.

'Heads!' I said.

The coin soared up and fell with a tinkle; everyone rushed toward it.

'You're lucky,' I said to Grushnitsky, 'you are to fire first! But remember that if you do not kill me, I shall not miss – I give you my word of honour.'

He coloured; he was ashamed to kill an unarmed man. I was looking at him intently: for a moment it seemed to me that he would throw himself at my feet, begging for forgiveness, but who could own having such a villainous design? . . . Only one resource remained to him – to fire in the air. I was sure he would fire in the air! Only one thing could interfere with it: the thought that I should demand another duel.

'It is time!' the doctor whispered to me, pulling my sleeve. 'If you do not tell them now that we know their intentions, all is lost. Look, he is already loading . . . If you do not say anything, I myself shall . . .'

'Not for anything in the world, doctor!' I replied, holding him back by the arm. 'You would spoil everything. You gave me your word not to interfere . . . What does it matter to you? Perhaps, I wish to be killed . . .'

He glanced at me with surprise.

'Oh, that's different! . . . Only do not bring complaints against me in the next world.'

In the meantime, the captain had loaded his pistols; he handed one to Grushnitsky, whispering something to him with a smile; the other he handed to me.

I took my stand at the apex of the platform, bracing my

left foot firmly against the rock and leaning forward a little, so as not to fall backward in the case of a light wound.

Grushnitsky stationed himself opposite me and at a given signal began to raise his pistol. His knees shook. He was aiming straight at my forehead.

Ineffable fury flared up in my breast.

Suddenly, he lowered the muzzle of his pistol and, going as white as a sheet, turned toward his second:

'I can't,' he said in a hollow voice.

'Coward!' answered the captain.

The shot rang out. The bullet grazed my knee. Involuntarily, I took several steps forward so as to get away, as soon as possible, from the brink.

'Well, friend Grushnitsky, it's a pity you've missed!' said the captain. 'Now it's your turn, take your stand! Embrace me first: we shall not see each other again!' They embraced; the captain could hardly keep himself from laughing. 'Have no fear,' he added, with a sly glance at Grushnitsky. 'All's nonsense on earth! . . . Nature is a ninny, fate is a henny, and life is a penny!'

After this tragic phrase, delivered with appropriate dignity, he withdrew to his place. Ivan Ignatievich, with tears, likewise embraced Grushnitsky, and now he was left alone facing me. To this day I try to explain to myself what kind of feeling was boiling then in my breast. It was the irritation of injured vanity, and contempt, and wrath which arose at the thought that this man, now looking at me with such calm insolence, had tried, two minutes before, without exposing himself to any danger, to kill me like a dog, for if I had been wounded in the leg a little more severely, I would have certainly fallen off the cliff.

For several moments, I kept looking intently into his face, striving to discern the slightest trace of repentance. But it seemed to me that he was withholding a smile.

'I advise you to say your prayers before dying,' I then said to him.

'Do not worry about my soul more than you do about your own. One thing I ask of you: shoot quickly.'

'And you do not retract your slander? You do not ask

my pardon? Think well: does not your conscience say something to you?'

'Mr Pechorin !' cried the Captain of Dragoons, 'you are not here to hear confession, allow me to tell you . . . Let us finish quickly, otherwise somebody may come driving through the gorge and see us.'

'All right. Doctor, come over to me.'

The doctor came. Poor doctor! He was paler than Grushnitsky had been ten minutes before.

I spaced on purpose the following words, pronouncing them loudly and distinctly, the way a death sentence is pronounced:

'Doctor, these gentlemen, no doubt in their hurry, forgot to place a bullet in my pistol. Please, load it again – and properly!'

'This cannot be!' the captain was shouting, 'it cannot be! I loaded both pistols: perhaps, the ball rolled out of yours . . . That is not my fault! And you have no right to reload . . . no right whatsoever. It is utterly against the rules; I shall not permit it . . .'

'All right!' I said to the captain. 'If so, you and I will have a duel on the same conditions.'

He faltered.

Grushnitsky stood, his head sunk on his breast, embarrassed and gloomy.

'Leave them alone!' he finally said to the captain who wanted to snatch my pistol out of the doctor's hands. 'You know very well yourself that they are right.'

In vain did the captain make various signs to him. Grushnitsky would not even look.

Meanwhile, the doctor had loaded the pistol, and now handed it to me.

Upon seeing this, the captain spat and stamped his foot.

'Brother, you *are* a fool!' he said. 'A vulgar fool! . . . Since you've relied upon me, you should obey me in everything . . . Serve you right! Perish like a fly . . .' He turned away and, as he walked off, he muttered: 'And still it is utterly against the rules.'

'Grushnitsky!' I said. 'There is still time: retract your

slander and I shall forgive you everything. You did not succeed in fooling me, and my self-esteem is satisfied. Remember, we were friends once . . .'

His face blazed, his eyes glittered.

'Shoot!' he answered. 'I despise myself and hate you. If you do not kill me, I shall cut your throat in a dark alley. There is no room in this world for the two of us . . .'

I fired . . .

When the smoke dispersed, Grushnitsky was not on the ledge. Only dust in a light column still revolved on the brink of the precipice.

All cried out in one voice.

'*Finita la commedia!*' I said to the doctor.

He did not answer and turned away in horror.

I shrugged my shoulders and bowed to Grushnitsky's seconds as I took leave of them.

On my way down the trail, I noticed, among the crevices of the cliffs, Grushnitsky's blood-stained body. Involuntarily, I shut my eyes.

I untied my horse and set out for home at a walk: a stone lay on my heart. The sun seemed to me without lustre; its rays did not warm me.

Before reaching the suburb, I turned off to the right, down the gorge. The sight of a human being would have been burdensome to me. I wanted to be alone. With slack reins, my head sunk on my breast, I rode a long while; at last, I found myself in a spot that was completely unknown to me. I turned my horse around and began to look for the road; the sun was already setting when I reached Kislovodsk, exhausted, on an exhausted horse.

My valet told me that Werner had called, and handed me two notes: one from Werner himself, the other . . . from Vera.

I unsealed the first one; it contained the following message:

'Everything has been arranged as well as possible: the body has been brought back in a disfigured condition, the bullet has been extracted from the breast. Everybody believes that his death had been caused by an accident;

only the commandant, to whom your quarrel was probably known, shook his head, but said nothing. There are no proofs against you whatsoever, and you can sleep in peace . . . if you can . . . Good-bye.'

For a long time, I could not make myself open the second note . . . What could she tell me? . . . A heavy presentiment agitated my soul.

Here it is, this letter, whose every word is indelibly graven in my memory:

'I write to you with the complete certitude that we shall never see each other again. Several years ago, when parting with you, I thought the same but Heaven chose to try me a second time. I did not withstand this trial: my weak heart submitted again to the familiar voice. You will not despise me for this, will you? This letter is going to be both a farewell and a confession: I feel obliged to tell you all that has accumulated in my heart ever since it loved you. I shall not blame you – you treated me as any other man would have done; you loved me as your property, as a source of joys, agitations and sorrows, which mutually replaced one another and without which life would have been dull and monotonous. This I understood from the first; but you were unhappy, and I sacrificed myself, hoping that some day you would appreciate my sacrifice, that some day you would understand my deep tenderness, not depending on any circumstances. Since then much time has passed. I penetrated into all the secrets of your soul . . . and realized that my hope had been a vain one. It made me bitterly sad! But my love had grown one with my soul; it became darker, but did not go out.

'We part forever; yet you may be sure that I shall never love another: my soul has spent upon you all its treasures, its tears and hopes. She, who has loved you once, cannot look without a certain contempt on other men, not because you are better than they – oh, no! – but because there is something special about your nature, peculiar to you alone, something proud and mysterious. In your voice, whatever you may be saying, there is unconquerable power. None is able to desire so incessantly to be loved; in none is evil so attractive; the gaze of none promises so much bliss; none knows better to use his advantages; and none can be so genuinely unhappy as you, because none tries so hard to convince himself of the contrary.

'I must now explain to you the reason for my hurried departure: it will seem to you of little importance, since it concerns me alone.

'This morning, my husband came into my room and related your quarrel with Grushnitsky. Evidently, I looked terribly upset, for he looked long and intently into my eyes. I nearly fainted at the thought that you must fight today and that I was the cause of it: it seemed to me that I would go mad . . . But now that I can reason, I feel sure that your life will be spared: it is impossible that you should die without me, impossible! My husband paced the room for a long time. I do not know what he was saying to me, I do not remember what I answered him . . . No doubt, I told him that I loved you . . . I only remember that toward the end of our conversation, he insulted me with a dreadful word and went out. I heard him order the coach to be got ready . . . I have now been sitting at the window for three hours, awaiting your return . . . But you are alive, you cannot die! . . .[21] The coach is almost ready . . . Farewell, farewell . . . I perish – but what does it matter? If I could be sure that you will always remember me – I don't say, love me – no, only remember . . . Farewell . . . Somebody is coming . . . I must hide this letter . . .

'You do not love Mary, do you? You will not marry her? Listen, you must make this sacrifice to me: for you I have lost everything in the world . . .'

Like a madman, I rushed out on to the porch, jumped on my Circassian horse which was being promenaded in the yard, and galloped off, at full speed, on the road to Pyatigorsk. Unmercifully I urged my exhausted steed, which, snorting and all covered with foam, carried me swiftly along the stony road.

The sun had already hidden in a black cloud that rested on the ridge of the western mountains; it had become dark and damp in the gorge. The Podkumok River roared dully and monotonously as it made its way over stones. I galloped on, breathless with impatience. The thought of arriving in Pyatigorsk too late to find her, beat like a hammer on my heart. To see her for one minute, one more minute, say good-bye to her, press her hand ... I prayed, cursed, wept, laughed ... No, nothing can express my anxiety, my despair! Faced by the possibility of losing Vera forever, I felt that she had become dearer to me than anything in the world – dearer than life, honour, happiness! God knows what strange, mad plans swarmed in my head ... And meanwhile I continued to gallop, urging my horse mercilessly. And presently, I began to notice that my steed was breathing more heavily; once or twice he had already stumbled on level ground. Three miles remained to Essentuki, a Cossack settlement where I might be able to change horses.

Everything would have been saved had my horse's strength lasted for another ten minutes! But suddenly, as we emerged from a small ravine at the end of the defile where there was a sharp turn, he crashed onto the ground. I nimbly jumped off, tried to make him get up, tugged at the bridle – in vain. A hardly audible moan escaped through his clenched teeth; a few minutes later he was dead. I remained alone in the steppe, my last hope gone; I tried to proceed on foot – my legs gave way under me. Worn out by the agitations of the day and by insomnia, I fell on the wet grass and began crying like a child.

And for a long time, I lay motionless and cried bitterly, not attempting to hold back the tears and sobs. I thought my chest would burst; all my firmness, all my coolness vanished like smoke; my soul wilted, my reason was mute and if, at that moment, anyone had seen me, he would have turned away in contempt.

When the night dew and the mountain breeze had cooled my burning head, and my thoughts had regained their usual order, I realized that to pursue perished happiness was useless and senseless. What was it that I still needed? To see her? What for? Was not everything ended between us? One bitter farewell kiss would not enrich my memories, and after it, we would only find it harder to part.

Yet it pleases me that I am capable of weeping. It may have been due, however, to upset nerves, to a sleepless night, to a couple of minutes spent facing the muzzle of a pistol, and to an empty stomach.

Everything is for the best! That new torment produced in me, to use military parlance, a fortunate diversion. Tears are wholesome, and then, probably, if I had not gone for that ride, and had not been compelled to walk ten miles home, that night, too, sleep would not have come to close my eyes.

I returned to Kislovodsk at five in the morning, threw myself on my bed and slept the sleep of Napoleon after Waterloo.

When I awoke it was already dark outside. I seated myself at the open window, unbuttoned my Caucasian over-coat, and the mountain breeze cooled my breast, which had not yet been appeased by the heavy sleep of exhaustion. Far away, beyond the river, through the tops of the dense limes sheltering it, there flickered lights in the buildings of the fort and of the suburb. Around the house, all was quiet. The princess's house was in darkness.

The doctor came in; his brow was furrowed; contrary to his custom, he did not give me his hand.

'Where do you come from, doctor?'

'From the Princess Ligovskoy. Her daughter is ill – a nervous breakdown ... However, that is not the matter, but this: the authorities are suspicious, and, although nothing can be proved positively, I would nevertheless advise you to be more careful. The princess told me today that she knows you fought a duel over her daughter. She learned it all from that little old man – what's his name? He witnessed your clash with Grushnitsky at the restaurant. I came to warn you. Good-bye. I suppose we shan't see each other again: you will be transferred somewhere.'

On the threshold, he stopped. He would have liked to shake my hand, and had I displayed to him the slightest desire for it, he would have thrown himself on my neck; but I remained as cold as stone – and he left.

That's the human being for you! They are all like that: they know beforehand all the bad sides of an action. They help you, they advise you, they even approve of it, perceiving the impossibility of a different course – and afterwards they wash their hands of it, and turn away indignantly from him who had the courage to take upon himself the entire burden of responsibility. They are all like that, even the kindest, even the most intelligent ones.

On the following morning upon receiving from the higher authorities the order to proceed to the fort of N—, I called on the old princess to say good-bye.

She was surprised when, to her question, whether I had not anything particularly important to tell her, I answered that I wished her happiness and so forth.

'As to me, I must talk to you very seriously.'

I sat down in silence.

It was obvious she did not know how to begin. Her face turned purple, her plump fingers drummed upon the table; at last, she began thus, in a halting voice:

'Listen, Monsieur Pechorin, I believe you are a gentleman.'

I bowed.

'I am even convinced of it,' she went on, 'although your behaviour is somewhat ambiguous; but you may have reasons which I do not know, and it is those reasons that you now must confide to me. You have defended my daughter from slander; you fought a duel for her – consequently, risked your life. Do not reply. I know you will not admit it, because Grushnitsky is dead.' (She crossed herself.) 'God will forgive him, and He will forgive you, too, I hope! . . . That does not concern me . . . I dare not condemn you, since my daughter, though innocently, was the cause of it. She told me everything – I think, everything. You declared your love to her . . . she confessed her love to you.' (Here the princess sighed heavily.) 'But she is ill, and I am certain that it is no ordinary illness! A secret sorrow is killing her; she does not admit it, but I am certain that you are its cause ... Listen, you may think, perhaps, that I am looking for rank, for huge riches. Undeceive yourself! I seek only my daughter's happiness. Your present situation is not enviable, but it can improve: you are a man of means. My daughter loves you; she has been brought up in such a way that she will make her husband's happiness. I am rich, she is my only child ... Tell me, what holds you back? ... You see, I should not have been saying all this to you, but I rely on your heart, on your honour ... Remember, I have but one daughter ... one....'

She began to cry.

'Princess,' I said, 'it is impossible for me to answer you. Allow me to talk to your daughter alone.'

'Never!' she exclaimed, rising from her chair in great agitation.

'As you please,' I answered, preparing to go.

She lapsed into thought, made me a sign to wait, and left the room.

Five minutes passed; my heart was beating violently, but my thoughts were calm, my head cool. No matter how hard I searched my breast for one spark of love for the charming Mary, my efforts were in vain.

Presently the door opened, and she came in. Good Lord! How she had altered since I saw her last – and had that been so very long ago?

On reaching the middle of the room, she swayed; I jumped up,[122] gave her my arm and led her to an armchair.

I stood facing her. For a long time we were silent. Her great eyes, filled with ineffable sadness, seemed to seek in my eyes something resembling hope; her pale lips vainly tried to smile; her delicate hands, folded in her lap, were so thin and diaphanous that I felt sorry for her.

'Princess,' I said, 'you know that I laughed at you? You must despise me.'

A feverish rosiness appeared on her cheeks.

I went on: 'Consequently, you cannot love me ...'

She turned away, rested her elbow on a table, covered her eyes with her hand, and it seemed to me that tears glistened in them.

'Oh God!' she uttered almost inaudibly.

This was becoming unbearable: another minute, and I would have fallen at her feet.

'So you see for yourself,' I said, in as firm a voice as I could and with a strained smile, 'you see for yourself that I cannot marry you. Even if you wished it now, you would soon regret it. My talk with your mother obliged me to have it out with you, so frankly and so roughly. I hope she is under a delusion: it will be easy for you to undeceive her. You see, I am playing, in your eyes, a most miserable and odious part, and even this I admit – this is all I'm able to do for you. However unfavourable the opinion you may have of me, I submit to it. You see, I am base in regard to you. Am I not right that even if you loved me, from this moment on you despise me?'

She turned to me as pale as marble; only her eyes glittered marvellously.

'I hate you,' she said.

I thanked her, bowed respectfully and left.

An hour later, an express *troika* was rushing me away from Kislovodsk. A few miles before reaching Essentuki, I recognized, by the roadside, the carcass of my gallant steed.[123] The saddle had been removed, probably by some passing Cossack and, instead of the saddle, there were two ravens perched on the dead beast's back. I sighed and turned away.

And now here, in this dull fort, I often scan the past in thought, and wonder why I had not wanted to tread that path, which fate had opened for me, where quiet joys and peace of mind awaited me? No, I would not have got used to such an existence! I am like a sailor born and bred on the deck of a pirate brig. His soul is used to storms and battles, and, when cast out on the shore, he feels bored and oppressed, no matter how the shady grove lures him, no matter how the peaceful sun shines on him. All day long he haunts the sand of the shore, hearkens to the monotonous murmur of the surf and peers into the misty distance. Will there not appear there, glimpsed on the pale line separating the blue main from the grey cloudlets, the longed-for sail, at first like the wing of a sea gull, but gradually separating itself[124] from the foam of the breakers and, at a smooth clip, nearing the desolate quay?

THE FATALIST

I ONCE happened to spend two weeks at a Cossack settlement on our left flank. An infantry battalion was also stationed there and officers used to assemble at each other's quarters in turn, and play cards in the evening.

On one occasion, having tired of boston and thrown the cards under the table, we sat on for a very long time at Major S——'s place. The talk, contrary to custom, was entertaining. We discussed the fact that the Moslem belief in a man's fate being written in heaven finds also among us Christians many adherents; each related various unusual occurrences in proof or refutation.

'All this does not prove anything, gentlemen,' said the elderly major. 'I take it, none of you witnessed the strange cases with which you corroborate your opinions?'

'None, of course,' said several, 'but we heard it from reliable people. . . .'

'It is all humbug!' said someone. 'Where are those reliable people who have seen the scroll where the hour of our death is assigned? And if predestination actually exists, why then are we given free will and reason, and why must we account for our actions?'

At this moment, an officer who had been sitting in a corner of the room got up and, slowly coming up to the table, surveyed all present with a calm and solemn gaze. He was of Serbian origin, as was apparent from his name.

Lieutenant Vulich's looks corresponded perfectly to his nature. A tall stature, a swarthy complexion, black hair, black piercing eyes, a large but regular nose, characteristic of his nation, and a sad chill smile perpetually wandering on his lips – all this seemed to blend in such a way as to endow him with the air of a special being, incapable of sharing thoughts and passions with those whom fate had given him for companions.

164

He was brave, spoke little but trenchantly; confided in none the secrets of his soul or of his family; drank almost no wine; never courted the Cossack girls (whose charm is hard to imagine for those who have never seen them). It was said, however, that the colonel's wife was not indifferent to his expressive eyes; but he would get seriously annoyed when one hinted at it.

There was only one passion of which he made no secret – the gaming passion. Once seated at the green table, he forgot everything, and usually lost; but continuous bad luck only served to exasperate his obstinacy. It was rumoured that, one night, while on active duty, he dealt out the cards at stuss on his pillow; he was having formidable luck. All of a sudden, shots were heard, the alarm was sounded, there was a general scamper for weapons. 'Set your stake for the whole bank,' cried Vulich, without rising, to one of the keenest punters. 'All right, I set it upon a seven,' answered the other, as he rushed off. Despite the general confusion, Vulich went on dealing all alone, and the seven came up for the punter.[125]

When he reached the front line, the firing there was already intensive. Vulich paid no attention either to the bullets or the swords of the Chechens: he was in search of his fortunate punter. 'The seven turned up on your side,' he shouted on seeing him at last in the firing line, which was beginning to force the enemy out of the forest, and, on coming closer, took out his purse and his wallet and handed them to the lucky gamester, despite the latter's protest that this was not an appropriate place for payment. Upon acquitting himself of this unpleasant duty, he dashed forward, carrying the soldiers with him, and most coolly kept exchanging shots with the Chechens to the end of the engagement.

When Lieutenant Vulich approached the table, everybody fell silent, expecting some eccentric stunt from him.

'Gentlemen!' he said (his voice was quiet though a tone below his usual pitch). 'Gentlemen, what is the use of empty arguments? You want proofs? I offer you to try out on me whether a man may dispose of his life at will or a fateful minute is assigned to each of us in advance . . . Who is willing?'

'Not I, not I,' came from every side. 'What an odd fellow! Who would think of such a thing! . . .'

'I offer you a wager,' I said in jest.

'What kind of wager?'

'I affirm that there is no predestination,' I said, pouring on to the table a score of gold coins – all there was in my pocket.

'I accept,' answered Vulich in a toneless voice. 'Major, you will be umpire. Here are fifteen gold pieces. The other five you owe me, and you would do me a favour by adding them to the rest.'

'All right,' said the major, 'but I don't understand, what is it all about? How are you going to settle the argument?'

Vulich without a word walked into the major's bedroom: we followed him. He went to the wall where there hung some weapons, and among pistols of various calibre, he, at random, took one down from its nail. We still failed to understand, but when he cocked it and poured powder into the pan, several officers, with involuntary exclamations, seized him by the arms.

'What do you want to do? Look here, this is madness!' they cried to him.

'Gentlemen,' he said slowly, freeing his arms, 'who is willing to pay twenty gold pieces for me?'

All were silent and stepped aside.

Vulich went to the other room and sat down at the table: we all followed him there. With a sign he invited us to take seats around him. He was obeyed in silence: at that moment, he had acquired some mysterious power over us. I looked fixedly into his eyes,[126] but he countered my probing glance with a calm and steady gaze, and his pale lips smiled; but despite his coolness, I seemed to decipher the imprint of death upon his pale face. I had observed – and many a seasoned warrior had confirmed this observation of mine – that often the face of a man who is to die within a few hours bears the strange imprint of his imminent fate, so that an experienced eye can hardly mistake it.

'Tonight you will die,' I said to him. He turned to me quickly, but answered slowly and calmly.

'Maybe yes, maybe no . . .' Then, addressing himself to the major, he asked: 'Is there a ball in the pistol?' The major, in his confusion, could not remember properly.

'Oh come, Vulich,' somebody exclaimed, 'surely it's loaded if it was hanging at the head of the bed. Stop fooling!'

'A foolish joke!' another joined in.

'I'll bet you fifty roubles to five that the pistol is not loaded!' cried a third.

New bets were made.

I became bored with this long procedure. 'Listen,' I said, 'either shoot yourself or hang the pistol back in its place and let's go home to bed.'

'That's right,' many exclaimed, 'let's go back to bed.'

'Gentlemen, please stay where you are!' said Vulich applying the muzzle of the pistol to his forehead.

Everybody sat petrified.

'Mr Pechorin,' he added, 'take a card and throw it up into the air.'

I took from the table what I vividly remember turned out to be the ace of hearts and threw it upwards. Everyone held his breath; all eyes, expressing fear and a kind of vague curiosity, switched back and forth from the pistol to the fateful ace which quivered in the air and slowly came down. The moment it touched the table, Vulich pulled the trigger . . . the pistol snapped!

'Thank God!' many cried. 'It was not loaded. . .'

'Let's take a look, anyway,' said Vulich. He cocked the pistol again, took aim at a cap that was hanging above the window. A shot resounded – smoke filled the room. When it dispersed, the cap was taken down. It had been shot clean through the middle, and the bullet had lodged deep in the wall.

For some three minutes, no one was able to utter a word. With perfect composure, Vulich transferred my gold pieces into his purse.

A discussion arose as to why the pistol had missed fire

the first time. Some maintained that the pan must have been clogged; others said in a whisper that at first the powder must have been damp and that afterwards Vulich added some fresh powder; but I affirmed that this last supposition was wrong because I had never taken my eyes off the pistol.

'You're a lucky gambler!' I said to Vulich.

'For the first time in my life,' he answered, smiling complacently. 'This is better than faro or stuss.'

'But then, it's a bit more dangerous.'

'Bye-the-bye, have you begun to believe in predestination?'

'I believe in it, but I cannot understand now why it seemed to me that you must certainly die tonight.'

This very man, who only a moment before had calmly aimed a pistol at his own forehead, now suddenly flushed and looked flustered.

'Well, enough of this!' he said, rising up. 'Our bet has been settled, and I think your remarks are out of place now.' He took his cap and left. This appeared odd to me – and not without reason.

Soon after, everyone went home – commenting variously upon Vulich's vagaries, and probably, in unison, calling me an egoist for having made a bet against a man who was going to shoot himself, as if without me he would not be able to find a convenient occasion! . . .

I was walking home along the empty alleys of the settlement. The moon, full and red, like the glow of a conflagration, began to appear from behind the uneven line of roofs; the stars shone calmly upon the dark-blue vault, and it amused me to recall that, once upon a time, there were sages who thought that the heavenly bodies took part in our trivial conflicts for some piece of land or some imaginary rights. And what happened? These lampads, lit, in the opinion of those sages, merely to illumine their battles and festivals, were burning as brightly as ever, while their passions and hopes had long been extinguished with them, like a small fire lit on the edge of the forest by a carefree wayfarer! But on the other hand, what strength of will they derived from the certitude that the entire sky with its countless inhabitants was looking upon them with mute but permanent sympathy! Whereas we, their miserable descendants, who roam the earth without convictions or pride, without rapture or fear (except for that instinctive dread that compresses our hearts at the thought of the inevitable end), we are no longer capable of great sacrifice, neither for the good of mankind, nor even for our own happiness, because we know its impossibility, and pass with indifference from doubt to doubt, just as our ancestors rushed from one delusion to another. But we, however, do not have either their hopes or even that indefinite, albeit real, rapture that the soul encounters in any struggle with men or with fate.

And many other, similar, thoughts passed through my mind. I did not detain them, since I do not care to concentrate on any abstract thought; and, indeed, what does it lead to? In my early youth, I was a dreamer; I liked to fondle images, gloomy or iridescent by turn, that my restless and avid imagination pictured to me. But what was left me of it? Nothing but weariness, as from a night battle with a phantom, and a vague memory full of regrets. In this vain struggle, I exhausted the ardency of soul and the endurance of will, indispensable for real life. I entered that life after having already lived it through in my mind, and I became bored and disgusted, like one who would read a poor imitation of a book that he has long known.

The event of the evening had made a rather deep impression upon me and had irritated my nerves. I do not know for certain if I now believe in predestination or not, but that night I firmly believed in it: the proof was overwhelming, and despite my laughing at our ancestors and their obliging astrology, I had involuntarily slipped into their tracks. But I stopped myself in time on this dangerous path; and as I have, for rule, never to reject anything decisively, nor trust blindly in anything, I brushed metaphysics aside and began to look under my feet. Such a precaution proved much to the point: I very nearly fell, having stumbled over something fat and soft, but apparently inanimate. Down I bent. The moon now shone right upon the road – and what did I see? Before me lay a pig, slashed in two by a sword. Hardly had I time to inspect it, when I heard the sound of footfalls. Two Cossacks came running out of a lane; one of them came up to me and asked if I had not seen a drunken Cossack chasing a pig. I informed them that I had not encountered the Cossack, and pointed to the unfortunate victim of his frenzied valour.

'The rascal!' said the second Cossack. 'Every time he drinks his fill of *chihir*',[127] there he goes cutting up everything that comes his way. Let's go after him, Eremeich;[128] he must be tied, or else . . .'

They went off; I continued my way with more caution and, at length, reached my quarters safely.

I was living at the house of an old Cossack sergeant, whom I liked for his kindly disposition, and especially for his pretty young daughter, Nastya.

As was her custom, she was waiting for me at the wicket, wrapped up in her fur coat. The moon illumined her sweet lips, now blue with the cold of the night. On seeing it was I, she smiled; but I had other things on my mind. 'Good night, Nastya!' I said, as I went by. She was on the point of answering something, but only sighed.

I closed the door of my room, lit a candle and threw myself on my bed; however, sleep made me wait for it longer than usual. The east was already beginning to pale when I fell asleep, but apparently it was written in heaven that I was not to get my fill of sleep that night. At four in the morning, two fists began to beat against my window. I jumped up: what was the matter? 'Get up, get dressed!' shouted several voices. I dressed quickly and went out. 'Do you know what's happened?' said, with one voice, the three officers who had come to fetch me. They were as pale as death.

'What?'

'Vulich has been killed.'

I was stupefied.

'Yes, killed,' they continued. 'Let's hurry.'

'Where to?'

'You'll find out on the way.'

Off we went. They told me all that had happened with an admixture of various remarks regarding the strange predestination which had saved him from inevitable death, half an hour before his death. Vulich had been walking alone in a dark street. The drunken Cossack, who had hacked up the pig, happened to pitch into him, and would, perhaps, have gone on without taking notice of him, had not Vulich stopped short and said: 'Whom are you looking for, man?' 'You!' answered the Cossack, striking him with his sword, and cutting him in two, from the shoulder almost down to the heart. The two Cossacks who had met me and who were on the lookout for the murderer, came along; they picked up the wounded officer, but he was already breathing his last and said only three words: 'He was right!' I alone understood the obscure meaning of these words: they referred to me. I had unwittingly foretold the poor fellow's fate; my intuition had not betrayed me; I had really read upon his altered face, the imprint of his imminent end.

The assassin had locked himself up in an empty hut on the outskirts of the settlement: we proceeded thither. A great many women ran, wailing, in the same direction. Here and there, some belated Cossack rushed out into the street fastening on his dagger, and passed us at a run. The commotion was terrible.

When we finally got there, we saw a crowd surrounding the hut: its doors and shutters were locked from within. Officers and Cossacks were eagerly discussing the situation; women were wailing, lamenting and keening. Among them I noticed at once the striking face of an old woman which expressed frantic despair. She sat on a thick log, her elbows propped on her knees and her hands supporting her head: it was the murderer's mother. Now and then her lips moved . . . Was it a prayer they whispered or a curse?

Meanwhile, some decision had to be taken, and the criminal seized. No one, however, ventured to be the first to take the plunge.

I walked up to the window and looked through a chink

in the shutter. White-faced, he lay on the floor, holding a pistol in his right hand; a bloodstained sword lay beside him. His expressive eyes rolled dreadfully; at times he would start and clutch at his head as if vaguely recollecting the events of the night. I did not read strong determination in this restless gaze and asked the major why he did not order the Cossacks to break down the door and rush in, because it would be better to do it now than later when he would have fully regained his senses.

At this point an old Cossack captain went up to the door and called him by his name: the man responded.

'You've done wrong, friend Efimych,' said the captain. 'There's no way out except to submit.'

'I will not submit!' replied the Cossack.

'Have fear of the Lord! Think, you're not a godless Chechen, but a decent Christian. Well, if sin has led you astray, there is nothing to be done; one can't avoid one's fate.'

'I will not submit!' fiercely cried the Cossack, and one could hear the click of a cocked pistol.

'Hey, my good woman,' said the captain to the old woman, 'talk a bit to your son, maybe he'll listen to you . . . All this only angers God. And look, the gentlemen have been waiting for two hours now.'

The old woman looked at him fixedly and shook her head.

'Vasily Petrovich,' said the captain, going up to the major, 'he will not surrender – I know him; and if we break the door open, he will kill many of our men. Hadn't you better give the order to shoot him? There is a wide crack in the shutter.'

At that moment, an odd thought flashed through my mind. It occurred to me to test my fate as Vulich had.

'Wait,' I said to the major, 'I shall take him alive.' Telling the captain to start a conversation with him and, having stationed three Cossacks at the door, ready to break it in and rush to my assistance at a given signal, I walked around the hut and went close to the fateful window. My heart beat violently.

'Hey you, cursed heathen!' the captain was yelling, 'are you laughing at us? Or do you think we shall not be able to subdue you?' He began to knock on the door with all his might. My eye against the chink, I watched the movements of the Cossack who did not expect an attack from this side. Suddenly, I wrenched off the shutter and flung myself through the window, headfirst. A shot sounded above my very ear, a bullet tore off one of my epaulets; but the smoke that filled the room prevented my adversary from finding his sword which lay beside him. I seized him by the arms; the Cossacks burst in, and three minutes had not passed before the criminal was bound and removed under guard. The people dispersed. The officers kept congratulating me – and indeed, there was reason enough.

After all this, how, it would seem, can one escape becoming a fatalist? But then, how can a man know for certain whether or not he is really convinced of anything? And how often we mistake, for conviction, the deceit of our senses or an error of reasoning? I like to have doubts, about everything: this inclination of the mind does not impinge upon resoluteness of character. On the contrary, as far as I am concerned, I always advance with greater courage when I do not know what awaits me. For nothing worse than death can ever occur; and from death there is no escape!

After my return to the fort, I related to Maksim Maksimych all that had happened to me and what I had witnessed, and I desired to know his opinion regarding predestination. At first, he did not understand the word but I explained it to him as best I could; and then he said significantly shaking his head:

'Yes, sir! this is, of course, a rather tricky matter! . . . However, those Asiatic pistol cocks often miss fire if they are not properly oiled or if you do not press hard enough with the finger. I must say, I also do not like Circassian rifles. Somehow, they don't seem to be suitable for the likes of us: the butt is so small you have to be careful not to get your nose burnt . . . But then, those swords they have – ah, they're really something!'

Then he added after some thought:

'Yes, I'm sorry for the poor fellow . . . Why the devil did he talk to a drunk at night! . . . However, this must have been what was assigned to him at his birth!'[129]

Nothing more could I get out of him: he does not care, generally, for metaphysical discussions.

TRANSLATOR'S NOTES

1. The English (London) versions known to me – all bad – are:

   1854 Wisdom and Marr, *A Hero of our own Time* (reprinted as *The Heart of a Russian*, 1912).

   1854 Pulszky, *The Hero of our Days*.

   1888 Lipman, *A Hero of our Time*.

   1928 Merton, *A Hero of our Time* (with a most unfortunate foreword by Prince Mirsky).

   1940 Paul, *A Hero of our Times*.

   And there have been others.

2. These chameleonic effects are nothing in comparison to the colorations of facial elements in the sloppier sort of French fiction of the time. I quote from Balzac's *La Femme de trente ans* (see note 54): '*Ses yeux de feu, ombragés de sourcils épais et bordés de long cils, se dessinaient comme deux ovales blancs entre deux lignes noires*' ('His fiery eyes shaded with thick eyebrows and bordered with long lashes appeared as two white ovals between two black lines'), Part I, description of Colonel Victor d'Aiglemont. Or: '*Et tout à coup une rougeur empourpra ses joues* [those of Hélène d'Aiglemont], *fit resplendir ses traits, briller ses yeux, et son teint, devint d'un blanc mat*' ('And suddenly a flush encrimsoned her cheeks, caused her features to glow resplendently, made her eyes shine, and her complexion turned a dull white'), Part V.

3. The MS title had been: *One of the Heroes of the Beginning of the Century*. The work was begun probably in 1838, was completed in 1839, and was first published in April 1840, after 'Bela', 'The Fatalist', and 'Taman' had appeared as separate stories in a magazine *(Otechestvennye Zapiski*, 1839, issues 2 and 6; 1840, issue 8). The author's introduction was written a year later for the second edition (1841), where it incongruously headed vol. 2, which, equally incongruously, contained the 'Second Part' ('Princess Mary' and 'The Fatalist'). Except in the position of the Introduction, Russian editions still follow this purely fortuitous arrangement: Part First: I 'Bela'; II 'Maksim Maksimych'; Introduction to Pechorin's Journal; I 'Taman'; Part Second: II 'Princess Mary'; III 'The Fatalist'.

   The Russian text I have used is Eykhenbaum's edition (Mikhail Yurievich Lermontov, *Polnoe sobranie sochinenii*, vol. 4, OGIZ, Leningrad, 1948).

4. I was travelling: Lermontov, or his representative, is travelling back from Georgia to Russia. The time is autumn, 1837. He is

taking the so-called Military Georgian road from Tiflis, capital of Georgia, to Vladikavkaz, a distance of about 80 mi. as the crow flies, but actually around 135 mi. At first, he drives north along the Aragva River, which rises northwest of the Pass of the Cross (almost 8,000 ft.) and flows south to the Kura. He enters Koishaur Canyon some 40 mi. north of Tiflis and, after having traversed the pass, reaches the village of Kobi (6,500 ft.), and pushes on north, through the villages of Kazbek and Lars to the town of Vladikavkaz (40 mi. from Kobi) along the Terek River. Stavropol, whither he is to proceed via Ekaterinograd, lies 160 mi. northwest of Vladikavkaz.

5. Springless carriage: the word for this primitive travelling contraption was, in Lermontov's time, still the old *telezhka* (which now means simply any small cart) or *telega* (now only connoting a peasant's wagon for hay, etc.).

6. A region in Southern Caucasus bounded by the Black Sea on the west and the Dagestan region on the east, with Tiflis (now Tbilisi), the capital.

   The gradual annexation of the Caucasus by Russia went on intermittently from the capture of Derbent (1722), by Peter I, to the capture (in 1859) of the chieftain and religious leader of the Lezgians, Shamil. The advance of the Russian Empire was realized by various means, from voluntary integration (e.g. Georgia in 1801) to a fierce war with the mountaineers, of whom the various Circassian tribes offered the toughest resistance. The war (mainly in Chechnya and Dagestan) was in full progress during the years Lermontov served in the Caucasus (1837, and 1840–1).

7. Aleksey Petrovich Ermolov (1772–1861), a celebrated Russian general, who, from 1818 on, conducted military operations in Chechnya, Dagestan, and elsewhere in the Caucasus, and built several forts along the northeast stretch of the Terek. He proved an able administrator. Retired in 1827.

8. *Shtabs-kapitan.* Maksim Maksimych's rank is between lieutenant and captain, and corresponds to the ninth rank (titulary councillor) in the civil service (see note 106). The lowest commissioned officer's rank in the military scale (corresponding to the one before last, thirteenth, in the civil service) is *praporshchik*, which is usually translated as ensign. This was Pechorin's rank when Maksim Maksimych first met him (see note 31).

9. A group of lavatic volcanic peaks, the tallest of which is 12,140 ft. high, southwest of Gudaur.

10. I do not know if this place really existed.

11. Webster spells it 'boza' in English. It is a fermented drink made of hemp seed and darnel meal; but the word may also mean any kind of new wine.

12. *Mirnoy knyaz'.* This term designated a local chieftain who took no sides in the war between the Caucasian tribes and the Russians.

NOTES

13. It will be noted that the story Maksim Maksimych eventually tells has little to do with his promise of it here, just as farther on (p. 26) the fact of Kazbich's wearing a coat of mail is not significant in the sense at which Maksim Maksimych darkly hints.

14. Although most of the Caucasus (deemed by Russians an Asiatic region) was by that time already 'Russia' in a political sense, the term is limited here to European Russia, the great plains extending northward from the Black Sea to the White Sea.

15. Pechorin: Maksim Maksimych refers to him as 'Grigory Aleksandrovich' here and elsewhere. Pechorin is Gregory, son of Alexander, and the junior captain (whose surname we never learn) is Maxim, son of Maxim (to anglicize these names). Maksim Maksimych's patronymic is a familiar contraction of Maksimovich. The 'Maksimych' is pronounced something like Mak-see-much, with the stress on 'see'. The mutual address between people in Russia is the use of name and patronymic as here. This is not inconsistent sometimes with an informal 'thouing'. There is a faint indication (p. 62) that Pechorin and Maksim Maksimych had switched to the familiar second person, and that Pechorin forgot its fraternal establishment between them when they met again.

16. Consecrated friend, convive, chum, buddy. It comes from the word for 'guest' in Turkic dialects. One is supposed to do anything for one's *kunak*, share with him one's home, and, if need be, avenge him. Maksim Maksimych does not live up to his 'kunakship'.

17. Meaning merely a Moslem in this context.

18. Probably, *shicha-pshina*.

19. Here and elsewhere, the Russian word is *barany* which specifically means 'rams'. I suspect it is loosely used for 'sheep'. 'Mutton' in Russian is *baranina*, and for a Caucasian a sheep is merely animated mutton, sheathed in useful wool.

20. That is to say west and north of Kuban River which takes its rise in a glacier at the foot of Mount Elbruz and flows north and west to the Sea of Azov, a distance of 560 mi.

21. Native bandits, dedicated breaknecks, guerrillas.

22. A kind of smock made of silk or cotton, generally belted and worn by Caucasians over the shirt. Over this, come two or three other garments, loosely opened and thus revealing the *beshmet*.

23. Neither this, nor the 'I recalled the coat of mail' (p. 26) is followed up.

24. Karagyoz or Karagöz: I suspect that the name of the horse is meant to mean 'Black Eye' in Turkish.

25. One should assume that Kazbich's situation in the ravine was on higher ground than the open country, where his horse was being pursued.

26. To this 'ancient song' (rendered by Lermontov in dactylic tetrameter with rhymes *bbaaccee*) the author appended the following note: 'I must apologize to my readers for transposing into rhymed

177

lines Kazbich's song which was given to me, of course, in prose;
but habit is second nature.'

The 'I' here (Narrator One, Lermontov's representative) is supposed to record faithfully not only the mannerisms of Maksim
Maksimych's speech, but Maksim Maksimych's rendering of the
mannerisms of other speakers (Pechorin, Azamat, Kazbich, etc.).
In the case of this 'ancient song', however, it is Narrator One
improvising on the version supplied by Narrator Two (Maksim
Maksimych).

27. Here and elsewhere, the listener's eagerness is a little overdone.

28. Maksim Maksimych seems to have forgotten that Kasbich (pronounced 'Khaz-beech' with the stress on the second syllable) never
bothered to tie his beautifully-trained steed (see p. 26).

29. There is some error in the Russian text at this point.

30. North of the eastern reach of that river. This was 'beyond' for a
Circassian, while the region south would be 'beyond' for a Russian.

31. *Gospodín práporshchik!* We do not know if Pechorin was reduced
to this lowest commissioned officer's rank in the infantry for his
mysterious St Petersburg escapade (before the events described
in 'Taman') or for his duel with Grushnitsky in 'Princess Mary'.

32. Pronounced something like 'Meets-kah' with the accent on the
first syllable. A vulgar abbreviation of 'Dmitri'.

33. Either Maksim Maksimych means that these Moslemized Circassians used a Turkish dialect allied to Turkish, or the author means
that Maksim Maksimych called 'Tatar' (in the loose sense of
'Asiatic') any Caucasian language. (In the original sense, Tatars
were Mongols.) The language of the Circassian tribes belongs to
the Iberian-Caucasian group and is not related to Turkish, though
certain familiar terms have been borrowed from the Turkish. One
feels that Lermontov himself was not too well acquainted with
these distinctions.

Further on (pp. 46 and 50) Kazbich is twice said to cry out
'something in his own tongue', Maksim Maksimych's remark that
he knows 'their' language when relating the visit to the neutral
chieftain is not very convincing since we are not told what language
is meant.

34. A town in northeastern Caucasus on the left (north) bank of the
eastern reach of the Terek River, in the Caspian depression, some
30 mi. west of the Caspian Sea.

35. Bela (the name means 'grief' in Turkish) is apparently a Circassian
(cherkeshenka, 'Cherkes girl'). Webster defines 'Circassian' as 'an
individual of a group of tribes in the Caucasus of Caucasian race,
but not of Indo-European speech, noted for their physical beauty.
They are tall, amiable and brave. The chief tribes are the Circassians proper and the Kabardians.'

36. Meaning Moslem girls of tribes living south of the Caucasian
Mountains, and in Dagestan.

37. The phrase I have rendered as 'dances of stars' is in the original *khorovody zvyozd*, 'the choral dances of stars', a formula stemming from Pushkin's 'Eugene Onegin', Two, XXVIII, 4 (1826).

38. This is, of course, a romanticist notion. It is completely untrue.

39. The allusion is to a blunder committed by Jacques François Gamba, French consul in Tiflis, who, in his work *Voyage dans la Russie méridionale et particulièrement dans les provinces situées au-delà du Caucase, fait depuis 1820 jusqu'au 1824*, 2 vols., Paris, 1826, translated *Krestovaya* as 'of Christopher' instead of 'of the cross'.

40. Names of cities in Central Russia that connote backwood, in-the-sticks provincialism.

41. The nickname of a mighty whistler appearing in Russian folk tales. He is a monstrous highwayman whose imitation of animal cries can overpower an army.

42. Peter I drove through the Caucasus in 1722 (see note 6.)

43. The full name of this Moscow club (founded in 1783) was, since 1810, The Russian Club of Nobility *(Rossiiskoe blagorodnoe sobranie)*. It was also known as *Dvoryansky Klub* or *Club de la Noblesse*. Its palatial white-pillared ballroom is often referred to in memoirs of the time.

44. The second half of September or the beginning of October, if we take into account the twelve-day lag of the Julian calendar ('Old Style'), used at the time in Russia, behind the universal Gregorian ('New Style').

45. Lermontov seems to employ here the word *polyana* (which really means 'small field', 'clearing', 'lawn') in the wrong sense of the Fr. *plaine*. Throughout the book, he has trouble finding the right words for natural objects – rocks, shrubs, streams, and so forth, hence the curious abstract quality of his landscape, despite the presence of colour words. The 'golden snows', for instance, are borne out by his own pictures of apricot-tinged, snow-capped mountains; and the adjective 'lilac' (Crimean shoreline) which occurs in 'Taman' was a new epithet in 1840.

46. There seems to be a misprint, or a reading based on an initial misprint, in the 1948 edition. I have used here Dudyshkin's otherwise unreliable edition of 1863. Unfortunately I have not been able to procure, for reference, the first and second editions (1840, 1841).

47. The good reader will note that there is no retrospective intimation here of the romantic adventures which Pechorin had with Mary and Vera only a few months before the 'Bela' episode. At the time, Lermontov had not yet written 'Princess Mary'.

48. A Circassian tribe inhabiting the northwestern coastal area.

49. Terek River (365 mi.) has its source from a small glacier in the Central Chain, on Mount Kazbeck. It skirts the Kazbek group and flows turbulently in a general easterly direction, through a series of gorges (of which the most famous is the Daryal Canyon),

along which the Military Georgian Road runs. Below Vladikavkaz, the Terek collects the waters of various mountain streams, flows north toward steppe country, then turns resolutely east and continues its course to the Caspian Sea.

50. The reference is to a Roman Catholic *mitra simplex* of white silk or linen.

51. The shrewd and disgruntled valet in Beaumarchais's comedy, *Le Mariage de Figaro* (1785).

52. I have translated as 'sacks' Lermontov's vague term *kotomki*. According to an English traveller (E. D. Clarke, 'Travels', vol. 2, p. 48), who sampled Circassian mountain honey in 1800, it is 'sewed up in goatskin with the hair on the outside'.

53. The 'medium height' probably implies a small man by our standards, as it seems to do a small woman in Vera's case (p. 95). Otherwise this descriptive item would be pointless. It is curious to note that in other fragments of fiction, Lermontov repeats this epithet. He was physically of smallish stature, with velvety eyes, broad shoulders and bow legs.

54. The allusion is to *La Femme de Trente Ans* in *Scènes de la Vie Privée* 1828–44, a vulgar novelette, ending in ridiculous melodrama, by the overrated French writer, Balzac. The Marquise d'Aiglemont reaches thirty in Part Three, and, when Charles de Vandenesse sees her for the first time, part of the description runs: '*Ce reste de coquetterie/"les soins minutieux qu'elle prenait de sa main et de son pied"/se faisait même excuser par une gracieuse nonchalance . . . [La] courbure de son cou, le laisser aller de son corps fatigué mais souple qui paraissait élégamment brisé dans le fauteuil, l'abandon de ses jambes, l'insouciance de sa pose, ses mouvements pleins de lassitude, tout révélait une femme sans intérêt dans la vie*', etc.

A little further, occur the famous, but actually insipid and commonplace pages ('*Son silence est aussi dangereux que sa parole*', etc.), wherein Balzac analyses the woman of thirty. No wonder Vandenesse '*resta silencieux et petit [?] devant cette grande et noble femme*'.

55. See note 15.

56. Oddly enough, Maksim Maksimych forgets that, as he had said himself (see p. 54), Bela was not to be mentioned.

57. It is hardly necessary to remind the good reader that these unrealistic blanchings and blushings, slight or otherwise, are mere code words used by novelists to convey one character's awareness of another character's emotion. Even Tolstoy, despite his incomparable genius for the vivid rendering of the physical, was not above the 'grew-slightly-pale' device which in the long run goes back to French novelistic formulas.

58. We never learn exactly how Pechorin died. His digestion was poor and his bile excessive, but otherwise he had a remarkably strong constitution. One suspects that the death he encountered on his way home from Persia was a violent one, and that Lermontov

withheld the mystery to make an additional story of it in some later volume (see also note 118.)

59. *Les Confessions de Jean Jacques Rousseau*, Genève, 1782 and 1789.

60. These 'Black-Sea Cossacks' (not to be confused with the other Cossacks mentioned in the book) were descendants of Ukrainians removed by Empress Catherine II from beyond the cataracts of the Dniepr to the Kuban region in order to repel the incursions of Caucasian and Turkish tribes.

61. Gelendzhik: A port on a small bay of the Black Sea about 80 mi. SE of Taman, in the extreme NW corner of the Caucasus. Taman village is a small port in Taman Gulf, an eastern inlet of Kerch Strait, about 250 mi. NW of Sukhum.

62. The hallway (or covered porch) of the second, smaller, cottage.

63. 'Then the eyes of the blind shall be opened.... And the tongue of the dumb sing.' Isaiah 35: 5–6. (The Revised Standard Version of 1952 adds 'for joy'.)

64. The word used here is *valuny* (sing., *valún*), which means 'boulders', not 'breakers', as indicated by the context. Lermontov's odd application of the word may have been influenced by a similarity to *volny* or *valy* (German, *Wellen*), 'waves', 'billows'. These *valuny* reappear as breakers on p. 163, in a poetical metaphor that links up the end of 'Princess Mary' with the 'Taman' seascape.

65. Ruins of an ancient Greek colony in the vicinity northeast of Taman village.

66. The Russian epithet *nechísto* implies some devilry; the 'evil' shades into the 'uncanny' and 'haunted'. 'There is something wrong about the place.' *Nechísto*, in its absolutely literal sense, means 'not clean', which is the way Pechorin first interprets it. It is interesting to note that the Cossack practically repeats line 15 of Zhukovsky's *Undina* (see next note).

67. A buoyant and frisky maiden meant to be eerie, a changeling of mermaid origin, well known to Russian readers from Zhukovsky's adaptation in rhymed dactylic verse (1833–6) of a romance by the German writer, La Motte Fouqué (*Undine*, 1811).

68. *Yunaya Frantsia*, in the Russian text. The *Jeune-France* was the Parisian dandy of 1830 who copied the London dandy of 1815. The movement (not to be confused with a later political organization, 1848) had but few repercussions in the literature of 1830–40. Eccentricity of language and manners, detestation of bourgeois smugness, a desire to scandalize people, etc., marked this rather sterile post-romanticist fad.

69. A reference to the fey Italian girl in Goethe's romance *Wilhelm Meisters Lehrjahre* (1795–6).

Lermontov knew French perfectly, German passably, and seems to have a little more English than his master in poetry and prose, Pushkin (1799–1837).

70. Pechorin borrows this epithet from Pushkin's novel-in-verse

Eugene Onegin (Five, XXXIV, 9) where Onegin gives Tatyana a 'wondrously tender' look.

71. Borrowed from the poem, *Le Déjeuner,* by the French elegiast, Millevoye (1782–1816):

> *Un long baiser...*
> *Vient m'embraser de son humide flamme*

72. Pechorin's description of the girl's attire is romantically vague. That kerchief or scarf was not her *only* garment.

73. I have left the dates as they are, in Old Style. They lag twelve days behind ours.

74. A famous mineral-springs resort in northern Caucasus. Another spa, Kislovodsk, is some 40 mi. to the west of it.

The Pyatigorsk mountains mentioned in the course of the story are: 1. Iron Mountain, Russian, *Zheleznaya Gora* (2,795 ft.); 2. Snake Mountain, *Zmeinaya Gora* or *Zmeyka* (3,261 ft.); 3. Besh Tau or Mount Besh (4,590 ft.); 4. Mount Mashuk (3,258 ft.); and 5. Bald Mountain (2,427 ft.). These mountains are situated north and east (Bald Mountain) of Pyatigorsk.

To the south, in the western part of the Central Chain (running from parallel 44° in NW Caucasus to parallel 41° in SE Caucasus), some 50 mi. south of Pyatigorsk, loom Mount Elbruz, the highest mountain in Europe (about 18,500 ft.), and Mount Kazbek (about 16,500 ft.).

75. The opening line of an allegorical short poem by Pushkin, *The Cloud* (1835), in amphibrachic tetrameter.

76. Here and elsewhere, the style of Pechorin's descriptions of Caucasian mountain views does not differ in any way from Lermontov's own prose rhythm (p. 17 and elsewhere).

77. The line of dots (here and elsewhere) was a stylistic device of the time denoting an interruption or pause, or ineffable things, with nonchalant or romantic connotations.

78. There existed a great social distinction between officers of the Guard and those of the Army.

79. A deleted passage in the draft corroborates one's suspicion that Pechorin in 1833 (like Lermontov in 1840) was expelled to the Caucasus because of a duel. Officers of the Guard were demoted to low ranks in the Army (Pechorin has sunk to the lowest degree of commissioned officer in 'Bela') for escapades of that kind, and Grushnitsky poses as a romantic exile by wearing a soldier's overcoat. Actually, he has not yet been promoted from cadet to officer. On the other hand, the much-prized soldier's St George's Cross that Grushnitsky sports does imply some act of courage in battle.

80. This sudden switch to the past tense is symptomatic (see note 84).

81. Grushnitsky's aphoristic remark might seem, at first blush, to be meant by Lermontov as an echo of a similar observation by Pechorin on a previous page (p. 85); actually, of course, Pechorin, in

tabulating the events of the day, jots down that phrase (p. 85) *after* his conversation with Grushnitsky (p. 86). This shifting of sequential levels of sense is typical of Lermontov's manner.

82. A kind of masculine bob.

83. A few moments after Grushnitsky has delivered himself of this aphorism ('I hate men in order not to despise them, since otherwise life would be too disgusting a farce'), Pechorin will deliberately echo it ('I despise women in order not to love them, since otherwise life would be too ridiculous a melodrama').

84. It would seem that Pechorin (who at the time may have thought of turning novelist) is experimenting, here and elsewhere, with the past tense, in an attempt to make of Werner a character in a story.

85. Lermontov, and other Russian authors before him, had a strange predilection for this trite Gallicism, an old cliché of French journalism, *Les augurs de Rome qui ne peuvent se regarder sans rire.* Cicero (in *De divinatione, Liber Secundus*, XXIV) says that Cato wondered 'how one diviner (*aruspex,* a soothsayer who foretold the future from an examination of the entrails of animals) could see another without laughing'.

86. 1. The sadness of sad things; 2. Their absurdity; 3. Our indifference to them.

87. At the height of Byron's vogue in Russia (1820–40), most educated people in Russia, where French was incomparably more widespread than English, read Byron's works in the prose versions of Amédée Pichot. These are wretchedly inexact, but read 'smoothly'.

88. This theme is not followed up.

89. *I bolee.* One wonders if this should not be *ne bolee* (no more).

90. *Nadulsya.* This has two possible meanings, the French *il se rengorgea* (as I think it is here) and the more usual 'he went into a huff'.

91. The omission of 'my' in the editions I have consulted is possibly based on an initial misprint.

92. This is defined by Littré as *'fièvre continue, peu intense dans ses symptômes, et qui suit une marche chronique. Souvent le mot est synonyme de fièvre hectique'* which is *'accompagnée d'amaigrissement progressif [et] survient assez souvent aux maladies du poumon'.*

93. Pechorin evidently means the oak scrub and juniper (or, as we say in America, 'cedar') that covers mountains at comparatively low elevations.

94. A kind of longish tunic worn by Circassians over the *beshmet* (see note 22).

95. The word (which is exactly rendered by the Spanish, *'barranco'*), is of Tatar (Turkic) origin and was used all over southern Russia.

96. This is a familiar reference to a passage in Griboedov's great comedy-in-verse *Woe from Wit* (*Gore ot uma*), completed in 1824, first edition published in 1833. The passage comes from Scene VII, Act One. Chatsky, returning after three years from abroad, asks Sofia about current fashions in Moscow, 1819:

> Does there still reign . . .
> At grand assemblies a confusion
> Of tongues, French and Nizhny-Novgorodan?

97. The Tatar population of the southern Russian steppes. Also the Nogay steppes in East Caucasus.

98. Grushnitsky's absence from the ball is due not to his wound, but to his not yet having got his commission.

99. Eykhenbaum's edition has *mazure*, which seems pretty meaningless, even for a Russian drunk. In Dudyshkin's edition of 1863, the word is spelled *mazurc*. The MS and the 1840–1 editions should be consulted.

100. It would have been rather difficult for Pechorin simultaneously to frequent the old princess, as Vera wants him to do, and to avoid meeting there Mr G—, who was a relation of the Ligovskoys. In fact, by p. 140 (three weeks later), Pechorin and Vera's husband are good friends.

101. *Begali slyozy v glazakh.* The same oddly un-Russian locution occurs in Chapter Four, lines 18–19, of Zhukovsky's *Undina* (see note 66).

102. *Ruka* as used here, in a not too felicitous image, may mean in Russian either 'hand' or 'arm'. The context suggests a middle course.

103. The reference seems to be to Pavel Kaverin (1794–1855), hussar, man-about-town, and Goettingen graduate, whom Pushkin, in an inscription to his portrait, in 1817, characterized thus:

> In him there always boils the heat of punch and war;
> A warrior fierce he was in fields of Mars;
> 'Mid friends, staunch friend, tormentor of the fair,
> And everywhere hussar!

He is also mentioned as a pal of the fictitious protagonist in *Eugene Onegin* (One, XVI, 6).

104. Jews in Russia were restricted in the choice of trade or profession; many of them became tailors; Grushnitsky's crack belongs to the stock-in-trade of literature.

105. *Biblioteka dlya Chteniya* (a magazine 1834–48), edited by Osip Senkovsky on the lines of the Parisian *Bibliothèque Universelle*. It contained, among other stuff, Russian adaptations of foreign novels.

106. An average rank in the civil service, the ninth in a scale where the lowest rung (fourteenth) is a Collegiate Registrator and the highest (first) a Chancellor (*Kantsler*), corresponding to Field Marshal in military service.

107. The whole interplay between Grushnitsky and the Captain of Dragoons is extremely unconvincing. Lermontov does not seem to have bothered about finding the right words here and keeps using the first comedy device that occurred to him.

108. Another curious link between Grushnitsky and Pechorin, who

utters here, with practically the same intonation, a dramatic phrase that on p. 85 he assigned to Grushnitsky as an example of the latter's post-Byronic style.

109. The owner of only fifty slaves was a needy landlord in pre-Emancipation Russia (i.e. before 1861), where a rich man might own a thousand peasants or more.

110. A carbonate mineral water, the name of which comes from *nartsane*, which means, in the Kabardian dialect, 'the drink of the giants' (Narts, mythical heroes sung by the tribes of the Northern Caucasus).

111. What is called in Southern Russia 'white acacia', and what Lermontov means here, as well as in the description of Bela's grave, is not the true acacia but the American Black Locust, *Robinia pseudoacacia* of Linnaeus, introduced into Europe by the French herbalist Robin in the seventeenth century.

112. This is from Griboedov's *Woe from Wit* (see note 96), Act Three, Scene III, Chatsky's retort to the toady Molchalin (but reads there somewhat differently than Pechorin has it):

When I have work to do, I hide from gaieties;
When it is fooling time, I fool:
To mix these two pursuits, a lot of men
Are apt. I am not one of them.

113. 'Grushnitsky every day carouses . . . He arrived only yesterday . . .' A strange discrepancy.

114. Tomashevsky (*Literaturnoe Nasledstvo*, issue 43–4, v. 1, 1941) has traced this and a few other passages in our book to the French novel *Gerfaux* (1838) by a disciple of Balzac, the forgotten writer, Charles de Bernard du Grail de la Villette (1804–50), whose name the otherwise admirable Russian commentator gives neither in full nor in French.

115. Pechorin quotes from *Eugene Onegin* the two closing lines of the Prefatory Piece, which first appeared, as a dedication of Chapters Four and Five, in 1828.

116. The allusion is to *La Gerusalemme liberata* (1581) by the Italian poet Torquato Tasso. He was read by Russians in French versions such as that of Prince Charles Lebrun, 1774.

117. The reference is to 'The Vampyre, a Tale', first published anonymously in the *New Magazine*, April, 1819, and attributed to Byron, in a separate edition, as a novel in July of the same year, but actually written by his physician, Dr John William Polidori. It was read by Russians in the French version of Chastopalli (joint pseudonym of Amédée Pichot and Euzèbe de Salle), who placed it among the *Oeuvres de Lord Byron* in their 1819 and 1820 editions of his works, after which it was dropped.

118. One wonders if perhaps Lermontov had planned to have Pechorin marry in Persia.

119. The reference is to Defauconpret's French version, under the

title Les *Puritains d'Ecosse* (Paris, 1817 and later editions), of *Old Mortality* by Walter Scott who, like all other English writers, was read by Russians in French.

120. An allusion to the various omens that preceded Caesar's assassination as related in Plutarch's *Parallel Lives* (circa AD 100), known to Russians in the French of Amyot's *Vies des hommes illustres* (1559).

121. The technical difficulty of having the lady leave Kislovodsk before the issue of her lover's duel is known, and of having her, simultaneously, be satisfied that he is spared is not solved here any too neatly.

122. Odd behaviour! Should we believe that Pechorin, a fashionable man, had remained seated after Mary had come in?

123. Cf. this to Pechorin's noticing Grushnitsky's corpse (p. 155).

124. *Otdelyayushchei, otdelyayushcheisya.* It is just like Lermontov and his casual style to let this long and limp word appear twice in the same, final, sentence.

125. In Lermontov's day, the fashionable banking game (*bank*) was a German variation of faro called *Stoss* (Russ., *shtoss*) or stuss. The player or 'punter' chose a card from his pack, put it down on the card table, and set his stake. The dealer or 'banker' unsealed a fresh pack and proceeded to turn the cards up from its top, one by one, the first card on his right hand, the second on his left, and so on, alternately, until the whole pack was dealt out. The dealer won when a card equal in points to that on which the stake had been set came up on his right hand, but lost when it was dealt to the left. When a doublet occurred – two similar cards turning up in the same coup – the punter lost half his stake at faro, the whole of it in stuss.

126. This scene curiously echoes that of the duel in 'Princess Mary' (p. 148), and there are other echoes further on (cf. p. 145, 'I myself am sufficiently bored', and p. 167, 'I became bored with this long procedure').

127. Caucasian new red wine, or must.

128. The second Cossack addresses the first by his patronymic ('son of Eremey'), and the same folksy familiarism is used on p. 172 by the Cossack captain in addressing the murderer (Efimych, 'son of Efim'). 'Vulich', which ends similarly, is, however, a surname.

129. It will be marked that Maksim Maksimych closes the book with much the same remark as the one he makes about Pechorin at the beginning (p. 23).

ABOUT THE TRANSLATOR

VLADIMIR NABOKOV (1899–1977), born in St Petersburg, was Professor of Russian Literature at Cornell University 1948–59. His many novels include *Lolita* (1955) and *Pale Fire* (1962). His translation with commentary of Pushkin's *Eugene Onegin* was published in 1964, and his *Lectures on Russian Literature*, posthumously, in 1981.

ABOUT THE INTRODUCER

T. J. BINYON is Senior Research Fellow in Russian at Wadham College, Oxford.

CHINUA ACHEBE
Things Fall Apart

THE ARABIAN NIGHTS
(2 vols, tr. Husain Haddawy)

MARCUS AURELIUS
Meditations

JANE AUSTEN
Emma
Mansfield Park
Northanger Abbey
Persuasion
Pride and Prejudice
Sanditon and Other Stories
Sense and Sensibility

HONORÉ DE BALZAC
Cousin Bette
Eugénie Grandet
Old Goriot

SIMONE DE BEAUVOIR
The Second Sex

SAUL BELLOW
The Adventures of Augie March

WILLIAM BLAKE
Poems and Prophecies

JORGE LUIS BORGES
Ficciones

JAMES BOSWELL
The Life of Samuel Johnson

CHARLOTTE BRONTË
Jane Eyre
Villette

EMILY BRONTË
Wuthering Heights

MIKHAIL BULGAKOV
The Master and Margarita

SAMUEL BUTLER
The Way of all Flesh

ITALO CALVINO
If on a winter's night a traveler

ALBERT CAMUS
The Outsider

MIGUEL DE CERVANTES
Don Quixote

GEOFFREY CHAUCER
Canterbury Tales

ANTON CHEKHOV
My Life and Other Stories
The Steppe and Other Stories

KATE CHOPIN
The Awakening

CARL VON CLAUSEWITZ
On War

S. T. COLERIDGE
Poems

WILKIE COLLINS
The Moonstone
The Woman in White

JOSEPH CONRAD
Heart of Darkness
Lord Jim
Nostromo
The Secret Agent
Typhoon and Other Stories
Under Western Eyes
Victory

THOMAS CRANMER
The Book of Common Prayer

DANTE ALIGHIERI
The Divine Comedy

DANIEL DEFOE
Moll Flanders
Robinson Crusoe

CHARLES DICKENS
Bleak House
David Copperfield
Dombey and Son
Great Expectations
Hard Times
Little Dorrit
Martin Chuzzlewit
Nicholas Nickleby
The Old Curiosity Shop
Oliver Twist
Our Mutual Friend
The Pickwick Papers
A Tale of Two Cities

DENIS DIDEROT
Memoirs of a Nun

JOHN DONNE
The Complete English Poems

FYODOR DOSTOEVSKY
The Brothers Karamazov
Crime and Punishment

GEORGE ELIOT
Adam Bede
Middlemarch
The Mill on the Floss
Silas Marner

WILLIAM FAULKNER
The Sound and the Fury

HENRY FIELDING
Joseph Andrews and Shamela
Tom Jones

F. SCOTT FITZGERALD
The Great Gatsby
This Side of Paradise

GUSTAVE FLAUBERT
Madame Bovary

FORD MADOX FORD
The Good Soldier
Parade's End

E. M. FORSTER
Howards End
A Passage to India

ELIZABETH GASKELL
Mary Barton

EDWARD GIBBON
The Decline and Fall of the
Roman Empire
Vols 1 to 3: The Western Empire
Vols 4 to 6: The Eastern Empire

J. W. VON GOETHE
Selected Works

IVAN GONCHAROV
Oblomov

GÜNTER GRASS
The Tin Drum

GRAHAM GREENE
Brighton Rock
The Human Factor

THOMAS HARDY
Far From the Madding Crowd
Jude the Obscure
The Mayor of Casterbridge
The Return of the Native
Tess of the d'Urbervilles
The Woodlanders

JAROSLAV HAŠEK
The Good Soldier Švejk

NATHANIEL HAWTHORNE
The Scarlet Letter

JOSEPH HELLER
Catch-22

ERNEST HEMINGWAY
A Farewell to Arms
The Collected Stories

GEORGE HERBERT
The Complete English Works

HERODOTUS
The Histories

HINDU SCRIPTURES
(tr. R. C. Zaehner)

JAMES HOGG
Confessions of a Justified Sinner

HOMER
The Iliad
The Odyssey

VICTOR HUGO
Les Misérables

HENRY JAMES
The Awkward Age
The Bostonians
The Golden Bowl
The Portrait of a Lady
The Princess Casamassima
The Wings of the Dove
Collected Stories (2 vols)

JAMES JOYCE
Dubliners
A Portrait of the Artist as
a Young Man
Ulysses

FRANZ KAFKA
Collected Stories
The Castle
The Trial

JOHN KEATS
The Poems

SØREN KIERKEGAARD
Fear and Trembling and
The Book on Adler

RUDYARD KIPLING
Collected Stories
Kim

THE KORAN
(tr. Marmaduke Pickthall)

CHODERLOS DE LACLOS
Les Liaisons dangereuses

GIUSEPPE TOMASI DI
LAMPEDUSA
The Leopard

D. H. LAWRENCE
Collected Stories
The Rainbow
Sons and Lovers
Women in Love

MIKHAIL LERMONTOV
A Hero of Our Time

PRIMO LEVI
If This is a Man and The Truce
The Periodic Table

NICCOLÒ MACHIAVELLI
The Prince

THOMAS MANN
Buddenbrooks
Death in Venice and Other Stories
Doctor Faustus

KATHERINE MANSFIELD
The Garden Party and Other
Stories

GABRIEL GARCÍA MÁRQUEZ
Love in the Time of Cholera
One Hundred Years of Solitude

ANDREW MARVELL
The Complete Poems

HERMAN MELVILLE
The Complete Shorter Fiction
Moby-Dick

JOHN STUART MILL
On Liberty and Utilitarianism

JOHN MILTON
The Complete English Poems

YUKIO MISHIMA
The Temple of the
Golden Pavilion

MARY WORTLEY MONTAGU
Letters

THOMAS MORE
Utopia

TONI MORRISON
Song of Solomon

MURASAKI SHIKIBU
The Tale of Genji

VLADIMIR NABOKOV
Lolita
Pale Fire
Speak, Memory

V. S. NAIPAUL
A House for Mr Biswas

THE NEW TESTAMENT
(King James Version)

THE OLD TESTAMENT
(King James Version)

GEORGE ORWELL
Animal Farm
Nineteen Eighty-Four

THOMAS PAINE
Rights of Man
and Common Sense

BORIS PASTERNAK
Doctor Zhivago

PLATO
The Republic

EDGAR ALLAN POE
The Complete Stories

ALEXANDER PUSHKIN
The Collected Stories

FRANÇOIS RABELAIS
Gargantua and Pantagruel

JOSEPH ROTH
The Radetzky March

JEAN-JACQUES ROUSSEAU
Confessions
The Social Contract and
the Discourses

SALMAN RUSHDIE
Midnight's Children

WALTER SCOTT
Rob Roy

WILLIAM SHAKESPEARE
Comedies Vols 1 and 2
Histories Vols 1 and 2
Romances
Sonnets and Narrative Poems
Tragedies Vols 1 and 2

MARY SHELLEY
Frankenstein

ADAM SMITH
The Wealth of Nations

ALEXANDER SOLZHENITSYN
One Day in the Life of
Ivan Denisovich

SOPHOCLES
The Theban Plays

CHRISTINA STEAD
The Man Who Loved Children

JOHN STEINBECK
The Grapes of Wrath

STENDHAL
The Charterhouse of Parma
Scarlet and Black

LAURENCE STERNE
Tristram Shandy

ROBERT LOUIS STEVENSON
The Master of Ballantrae and
Weir of Hermiston
Dr Jekyll and Mr Hyde
and Other Stories

HARRIET BEECHER STOWE
Uncle Tom's Cabin

JONATHAN SWIFT
Gulliver's Travels

JUNICHIRŌ TANIZAKI
The Makioka Sisters

W. M. THACKERAY
Vanity Fair

HENRY DAVID THOREAU
Walden

ALEXIS DE TOCQUEVILLE
Democracy in America

LEO TOLSTOY
Anna Karenina
Childhood, Boyhood and Youth
The Cossacks
War and Peace

ANTHONY TROLLOPE
Barchester Towers
Can You Forgive Her?
Doctor Thorne
The Eustace Diamonds

ANTHONY TROLLOPE *cont.*
Framley Parsonage
The Last Chronicle of Barset
The Small House at Allington
The Warden

IVAN TURGENEV
Fathers and Children
First Love and Other Stories
A Sportsman's Notebook

MARK TWAIN
Tom Sawyer
and Huckleberry Finn

JOHN UPDIKE
Rabbit Angstrom

GIORGIO VASARI
Lives of the Painters, Sculptors
and Architects

VIRGIL
The Aeneid

VOLTAIRE
Candide and Other Stories

EVELYN WAUGH
The Complete Short Stories
Brideshead Revisited
Decline and Fall
The Sword of Honour Trilogy

EDITH WHARTON
The Age of Innocence
The Custom of the Country
The House of Mirth
The Reef

OSCAR WILDE
Plays, Prose Writings and Poems

MARY WOLLSTONECRAFT
A Vindication of the Rights of
Woman

VIRGINIA WOOLF
To the Lighthouse
Mrs Dalloway

W. B. YEATS
The Poems

ÉMILE ZOLA
Germinal

This book is set in EHRHARDT. The precise origin
of the typeface is unclear. Most of the founts were
probably cut by the Hungarian punch-cutter
Nicholas Kis for the Ehrhardt foundry
in Leipzig, where they were left
for sale in 1689. In 1938 the
Monotype foundry pro-
duced the modern
version.